TAKE ME TO HEART

It was his eyes that spoke loudest, pulling at her insides like heavy vises clasped about the soul of her being. When he was close to her, she didn't need to see him to know that he was staring. She could feel his prying eyes upon her, burning, caressing, promising. He would stand close, causing her to shiver, and he'd nourish himself upon her fear, hungriest when she was most uneasy, feasting on her nervousness.

Pulling off Route 7 into Danbury, she wanted to turn the car around, to ignore his invitation. A quick phone call, a well-tuned lie, and she could head back to the security of her apartment and a good book, but his cries were loudest now, pulling her closer, sensing she was near. At his front door, she had barely hesitated before it swung open and he stood before her, ushering her inside.

"Welcome."

"Thank you," she responded cheerfully. "How are you?"

"Better now that you're here. You didn't have any problems finding the place, did you?"

Marguerite blushed ever so slightly. He didn't need to know that she'd studied two maps and had spent over an hour memorizing the route from her front door to his. "No, not really."

TAKE ME TO HEART

Deborah Fletcher Mello

BET Publications, LLC
http://www.bet.com
http://www.arabesquebooks.com

ARABESQUE BOOKS are published by

BET Publications, LLC
c/o BET BOOKS
One BET Plaza
1900 W Place NE
Washington, DC 20018-1211

All Kensington Titles, Imprints, and Distributed Lines are available at special quantity discounts for bulk purchases for sales promotions, premiums, fund-raising, and educational or institutional use. Special book excerpts or customized printings can also be created to fit specific needs. For details, write or phone the office of the Kensington special sales manager: Kensington Publishing Corp., 850 Third Avenue, New York, NY 10022, attn: Special Sales Department, Phone: 1-800-221-2647.

BET Books is a trademark of Black Entertainment Television, Inc. ARABESQUE, the ARABESQUE logo, and the BET BOOKS logo are trademarks and registered trademarks.

First Printing: December 2003
10 9 8 7 6 5 4 3 2 1

Printed in the United States of America

For my husband,
Allan Anthony Mello

ACKNOWLEDGMENTS

First and foremost, I give thanks to God for His many blessings, for only through Him are all things possible.

I want to thank my parents, Walter and Corrine Fletcher, for their invaluable lessons on life and love. You two are truly an inspiration.

To my grandmother, Susie Cole, my sister, Tealecia Fletcher, and my uncle, Dr. William T. Fletcher, your love and support continues to be a great source of comfort.

To my best friend, Angela D. Thomas, if I had a twin spirit she'd be you. Your invaluable wisdom and well-tuned humor have made this trip well worth the journey. Everyone should have at least one best friend like you. I am blessed that you are mine.

Much love to my "other" mothers, Sarah Jenkins and Louise Thomas. May you both know just how much your love and kindness has meant to me.

Gratitude also to my sister-friends, Jackie Liggins, Janet Knight Ledbetter, and Yvonne Gatewood, for all the encouraging words and support.

And, most especially, I want to thank my son Matthew, who has believed in me when I could barely find strength to believe in myself. You, young man, are living proof that dreams do come true.

1

Aretha Franklin played on the stereo. Smooth, silky, gossiping Aretha, singing of love and desire. That get-down, nasty kind of love that reminded Marguerite Cole of new leather christened by the lust of furtive hands searching where she should have posted a no-trespassing sign.

It felt good to her, the music blasting in the background, as she primped in the mirror testing out a new shade of blush across her high cheekbones. The color was mocha cinnamon, a blend of red clay and chocolate that sat harshly against the warm brown of her skin. Cursing, she wiped the offending color from her face. The stark white ball of cotton absorbed the blush hesitantly, seeming non-approving as she smeared it from one medium to the other.

Aretha was preaching. Snapping her fingers, Marguerite danced around the commode to the shower. Turning on the faucet, she shimmied from side to side as she waited for the chilling flow of water to turn warm, showering a sheer mist of steam upon her skin and the porcelain of her baby-blue bathroom. In the background, Aretha was now confessing her love.

Dropping her peach silk robe to the floor, Marguerite stepped into the stream of water. Its wetness flowed wickedly over her flesh, kissing the tattooed shoulder, the sepia nipples, settling around her manicured toes. She held her head slightly askew, not wanting to dampen her new extensions. The synthetic braids twisted atop her head like a regal crown had taken twelve strained hours of pulling at her own over-processed, chemically straightened, russet strands to achieve. If nothing else, the discomfort had not only appeased some deep-seated sense of ethnicity she professed to feel, but had afforded her at least six weeks of freedom from her curling iron and rollers.

As the avocado-scented suds washed over her skin, she wondered if this date was going to be a mistake. This too-smooth brother in his tailored suits and expensive leather shoes, who looked at her hungrily and spoke her name with a self-assurance that already had her wrapped within the sheets of his bed, scared her. He had taunted her with a dimpled smile, and thick eyebrows that rose suggestively when he leaned down to whisper in her ear, pressing the chocolate of his complexion hotly against her own caramel cheek.

She could taste him the first time he walked into the office, boldly announcing his name and that of his company. His blackness had surprised the office manager, a timid Asian man, who had greeted him coolly, a shaky hand extended into a limp handshake. From where she sat behind the security of her oak desk, she had observed the solid build, the thick shoulders, and high behind. She had also noted how the temporary receptionist, a too-thin, porcelain-white blonde, had eagerly taken his gray wool overcoat from him, lightly brushing the length of his arm with chipped nails, with an "I'm available" smile outlined in pale pink lipstick upon her alabaster face.

When her secretary buzzed her on the intercom, summoning her to the conference room, she had risen from her seat with some trepidation, her instincts screaming at her to sit back down and feign illness. Instead, she had ventured down the hallway toward the conference room, painfully aware that her firm hips were swaying too freely, her long legs were peeking too boldly from beneath her gray wool skirt, and the matching double-breasted blazer was buttoned too neatly across her full chest, accentuating her small waist.

When she entered the elongated room, textured in rich mahogany and rose-colored upholstery, she had extended a newly manicured hand that he had held longer than necessary, his dark eyes piercing her insides with promises of more to come. He had licked his lips lightly as he watched her from across the table, and she had twisted in her seat nervously, feeling deliciously naked as the deep vibrato of his voice tap-danced up her spine.

That had been the first of many meetings as he had negotiated a contract to upgrade the computer services for her firm. Business meetings had carried over into lunch dates as he'd pressed urgently for more; more meetings, more of her time, more of her. Six months later, when the contracts had been signed and the installations completed, he had sat in her office, boldly confident, slightly arrogant, exuding a raw, carnal yearning that reeked of a tactile potency. The business was finished and he was manipulating a move to something more personal. Together they'd negotiated dinner as he allowed her to set rules he intended to break, making promises she knew were to be soon forgotten. Now she stood shivering under a plush terry towel intimidated by the prospects of what lay ahead of her.

Wiping the moisture from her firm flesh, she studied her body as she imagined he might if given the opportunity. She was flush from the heat in the room, the warm color accentuating her cheeks. Her breasts, neither too large nor too small, stood imposing, not yet bruised by age or childbirth. The nipples were inverted, a curse of nature, the dark aureoles full like ripe raspberries. Her stomach was flat, her buttocks full. Large thighs rubbed gently together paying homage to the dark pubic hair curled tightly below a slightly protruding navel. A belly-button ring in sterling silver lay neatly against the smooth line of her abdomen.

She massaged her firm flesh with a peach-scented moisturizer, starting at the tip of her toes and working her way up the length of her torso to just beneath her chin. Her skin soaked up the creamy emollient like a sponge absorbing water, and she lathered the lotion on generously. The cooling balm against the warmth of her flesh felt comfortable beneath the palm of her hand.

She slipped into a lemon-yellow camisole and matching thong, adjusting the strap against the crevice of her buttocks ever so carefully. Pulling a mustard-colored velvet jumpsuit over her undergarments, she concealed the lace-edged top that pushed her breasts up, deepening her cleavage.

Straining her arms behind her, she pulled at the extended zipper, closing the soft fabric comfortably around herself like a newborn encased in a bunting. Short brown leather boots, a faint touch of gold, delicate drop earrings, and a slim ring of bangles around her wrist finished the look.

Reaching for the telephone, she pulled the receiver to her ear and blindly dialed seven digits. As the phone rang, she studied herself in the full-length mirror across the room. The thought of changing into something more businesslike briefly crossed her mind.

"Hi, Mrs. Donald," she said, responding to the greeting on the other end. "Very well, thank you. Is Sharon home? Yes, ma'am. I'll hold."

The pause was brief. "Well, it's about time," said Sharon. "I have left five messages for you. Where in the world have you been?" her best friend asked, shouting softly into the phone.

"Don't have time to explain. I'm going on a date."

"A what?"

"A date. You remember that. One woman, one man. Dinner, maybe dancing or a movie. A lot of small talk and if you get real lucky, a kiss on the cheek when it's over."

"Can't say that I do. It's been so long," Sharon Donald responded sarcastically. "Who is he, and please tell me the brother carries a briefcase to work every day."

"A business associate. Dexter Williams. He's the guy I told you about that we did the hardware deal with, remember?"

"Yes, I do, but I don't recall you saying he was dating material."

"He may not be, but we shall soon find out. I just wanted to let you know, though, that I hadn't forgotten about you."

"Uh-huh."

"I've got to go. I'm supposed to meet him in Danbury in one hour."

"Meet him? I thought when you had a date the man was supposed to pick you up at your door."

"Not this man. I want to have my own car just in case he turns out to be a knife-wielding psychopath."

"I hear that, but why Danbury? That's over an hour away."

"I know, but that's where he lives. Besides, I don't want anyone I know to see me with him."

"Why not? You said the brother was too fine."

"I just don't. Why didn't you want anyone to see you with Charles?"

"Never mind." Sharon grinned into the handset. "You just call me when you get home and don't forget any of the details."

"I promise. See you later." Marguerite dropped the receiver back onto its cradle, then paused again in front of the full-length mirror for one last look. She decided it was too late to change. The outfit would just have to do. The body suit fit like a glove, falling in a smooth line over her hips and rotund behind, flattering the envious curves of her figure. Studying her reflection, she cursed her big legs and large feet, the size-ten snakeskin boots shining with newness. Her grandmother called her legs "sturdy." "Girl, runnin' or walkin', them big sturdy legs will carry you far," the old woman often told her.

Her eyes were the color of light nutmeg, intruding on a canvas of clear, chestnut skin, her coloring warm and rich with history. Her mulatto features had a distinct character, evidence of her mixed breeding. The almond eyes, thin nose, full lips, and wide forehead confirmed many a tale told in hushed whispers behind closed doors. The thin braids hung wildly, held captive at the base of her neck with a brown print hair band. She knew she looked good. She felt even better. What was to be would be. As she gathered car keys and her purse, locking the door behind her, she could hear him calling to her, "Take me to heart."

2

The sun was setting in front of her, the flaming glow swallowing the sky as she drove. She loved to drive, but she hated that she was driving to Danbury to meet a man who was probably not right for her. But as the sun was calling out for the dark sky to pull up its black cover and tuck it under its chin, so did he call out to her.

It was his eyes that spoke loudest, pulling at her insides like heavy vises clasped about the soul of her being. When he was close to her, she didn't need to see him to know that he was staring. She could feel his prying eyes upon her, burning, caressing, promising. He would stand close, causing her to shiver, and he'd nourish himself upon her fear, hungriest when she was most uneasy, feasting on her nervousness.

Pulling off Route 7 into Danbury, she wanted to turn the car around, to ignore his invitation. A quick phone call, a well-tuned lie, and she could head back to the security of her apartment and a good book, but his cries were loudest now, pulling her closer, sensing she was near. At his front door, she had barely hesitated before it swung open and he stood before her, ushering her inside.

"Welcome."

"Thank you," she responded cheerfully. "How are you?"

"Better now that you're here. You didn't have any problems finding the place, did you?"

Marguerite blushed ever so slightly. He didn't need to know that she'd studied two maps and had spent over an hour memorizing the route from her front door to his. "No, not really."

"Well, make yourself comfortable. John and I were just talking about last night's Redskin's game," he said, gesturing toward a tall white man who had risen from his seat to extend a hand in her direction.

Marguerite smiled. "Hi. It's nice to finally meet you."

"You too," John, the roommate, business associate, and best friend, said, greeting her warmly. "Would you like a glass of wine?"

"Thank you. I'd love one."

Marguerite made herself comfortable on an oversized gray recliner, taking in her surroundings. The living room was a warm mixture of eclectic furniture, the colors a muted blend of taupe and tan with a sporadic use of bright colors thrown about. A glass-topped, marble-filled coffee table cast a faint illumination of colored shadows from the center of the room. The glass baubles in a myriad of colors were quite intriguing, and Marguerite studied them with some intensity. The three-bedroom condo smelled faintly of lemon cleaner, a light oily scent that pleasantly tickled her nostrils.

Pulling her aside, John gave her a tour of their home, showing her from room to room as he extolled the virtues of the dark shadow who watched her too closely. Side by side the two men had stood, like opposite ends of a spectrum, he a dark prince, tall and bronzed, his friend a fair-haired blond with strong Nordic features. They were both pleasant to look upon, like famed statues blessing their on-lookers with the pleasure of gazing upon their beauty. They had made her comfortable, and she had laughed heartily at their bad jokes and off-color tales as the three sat sharing a bottle of light Chardonnay.

"So tell me, Marguerite," John said, "how long have you been with Braedman and Associates?"

"Almost four years now. It seems like an eternity since I started there as a marketing manager."

"It's an interesting organization," Dexter inter-jected, reaching to refill her glass. "Almost a mini Peyton Place. I have never seen people so into everyone else's business."

Marguerite laughed. "Why do you say that?"

"Well, I heard enough office gossip during the short time I was there to fill a book. Maybe two books, and it was killing them to know what was going on between me and you."

"Well, there was really nothing for them to know, now was there?"

Dexter chuckled, detecting from the tone in her voice that he'd touched a nerve. He shrugged, reaching for his wineglass.

Shaking her head, Marguerite smiled warmly, cutting her eyes at him ever so slightly. "It is bad, though. It definitely took some getting use to."

John looked from one to the other, noting a faint touch of tension rising between them. "The company is relatively new, isn't it?"

"They were a spin-off of Hall, Hall, and Braedman

Marketing. When Elias Hall passed away, the other two partners went their separate ways. The rumor mill says it was because the younger Hall—I think his name was Tyler, Tyler Hall—was having an affair with Earl Braedman's first wife. She's that actress, Jaden Thames."

Both men laughed. "See?" said Dexter. "The business started with office gossip. I told you those people gossip about everything."

Marguerite joined in the laughter.

Regaining his composure, Dexter rose from his seat extending a hand to Marguerite. "We should be heading to dinner."

As he pulled her to her feet, she noted how soft his hands were, the tanned palms sliding gently against her own flesh. She caught her breath at the sudden sensation that filled her midsection. Nodding, she muttered faintly, her words barely discernible, then turned to say good-bye to John.

"It was a pleasure meeting you," she said.

"It was nice meeting you, Marguerite. I hope we'll see each other again real soon."

As she exited Dexter's home, Marguerite suddenly welcomed the cool evening air. She inhaled deeply, gulping in deep breaths as though she'd not been able to breathe for a long time. As he guided her toward his car, a black Lincoln Navigator, she thought again about not going through with this date. She was comfortable with him in the presence of others, but there was something between them when they were alone. Something that played wickedly with her emotions.

As they drove to the restaurant, she and Dexter talked business, a topic both were comfortable with. Her sensitivity was running high, egged on by the wine, and when he clasped her hand in his as they walked into the restaurant, her knees quivered, threatening to drop her helplessly to the floor. She fought to contain the sudden rush of tears that rose threateningly to her eyes. What in the world was wrong with her? she mulled in silence hoping that he had not noticed. It was not until she had consumed a double vodka tonic that she could feel a calm wash over her.

"So, tell me more about yourself," Dexter said as he bit into a salted bread stick. "Anything. I always seem to be the one doing most of the talking."

"I'm not much of a talker. I like to sit back and take it all in."

"Well, tell me something anyway. Something I don't know," Dexter added.

Marguerite smiled. "There's really not much to tell. I'm an only child born right here in Connecticut. My mother died when I was a baby and my grandmother raised me. I love music, slow, easy stuff mostly. I'm an avid reader, and I must confess to enjoying a good soap opera, or anything else that will take me away from the realities of life for a few brief moments."

Dexter laughed lightly.

Marguerite continued. "I despise cats, the cellulite on my thighs, and women who whine about having no man and no money get right on my nerves. So, that's the edited, classified-ad version of my life."

He laughed again, nodding. "Interesting. And why do you dislike women who whine?"

"Because I have done enough whining of my own to have heard it all and it's not a pretty sight."

"Now I know a beautiful woman like you doesn't have a problem with men. I imagine I'm going to have to beat them off with a stick to be with you."

She laughed. "I only have a problem with those tired brothers with truly pathetic 'you're so beautiful' lines. They grate on my last nerve."

He smiled. "So tell me, why do I make you so nervous?" he asked, his expression smug.

She raised her eyebrows slightly, turning her attention back to the linguine carbonara on the plate before her. "Who says you do?"

Reaching over the table, he ran his hand along her arm, brushing the back of her hand with his palm. "Just a feeling I get."

Pulling her hand away, she reached for her wineglass, tipping the crystal to her lips. As she did, she looked into his eyes. The cavernous orbs whispered her name, blowing a gentle breeze along the back of her neck. His eyes smiled seductively.

She watched as he stabbed a clam with his fork, pulling the gelatinous morsel to his mouth, holding it in front of him like a prized catch. Easing his tongue past his lips, he licked lightly at the garlicky coating, the warm butter flowing gently over his tongue, tempting, mesmerizing. Wrapping his tongue around it like a snake inhaling its prey, he pulled the delicacy into his mouth and chewed it slowly, each bite steady and rhythmic. The sensuous motion both intrigued and disgusted her, lighting a low flame between her tightly pressed thighs.

Placing her glass on the table, she shook her head.

"Is something wrong?" he asked, dabbing at the side of his mouth with a napkin.

"No," she sighed, avoiding his eyes. "I'm just tired. It's been a long day."

"No wonder you're so tense. You look like you could use a massage."

"Is that an offer?"

"If you want it to be."

"How do I know you're any good at it?"

"You know," he responded confidently.

"I do?"

"Well, if you don't, there is only one way to find out."

"You are just so sure of yourself, aren't you?"

"Aren't *you*?"

She retreated into the pregnant silence that followed, studying the last drops of wine in her glass as he gestured to the waitress for the check.

"Thank you," she said. "I had a nice time tonight."

"The night's not over yet," he said as they left the building. "There's someplace I want to take you."

"Where?"

"It's a surprise."

"I don't like surprises."

"You'll like this one."

Shaking her head, she sat back in her seat, feigning disinterest.

As they drove, she studied him in the darkness, the passing streetlights reflecting inside the car her sole source of light. His features were crisp, chiseled neatly in dark clay. His hair was cropped short, the sides faded slightly toward the back. Two diamond studs penetrated one earlobe; a faint shadow of a beard peeked from his pores.

Her heartbeat increased ever so slightly. "This man is beautiful," Marguerite thought. She took a deep breath, intoxicated by his presence. She could feel the warm mist of perspiration rising to the palms of her hands, and she nervously brushed them atop her thighs, the fabric of her jumpsuit pleasing to the touch.

As he pulled onto a darkened road, she wanted to be afraid, but could find nothing to fear but herself and the rising desire growing within her. At the top of the hill, he stopped the car and got out, grabbing a blanket from the backseat. Walking over to her side, he opened the door and helped her out, wrapping his arms easily about her shoulders. The night air was beginning to change, the mild coolness giving way to an even cooler, chillier breeze.

Walking back around to the other side of the car, he pulled her along beside him until they reached a small clearing that looked out upon an airport below. The bright lights beneath them flicked eagerly, hugging the ground. Settling down on the blanket, he pulled her close, laying her head upon his shoulder, wrapping his arms protectively around her body.

"This is one of my favorite places," he said. "I come up here to think. I love to just sit and watch the planes landing and taking off."

Marguerite nodded, understanding. "I can remember when I was a little girl wanting to be a jet pilot. I use to get such a rush imagining myself in control, soaring through the clouds."

"Why didn't you make the dream come true?"

"Bad eyesight. Too many years of glasses and contact lenses."

He laughed. "Personally, I'm afraid of heights. I like to watch the planes, but I'm not thrilled about being in one."

She laughed with him.

"So tell me, what made you finally decide to go out with me tonight?" he asked. "I've been trying to get together with you for months now and you have made it difficult at best."

She shrugged. "I try not to mix business and pleasure. I found out the hard way that it can complicate things."

He nodded. "You want to talk about it or him?"

"No. It's been long forgotten and I buried him ages ago," she said, the dark night hiding the tense expression that crossed her face.

"Good. I want to be sure I have your full attention."

In the darkness, she could feel him staring, those eyes devouring her. Staring at the runway, she tried to ignore his lips as they brushed lightly against her cheek, planting delicate kisses down the length of her face. Clasping her face between his massive hands, he pulled her to him, pressing his lips firmly against hers.

As he dropped onto his back, she fell across his body, his hands gently stroking the length of her spine. The kiss was tender, the passion rising as their lips melted like warm butter, one into the other. As his mouth searched hers, his tongue dancing a slow waltz with hers, she marveled at how sweet the connection was. His body felt good next to hers, and she pressed herself into him, pushing him against the hard earth. Reluctantly, they pulled apart, her lips still tingling with the feel of his. Rolling, he lay beside her, nuzzling his face into her neck.

"I have wanted to do that for some time," he said breathlessly, running the tip of his fingers down the length of her arm. He could feel the length of his manhood growing, his rising desire becoming clearly evident. Unable to gain control over the sudden sensation, he eased himself away from her, the movement ever so gentle. He was hoping she'd not notice his sudden discomfort. He dropped his hand down to his side, resisting the temptation to pull at his crotch.

In the darkness she nodded, then kissed him again, the faint taste of garlic and butter painted lightly upon his lips. Dexter suddenly felt as if he was going to burst, and as quickly as the sensation was starting to overwhelm him did he push her gently away. He kissed her cheeks, her nose, brushed his lips across her forehead, down to her neck. Sighing heavily, he rose, extending his hand down toward her.

"It's getting late and you have a long ride home," he said, hoping that his sudden anxiety was not evident in his voice. He pulled her easily from the ground, helping her to her feet.

In the darkness, she blushed profusely, the flaming color rising to her cheeks. She was thankful he could not see her embarrassment. She was thankful that he could not read her disappointment. She had wanted more, and if he had attempted to pull at her zipper, she would have given in eagerly, baring herself willingly under the star-filled sky. She would have welcomed the crisp evening air blowing whispers across the roundness of her buttocks, the brown of her skin illuminated only by the white lights below and the faint crescent of the moon above. She gasped lightly, imagining her long legs wrapped across his back, her breasts pressed against his firm chest. Thankful she was indeed for the darkness that hid her desire from his scrutinizing gaze.

He wrapped his arm around her shoulder once again, his hip brushing against her waist as he led her back to his car. As she eased down into the seat, she searched her thoughts for something appropriate to say, something light and witty to ease out of the silence that had encased them. But she could think only of the fullness of his lips, the softness of his hands against her skin, and there were no words she could roll off her tongue that would not reveal her longing.

In the other seat he played with the radio, quickly switching from one station to another until the dulcet tones of Macy Gray flooded the car. She extended her hand, gesturing for him to let it go on. It was one of Macy's newest cuts. Marguerite loved the song even though she didn't have a clue about its title. Closing her eyes, she leaned back into the leather seat, folding her arms across her chest. Her head spun lightly as she concentrated on the music. She had not been blessed with a pleasant singing voice, and so she rarely sang, not wanting to offend anyone. It had been an ongoing joke in her family that she'd been blessed with concrete pipes for vocal cords. In the background, though, she could hear him singing along with the tune, and she noted that he had a beautiful voice, the strong tenor overtones rising from deep within. Marguerite, keenly aware of his presence, could feel him stealing glances at her.

"Why do you do that?"

"What?" he asked, slightly taken aback.

"Watch me like you do."

He laughed. "Was I watching you?"

"Yes, you were watching me," she said, opening her eyes as she shifted her body to face him. "Why do you do it?"

"Because you excite me," he said matter-of-factly. "I enjoy looking at you. I enjoy watching you get nervous when I do."

"Why?"

"Because it excites you."

Pondering his remarks, she paused briefly, then thought better about responding. Instead, she leaned back against the seat as he smiled into the darkness, reaching to brush his hand against her cheek.

Back at his condominium, he pulled his car alongside hers.

"Thank you," she said politely.

He nodded. "Come inside for a drink?"

She shook her head. "I've already had too much to drink."

"A cup of coffee then. I don't want you driving if your head isn't clear."

She thought about it briefly. She could use a cup of coffee to clear her head. "Thank you," she responded. "If it won't be too much trouble."

Inside, a digital clock purred softly, a faint light gleamed from a back bedroom, and a freshly lit fire burned briskly in the fireplace. She was lured to the warmth of the flames that crackled in swirls of reds and yellows with a faint hint of blue. "Where's John?" she questioned, sensing they were alone.

"He's spending the night at his girlfriend's. He's in transition at the moment. You see, he and Debbie

are getting married next month. They were living together, but when her mother came from Iowa to
help with the final plans, he moved in here with me
to keep the old woman from getting too upset. When
Mom's not around, he sneaks back over to get some."
Marguerite could feel him smiling. "Do you take
cream and sugar in your coffee?" he asked.

"No. I take it black, please." As he moved about
the kitchen, she turned on the stereo. "Do you like
to listen to anything in particular?" she asked as she
scanned the mess of tapes and CDs that lay strewn
on top of the shelf.

"No. Anything's fine with me," he called back.

Selecting an old Kenny G tape, she inserted it into
the lower portion of the impressive stereo system and
pushed the play button. She quickly eased into the
blast of jazz that dripped from the speakers. Sinking
to the carpet in front of the fireplace, she relished
the warmth of the flames. "Convenient of John to
leave you a fire," she said, hoping that her tone em-
bellished just the right touch of sarcasm.

He laughed. "Despite what you might think, we
did not plan this. We do it to warm the house at
night. It can be pretty expensive to heat this place,
and for the price of a Duraflame log we can usually
keep the temperature fairly comfortable without
having to turn the heat on."

"Uh-huh," she responded as he brought her a
large mug filled with dark brew. The smell was rich
and pungent and she inhaled deeply, the aroma filling her lungs. She sipped the fluid cautiously,
savoring the vibrant flavor. Taking a seat beside her,
Dexter sipped at his own mug, capped with rich
cream and a shot of Bacardi.

"Yours smells better than mine," she quipped, the familiar scent of rum teasing her nostrils.

"I don't have to drive myself home," he responded, extending his long legs out in front of him.

Focusing on the fire, she felt comfortable, the warmth of the flames and the lilt of the music intoxicating. Kicking the boots from her feet, she wriggled her toes, which had been begging for release, stretching the length of her arches. Spinning her legs around, she stretched the length of her body across the floor, laying her head into the crevice of his lap. Smiling down at her, he reached for her hand, pulling it to his lips. "It's nice to see you finally relax," he said, kissing her palm lightly.

She smiled back, stroking his chin, the impending growth ticklish against her fingertips. Pulling her knees up to rest the bottoms of her feet on the floor close to her buttocks, she dropped her hand to her stomach, lightly stroking the plush velvet of her jumpsuit between her fingers.

Neither spoke. Jazz conversed with the silence, the saxophone dancing in the darkness. With her eyes closed, she felt him playing with her hair, pushing the minute braids away from her face. She leaned into his hand as he traced the outline of her features, trailing his fingers across her eyes, past her nose, along her lips. The movement was sensual and exciting. The passion between them was rising, starting to fill every crevice of the room.

Leaning over her, he kissed her lightly, savoring the sweetness of her lips. His mouth was warm and enticing, dancing an easy glide across hers, taunting her tongue with his own. Easing her up slightly, he shifted his body to lie beside her, extending the length of his frame alongside hers. Losing herself in the embrace, she became acutely aware of his hands, which had reached timidly for her breasts, caressing the fleshy tissue easily through the fabric of her jumpsuit. Circling his arm beneath the small of her back, he nuzzled her neck, tracing the line of her ear with his tongue. His breath blew hotly against her flesh, fanning the flames that burned inside her.

Wrapping him in her thin arms, she pulled him closer, trailing her nails down his back. Rising up on his arms, he looked down at her, the light from the flames highlighting her beauty. "Stay with me tonight," he commanded, pulling at her with his eyes. "Please, stay with me." Raising her torso up to meet his, she pulled him back to her with her lips, answering him with her tongue.

As he pulled at the zipper of her jumpsuit, she could feel the rise of his masculinity pressing against her. Reaching for him, she grasped him firmly, stroking the length of him through his pants. Not moving, he leaned his forehead into her shoulder, relishing the sensation of her hands. Rising, he pulled her to her feet, dropping the confines of her clothing to the floor beneath them.

As she stepped out of her garments, kicking them aside with her feet, her breathing was deep, starting down low within her midsection, racing to blow past her parted lips. Her chest heaved ever so slightly as she studied the depths of his eyes. Dexter stood at arm's length, slowly appraising her body, his gaze reflecting his pleasure. He licked his lips lightly, and Marguerite felt as though she would fall to the floor if he didn't wrap his arms back around her. As though sensing her thoughts, he pulled her tightly to him, nestling his face between the deep rise of her cleavage, caressing the round of her backside as he entwined his fingers under the elastic of her thong. As his fingers combed through the softness of her, it was like an electrical charge she could not control. The sensation ripped her breath away. Gasping for air, she kissed him hungrily, pushing her tongue past the line of his teeth.

Sweeping her up into his arms, he carried her back to his bedroom. Kicking the door open with his foot, he dropped her gingerly onto the water bed, the huge bed frame pervading the entire room. As she rocked atop the warm cushion, she watched him strip out of his clothes, neatly folding each piece and laying it across the back of a chair.

His skin shone dark like expensive mahogany freshly polished with lemon oil. Two scars graced his chest alongside his right nipple. A faint brush of hair coated his upper body. The muscles along his back and shoulders rippled like wet sand dampened by an evening rain. Marguerite found him beautiful, and her wanting had taken control of her sensibilities.

Rising up onto her knees, she reached for him, kissing the flesh on his torso. Running her tongue across his chest, she looked up toward him, her desire etched in the furrows of her brow. Pushing her back onto the bed, he lay down beside her, searching out her mouth with his. "I'm about to explode I want you so bad," she whispered, biting lightly at his lip.

Dexter nodded, his heart racing to keep up with the adrenaline pumping through his veins. "Oh, Marguerite," he muttered, pressing his body against hers. Rolling above her, he plied her legs open easily, easing his way slowly. Marguerite gladly welcomed him as he rotated his hips, teasing her, his rhythmic strokes long and slow. Her body begged for more as she thrust her hips upward, meeting him stroke for stroke. Like two musicians, they played each other beautifully, the tempo of their rhythm rising to an intense crescendo at the exact same moment. As the spasm of their orgasms flooded through both of them, Marguerite was suddenly rocked by the reality that he wore no condom and she had used no birth control.

3

Dexter Williams rose with a start, reaching toward the other side of the bed for the warmth of her body. The room was quiet. It was dark outside, the sun still lost somewhere among the clouds. Finding his bed empty, he rose quickly, calling out her name. Getting no answer, he walked to the front window, searching the outer parking lot for her car. It was gone. Leaning against the window frame, he sighed heavily, the moonlight outside gently illuminating his naked body, the sheer curtains brushing lightly against his backside.

Stepping back out of the curtains, he yawned widely, stretching his massive arms high above his head. The fire had burned out hours ago, and the room had taken on a mild chill. Dexter shuddered, wrapping his arms around his torso. Making his way back to his bed, he wiped the sleep from his eyes, climbed under the covers, and adjusted the pillows beneath his head. Tapping his fingers lightly atop the mattress, he fought the urge to pick up the telephone and call her even though he wanted to know why she had left without so much as saying good-bye.

He inhaled deeply, the scent of her perfume and

sex gracing his body. "Sweet Marguerite," he said aloud. "What am I going to do with you?" He smiled into the darkness. He'd fallen for her the moment he'd met her, and he had fallen hard. Their first meeting had not been what he had at all expected. She ran the show with an iron fist, but beneath the staunch business demeanor she exuded raw passion.

He had not met a woman who was so intensely sensual without trying to be. It was no effort for her. It was how she walked and talked, how she held her head when she was listening intently to his ramblings, how she smiled and laughed. It was what she was.

He'd laid the charm on heavy, his behavior almost overbearing. He'd been desperate to move her past their cool business agenda toward something more personal, and she had fought him tooth and nail. Tonight had been a bonus he had only fantasized about, and she had left him hungry for more. He sighed again.

Reaching for the phone, he palmed the receiver, debating whether to call, then dropped it onto the bed beside him. "This is crazy," he thought. "She makes me feel like I'm a teenager all over again." He pulled the covers tighter around him, warding off the early morning chill.

At thirty-nine, he had never imagined any woman having the effect on him that Marguerite did. His own arrogance had put him above such a loss of control. He'd always played women the way a good musician would play an instrument. They danced to the beat of his music, not he to theirs. A permanent relationship was not something he had ever wanted.

Momentary pleasure was all he'd ever needed. Marguerite was an exception to the rules he played by, and though he did not want to admit it, it had been she who had seduced him tonight. It was she who'd been in total control, and she had pulled his strings much like a puppeteer makes a marionette dance.

Picking up the receiver again, he dialed her number quickly, fighting the nervousness that rose within his stomach. Pulling the receiver to his ear, he waited anxiously as it rang on the other end.

Bright sunshine shone into her bedroom rousing her from a deep sleep. She stretched lengthwise, pushing her arms out high above her head. The digital clock on the table beside her read ten-twenty. She cursed under her breath.

The light on the answering machine blinked incessantly, indicating five calls had come in for her. Reaching toward the machine, she pushed the play button, then rotated the knob to turn up the volume.

"Marguerite, it's Aunt Leah. Call me, honey, when you get a chance. It's important. Love you."

Beep.

"Hi, it's Dexter. Why'd you leave? I missed waking up next to you. Everything okay? Call me. Please?"

Beep.

"Where are you? It's Sharon. Call me."

Beep.

"Girl, where the hell are you? I'm just checking to make sure you made it home okay. Call me!!!"

Beep.

"Marguerite? Are you home? If I don't hear from you soon I'm going to call the police. He was some sort of freak, wasn't he? You are sitting in some jar in his refrigerator, aren't you? Call me!!!"

Beep.

She turned the volume back down. Stretching once again, she yawned widely, kicking the covers from around her feet. A wicked film graced the inside of her mouth, and the braids atop her head were irritatingly tangled. A full bladder pulled her to her feet and guided her into the bathroom. When she'd finished, she rinsed her mouth with mouthwash, then brushed and flossed each tooth till they all gleamed. After splashing her face with cool water, she turned on the shower and stepped beneath the warm spray.

Shaking her head, she cursed again. The water felt good, but did nothing to wash away the feelings of dread that flooded her. "What was I thinking?" she shouted at the faucet, the spray of water rinsing her words down the drain. She swore, loudly, the profanity echoing around the tiled walls.

After slipping into a red sweatshirt, CONNECTICUT emblazoned across the front in shades of gray, and a pair of black leggings, she reached for the telephone, curling up against the headboard, a mountain of pillows supporting her slight frame.

"Hey, Sharon."

"Where are you? I've been calling you since seven-thirty this morning."

"I'm home. I turned the volume down on the machine after I got in so that I could get some sleep," she responded.

"Mmmm. What did you do?" her friend asked knowingly.

"Nothing. It was just a long night."

"You slept with him, didn't you?"

"No," she lied, poorly.

"Bull."

"Screw you."

"I wish someone would. Was he good?"

"Damn good." They both laughed.

"I want details."

Marguerite shook her head. "Nothing to tell."

"You are such a witch."

"I'm serious. There's just nothing to tell."

"When do we get to meet him?"

"We?"

"The family. Me, your granny, the rest of the old people."

"Please," Marguerite responded, exasperated.

"Yes, please. If you slept with him, I know somebody's going to meet him."

"Can we change the subject, thank you."

"Fine. I just hope you remembered protection. I am too young to be an auntie yet and there are too many diseases out there waiting to be caught."

Marguerite shuddered, intense anxiety sweeping through her. "Of course," she lied again. "So what else is up?" she asked quickly, changing the subject.

"Not much. I've got that coalition thing tonight, but that's about it."

"Oh, yeah, the cocktail party for the art show, right?"

"Yeah. I finally found a dress. Still ain't got no date, though."

"What about Randy, or is this his weekend with his mommy?"

"Yep. The old bat sees him more than I do. Almost incestuous, if you ask me."

Marguerite smiled. "Well, look, I've got to go. Leah called and I've got to call her back. Call me tomorrow when you get home from church."

"You want to go with me? Maybe confess your sins?"

"No, thank you."

"Uh-huh. Do you think he'll call again?"

"He already has, thank you very much."

Sharon laughed. "I'll pray for you."

"Good-bye."

Depressing the hook, she dialed Dexter.

"Hello," he answered softly, his thick voice barely audible.

"Hi," she responded, suddenly embarrassed that she had called.

"I was worried about you. What happened?"

"Everything's fine. I just needed to get home."

"You could have woken me to say good-bye," he responded, a hint of attitude in his voice.

"You were sleeping too peacefully. I didn't want to disturb you."

There was a slight pause before he continued.

"I had a great time last night. You were too good to be true."

Marguerite could feel herself blushing profusely. "Thank you. I had a good time too."

"When can I see you again?"

Marguerite stuttered slightly. "I—I . . . don't . . ."

"Don't you want to see me again?"

Marguerite sighed heavily, then took a deep

breath before proceeding. "Yes, I do. But what happened last night shouldn't have. I don't usually sleep with any man on the first date."

Dexter laughed lightly. "Well, that's good to know, but it's not like it was our first date. You and I have been dating for months now."

"Lunch dates don't count."

"Well, then, I guess that makes me special, right?"

Marguerite smiled. "Exceptionally so, I guess."

"I need to ask you something. We got so wrapped up in the moment that neither of us was thinking too clearly last night."

"What?" Marguerite asked, shifting uncomfortably against the headboard.

"Do you use any type of birth control? I mean, are you on the pill or anything?"

Hesitating, Marguerite briefly thought about repeating the lie she'd just told Sharon, but thought better of it. It was not in her nature to lie so callously about things of such importance. It was different with Sharon, who knew her better than anyone else. With Sharon, the truth always came out once they were face-to-face. Sharon understood her not wanting to share everything all of the time. This was new territory for her and Dexter, and she didn't want to start it off by being dishonest.

"No," she answered. "That's another reason last night shouldn't have happened, but like you said, we weren't thinking straight."

She could feel him nodding into the receiver.

"Well, we're both to blame. I should have been wearing a condom. We'll just deal with whatever happens when and if we have to," he responded matter-of-factly. "But in case you were worried, I'm

HIV-negative. I broke down and got tested a few months ago not long after I met you. Just in case, you know?"

Marguerite nodded again, a cool chill shaking her lightly. "I've never thought about being tested. My experiences have been very limited, but I guess that's something I should go do."

"It's better to be safe than sorry. I'll go with you if you want."

Marguerite nodded into the receiver. "We'll see."

"Marguerite, no matter what may or may not happen, I want you to know that I'm going to be here to support you. If we do have to pay the price for what happened, you and I will be doing it together, so please know you can count on me."

His tone was caressing, and Marguerite did feel comfortable about trusting him. That fact unnerved her ever so slightly, but she did not want him to hear that in her voice. She cleared her throat, coughing lightly.

"Thank you, Dexter, but let's not get ahead of ourselves. We'll just have to wait and see what happens."

Dexter smiled on the other end. "Okay. Now, when do I get to see you again, lady?"

Marguerite giggled. "Well, my schedule is fairly full these days, Mr. Williams, but I guess I can squeeze you in sometime soon."

"Well, that's very good of you, Ms. Cole. How does this evening look, say around six?"

"No, I think I'm busy," she said teasingly.

"Seven?"

"Still busy."

"Seven-thirty then."

Marguerite giggled. "I guess if I have to, then seven-thirty will have to do. But don't be late, sir."

Dexter smiled into the telephone. "Not me, Ms. Cole. I promise to be very punctual. I'll see you at seven-thirty."

"I'm looking forward to it."

"Not as much as I am, madam. Not as much as I am."

After giving him directions, Marguerite hung up the telephone. As she inhaled deeply, her body shook uncontrollably, the memories of the previous evening flashing before her like scenic snapshots taken on one's vacation. She liked this man. She liked this man a lot, and she wasn't quite sure what to do about it.

Heading into the kitchen to get herself something to eat, she picked up the cordless phone in the living room and dialed her aunt. As the phone on the other end rang, she dropped two slices of bread into the toaster and reached into the refrigerator for the butter and jam.

"Hello?"

"Hi, Aunt Leah."

"Hi, Baby Girl. How are you, sweetheart?"

"Fine, thank you. I just got your message. Is everything okay?"

"No, honey. We had to take Miss Mae to the hospital last night. She wasn't doing too well."

"What happened?" Marguerite gasped, dropping the butter knife in her hand to the counter. Panic swept through her as she thought of something having happened to her grandmother while she'd been in some man's bed.

"She was complaining about chest pains and

having a hard time breathing. I didn't like the way she looked, so I took her to the emergency room. They released her this morning, but she's got to go in next week for some tests. I thought you would want to know. She's being very stubborn, though. I doubt that she will listen to a word the doctor's told her."

Marguerite sighed. "I'll go over and see her right now."

"I took her to Pat's house. She'll be there for most of the day at least. You know she doesn't want to stay there, though, but I couldn't leave her alone in that big house."

"Well, I can go stay with her, Aunt Leah."

"That's up to you, sweetie. You know if she'd let any one of us stay, it would be you. She complains that Pat and I get on her nerves."

Marguerite laughed. "She says the same thing about me."

"That's true," Leah said, laughing with her. "Well, you talk to her. I have to go to Trumball, but I'll be back by one-thirty, and I'll come right over to Pat's. We can decide then. See you later."

"Yes'm. See you later."

As Marguerite hung up the telephone, she cursed under her breath. This would mean breaking her date with Dexter. She should have returned her aunt's call first, she thought, tension rising along the back of her neck. Glancing at the clock, Marguerite pondered whether or not to call Dexter right back or wait until after she saw her grandmother. She decided to wait. Having lost her appetite, she brushed her breakfast into the trash can, wiped the bread crumbs from the counter,

then placed the butter and jelly back into the refrigerator. Pondering what was waiting for her, she
inhaled deeply, unsure of what she should do, then
opting not to give it another thought, she reached
for her jacket and purse and raced out the door.

4

Pulling into her Aunt Pat's driveway, Marguerite sighed heavily. "Looks like a family reunion," she muttered under her breath as she took inventory of all the cars parked in front of her aunt's spacious North Stamford home. Her grandmother's first cousin, Miss Minny, had parked her faded blue Chevy Impala directly behind her Uncle William's latest jet-black Cadillac. Marguerite knew that if Miss Minny was there, then at least one of her two hateful offspring, Michael or Delores, was there also. She laid odds that it was Delores. The steel-gray Volvo of Sharon's mother, Helen Donald, sat off to the side out of the way of any traffic.

Marguerite pulled her own ice-blue BMW in behind her Uncle Clarence's Honda Accord, and wondered if his latest lover had come with him. Across the street, she recognized the new Ford Taurus her Aunt Leah's husband, Martin, had just purchased, and she instinctively knew that at least two of his old cronies had accompanied him, it being Saturday and Saturday being his "I do what I darn well please" day.

Approaching the front door, she cursed under her breath as the obnoxious beep of her car alarm being set sounded behind her. "Hi, everyone," Marguerite called out through the crowded two-story Tudor-style home. As she pulled her coat from around her shoulders, she waved with feigned enthusiasm at all the menfolk who sat in the den, gathered about the television, their empty glasses and beer cans scattered about the pine tables.

In the living room, Mae Cole sat comfortably in an oversized easy chair, her plump legs lifted high up into the air, the other women seated beside her. "Hey, Mama," Marguerite said, kissing her grandmother warmly on the cheek. "What have you gone and done to yourself now, old woman?"

"Humph," Miss Mae clucked loudly. "Ain't nothin' wrong wit' me. These girls just think they gon' run me to my grave sooner than I'se ready to go and I ain't havin' none a it."

Marguerite laughed, then made her way about the room dutifully kissing and hugging her relatives.

"Where you been, Miss Freshy?"

"Pardon?" Marguerite responded, eyeing Miss Mae cautiously.

"Where you been, I said. I know Leah been trying to get you since late last night and there ain't been no answer. So where you been? And don't try tellin' me you was with my Sharon 'cause Helen done told me she ain't seen you."

Marguerite rolled her eyes. "I went out for a while, then I was home. I just had the volume on the answering machine turned down so I could get some rest."

"Rest from what?"

"Leave dat chile alone," Miss Minny piped in, a

thin thread of spittle falling down her wrinkled chin. "She grown now, so you leaves her be."

"Mind yo' business now, Minny. Ain't no one talkin' to you."

"You da one need to be mindin' they own business, Mae. Always fussin' at these chilen."

As her Aunt Pat brushed past her, she slapped at Marguerite in jest. "Now you've done it. Those two just got settled down from the last argument, and you've got them started again."

Marguerite shrugged. "Sorry."

Mrs. Donald hugged her warmly. "I hear you had a big date last night, Miss Marguerite. How was it?"

"Marguerite had a date," Miss Minny's daughter, Delores, quipped. "You hear that, Mom? Marguerite had a date last night."

"Yes, Marguerite had a date last night," Marguerite muttered, settling herself down beside Miss Mae. "My date was just fine, thank you very much."

"I know this boy?" Miss Mae asked.

"No, Miss Mae. He's just someone I know from work."

Miss Mae eyed her curiously. "When you gon' bring him by so I'se can meet him?"

"Soon, Mama."

"When?"

"I don't know when, but it'll be soon."

"When you gonna see him again?" Delores asked, shoveling a fistful of freshly popped popcorn into her mouth.

Marguerite tossed her an icy mind-your-own-business look, then shrugged.

"Well, you gonna see this boy again or not?" Miss Mae continued, asking what Delores didn't dare.

"Yes, I am. In fact, I was supposed to see him tonight."

"So?"

"So, I know you want to go back home tonight and someone is going to need to stay with you. I'll just make plans to meet him another time."

Miss Mae sucked her teeth loudly. "Now I sure don't need no baby-sitter, Miss Freshy," she stated emphatically.

"No one said you did, Mama. I just don't want you to be by yourself," Marguerite said, looking to her Aunt Pat for assistance.

"Marguerite's right, Mom," Pat interjected. "After last night, you should not be by yourself. You can always stay here with us tonight, you know."

Miss Mae rolled her eyes, sucked her teeth, then flicked her head with irritation. "I will be just fine. I do not need any of you watchin' and waitin' for me to drop dead."

Pat threw her hands into the air. "She's impossible."

"Always been like dat," Miss Minny piped in. "Been mean and evil ever since she was a little bitty thing."

"How you know?" Miss Mae asked.

"'Cause ya was always up to no good. Never had nothin' nice to say 'bout nobody. You was just evil, evil, evil," Miss Minny cackled toothlessly.

As the two drifted off, reminiscing about some escapade they'd shared decades ago, Marguerite inhaled deeply. She usually welcomed these impromptu family gatherings, but today was not one of them. She wasn't interested in Miss Minny's arthritis, and didn't particularly care about Delores's latest job loss. She didn't want to hear that her aunt had been given another promotion, nor did she want to pretend to be interested in what Uncle This said to Cousin That or how so-and-so hadn't talked to his brother since 1942.

She watched as her grandmother fluttered her dark eyelashes, rolled her brown eyes, and pretended to be interested in one of Delores's boring stories, knowing that the old woman felt like she did. Miss Mae loved her children, but she preferred the quiet of her own home, and had taught Marguerite to relish the sanctity of her own aloneness. Miss Mae had also taught her the grace of pretense when one had no other choice but to oblige those you loved most.

Marguerite turned her attention to each of her grandmother's children. Patricia, the eldest daughter, was the product of Miss Mae's first sexual encounter, a quick moment of childish groping with a man old enough to be her father. At the sweet age of sixteen, Miss Mae had brought Patricia into the world without shedding a tear or allowing a scream to ease past her lips. She had wrapped her brown bundle in the tattered sheets left by the midwife, and had risen just hours later to go help her own mother finish plowing the left field before the day's sun settled into darkness.

Patricia had grown up strapped to her mother's back, in the dusty heat of a South Carolina sun. The vast fields of an old farm had been her only playground, and she had learned how to walk among the tall cornstalks that blew gently under a Southern breeze. At the age of fourteen, Pat had left school to help her mother raise her younger siblings, who had been brought into the world under more acceptable circumstances. Her brother Clarence had been born when Pat was eight, and the twins the week before her fourteenth birthday. When the twins no longer required constant attention, she had secured a high school equivalency diploma, then had put herself through community college to obtain a teaching certificate.

Patricia had taught for years before deciding she wanted children of her own. After enduring two abusive marriages before settling on her third husband, she was still childless, except for the thirty or so small faces that faced her every morning from September to June to be taught the fundamentals of reading, writing, and arithmetic. She blamed her childless state on her husband William, who sought only to pass his time in the solace of a liquor bottle. Marguerite now watched as Patricia played hostess, setting large platters of food upon the dining room table and directing the men to go help themselves to some lunch.

In the other room, her Uncle Clarence, Miss Mae's only son, stood bored, his broad shoulders solid and square. His balding crown, the last strains of hair peppered with gray, contradicted his effeminate mannerisms and soft attributes. Miss Mae had deemed him "special," never acknowledging his homosexuality or his choice to never pass on the family name to a son of his own.

His father, Clarence Bernard Cole, had been Miss Mae's greatest love. The one man who had courted her, married her, and loved her as passionately as she did him. The man who had taken her eldest daughter as his own, giving her his name and all the love he could muster from within himself.

Clarence was a carbon copy of his father, his features strong, his coloring vivid. He had been his father's pride and joy until the day he'd been caught in an unmanly embrace with Deacon Bishop's son, Edward. His father had cursed him that day, and even on his deathbed he could not find it within himself to take his son back into his heart, having locked the boy out of his soul. It had been his only act that had ever driven a rift between him and Miss Mae.

Clarence had fought the usual prejudices faced by anyone who dared to be different, and he had always been Marguerite's favorite, forever challenging her to do and be more than she herself imagined she could be. She rose from her seat on the floor to go speak with him

"Hi, Uncle Clarence," she whispered, kissing him on the cheek.

"Hey, Baby Girl. How's it going?"

"Good. How are you?"

"I'm real good. I leave for London tomorrow, so I couldn't be better."

Marguerite laughed. "Who with this time?"

"Now," her uncle said with a chuckle, "you don't ask about my date and I won't ask who you spent the night with last night."

Marguerite could feel the color rising to her cheeks. "Is it stamped on my forehead or what?"

Her uncle laughed. "No, honey, it just runs in the family."

Their giggling was interrupted by her Aunt Leah's entrance. As the woman swept into the room, planting kisses and hugs on all those who stood still, Marguerite was suddenly struck by thoughts of her own mother, Leah's mirror image. Greer Cole had given birth to her, dropping her illegitimate bundle eagerly into a world of political rallies and marches, police raids and gang assaults. After much prodding, she had hesitantly abandoned her infant into the arms of Miss Mae to follow the righteous bantering of Marguerite's activist father, a man who sought only to fight for the freedoms offered by Newton and Cleaver and Seales and Hilliard. He had fought endlessly, wielding his anger against all who questioned the depth of his blackness and the magnitude of his heritage, belied by his milky complexion and too straight hair.

Greer's life had been cut short by a stray bullet piercing her heart as she had stood gazing into the innocent eyes of another's daughter, pondering the existence of her own child. Marguerite had been a precocious two years old at the time, and now her only memories of her mother were found within the faded pages of Miss Mae's photo albums.

Marguerite had no knowledge of her father. His last check had come when she was twelve: fifty-five dollars spent on too much candy, a striped green-and-white dress, and a pair of black patent-leather shoes.

"Marguerite Cole? What in the world have you done to your hair?" Leah screeched, startling her out of her thoughts.

"You're in for it now," Clarence whispered in her ear, extricating himself from the conversation.

"Miss Mae, did you see what this girl has gone and done to her hair?" her aunt called out.

Marguerite's hands rose to her mass of braids.

"What is the matter with my hair?" she asked self-consciously.

"Mmm," Leah murmured. "If you can't figure it out, I can't tell you."

"I like her hair," Delores said, still filling her cheeks with food. "Her hair looks fine to me. Mama, do you like Marguerite's hair?"

Both Leah and Marguerite rolled their eyes as Miss Minny turned to stare at her.

"Mae, don't she look like Beulah's chile? The one dat didn't like to comb her hair. What dat chile's name?"

Miss Mae chuckled. "You talkin' 'bout Junie. Lord, lord, lord, that girl didn't like to comb her hair. She'd start screamin' when you told her to go get the brush. Beulah use ta tear Junie's behind up to get her to sit still."

The two old women laughed heartily.

"Well, I like my hair," Marguerite stated. Her Aunt Leah continued to shake her head.

"Baby Girl," her grandmother called out to her. "Come here."

"Yes, Mama?"

"I'm gone stay here wit' Pat tonight, so you go on your date."

Surprised, Marguerite looked from Pat to Leah and back to Miss Mae. "Excuse me?"

"You heard me. I'se stayin' here tonight. Now you just call dat boy and tell him to pick you up here so I can meet him."

Marguerite smiled. "I don't think so, Mama. I am not about to subject the poor man to this crowd."

Her Uncle Clarence wrapped his arms about her

shoulders. "Don't do it, Baby Girl. These women are vicious."

"You hush, Clarence," her grandmother clucked. "And I ain't stayin here at Pat's if she don't bring him by."

"That's blackmail, Mama," Clarence continued, grinning.

"No, it ain't." Miss Mae shifted in her seat, a smug grin spreading across her face. "That just be the way it's gonna be."

"Oh, well," Marguerite uttered. "I guess you and I'll be going home tonight then."

Her grandmother flipped her hand in Marguerite's direction, laughing. "She just like me, ain't she, Minny?"

"Close, but she still ain't nearly as mean and evil as you is, Mae."

The room laughed.

"Well, tell us something about him at least," her Aunt Pat said, finally resting herself on the sofa. "Is he cute?"

"Probably too pretty," Miss Mae interjected.

Marguerite ignored her. "He's very good-looking. He's thirty-nine years old. He owns his own computer consulting firm. He's originally from Arizona, and I have no intentions of allowing you people to torture him any time soon. Any other questions?"

"She a little snippy too, ain't she," Miss Minny said.

"Right fresh she is," Miss Mae responded. "You ain't too big to get slapped, Miss Freshy," her grandmother said, directing her comment in Marguerite's direction.

Marguerite laughed and took her seat back beside the older woman. "Then beat me good so I can go."

Miss Mae patted Marguerite lightly atop her head. "If you gon' be like that, then I'se definitely goin' to my own house tonight."

"That's fine," Marguerite responded. "I'll be more than delighted to take you and stay with you."

Miss Minny chuckled loudly, a wide, toothless cackle. "I guess dey is like two peas in a pod. I swear, Mae, you has made that chile just as mean as you."

Miss Mae sucked her teeth. Clarence shook his head, laughing to himself.

Leah, coming to grasp a handful of Marguerite's braids in her thin hands, looked from her mother to her niece. "Now, Mama. You already said you were going to stay here with—"

"Well, I've changed my mind," Miss Mae interrupted, closing her eyes. "And all a you girls is gettin' on my last nerve."

"Well, that's nothing new," Pat murmured under her breath as she rose to clear away the dirty dishes.

Marguerite looked at her watch. "Aunt Pat, may I please use your phone?" she queried, rising to her feet. "I need to cancel my date."

Her aunt nodded, motioning for Marguerite to go upstairs. In the privacy of her aunt and uncle's bedroom, Marguerite dialed Dexter's number and waited anxiously for him to answer the telephone.

"Hello?"

"Hi, it's Marguerite."

"Hi. I was just about to walk out the door. What's up?"

"Just a minor change in plans. My grandmother had a bit of a scare last night. They had to take her to the hospital and I don't want her to be by herself tonight. I need to stay with her at her house. If you don't mind hanging out with an old lady until she falls asleep, I would still love to see you. Otherwise, I'm going to have to reschedule."

"Not at all. I'm anxious to meet her."

"Well, don't be too anxious. She's in one of her moods, and you may not want to see me again once she gets through with you."

Dexter laughed. "Well, I'm sure I'll have no problems winning her over. I am just such a likable kind of guy that she is going to love me. So, how do I get there?"

Before heading back downstairs, Marguerite paused in front of her aunt's mirror. Staring at her reflection, she ran her hands lightly through her hair and wondered what Dexter thought of her braids.

5

John laughed as Dexter searched the front hall closet for his black leather shoes. "So, she actually agreed to see you again, huh?"

Dexter smiled, throwing a sneaker in the direction of his friend's head. "Did you think she wouldn't?"

John shrugged, grinning broadly. "Personally, I don't know what she sees in you. I mean, she's a beautiful woman. She could probably do a lot better than you, my friend."

Dexter flipped his middle finger at him. "With a friend like you, I sure don't need any enemies." They both laughed.

"So what time did she leave?"

"I don't remember. It was late, though."

"Uh-huh. And how far did you get?"

Dexter raised his eyebrows while still digging through the mess at the bottom of the closet. "Why? You jealous?"

"Hey, I just wanted to know if you got lucky or not. I sure wouldn't have minded if it had been me. That woman had a body that could make a man cry."

Dexter stood tall, shoes in hand. "There's a lot more to that woman than you will ever know," he said, sitting down on the sofa to pull them onto his feet.

"So what are you saying? You didn't get lucky?"

"I'm saying don't go there. That woman is going to be my wife, and I will not have you or any other puny white man disrespecting her. What she and I did or did not do is my business, not yours."

John nodded. "The brother is a bit sensitive. I do believe it must be love." He smiled, extending his hand toward Dexter. "Peace be still, my friend. You know I would never purposely disrespect you, nor would I purposely disrespect your lady. And I can't help it if I'm a puny white man. So, we still be cool?"

Dexter met his friend's intense gaze, clasping the man's hand with his own. "We're still cool and you are one sick brother," he said with a laugh.

"Hangin' around you too long, and I'm glad you got lucky last night. I don't think I could have taken you too much longer if you hadn't gotten some sex from somewhere soon." He smiled.

Dexter shook his head, smiling also. "I'm going to hurt you one day." He laughed. "I don't care if you are my best friend. Keep your nose out of my business."

John smiled back. "Oh, before I forget, Shepard called looking for you. He wants you to call him."

Dexter nodded his head. "Did my big brother say what he wanted?"

"Said he's going on a trip or something and wanted to ask for a favor."

"Thanks, I'll call him tonight."

John rose, heading for the door. "I'm horny now. Think I'll go over to Debbie's and send her mother shopping or something. Talk to you later."

"Yeah," Dexter called out after him. "Get some for me too."

"Go get your own," John responded, his hand on the doorknob. "Yours is probably better than mine is anyway."

"Told you to get yourself a black woman," Dexter said, pulling on his jacket.

"Wish I could." John laughed, closing the door behind him. "But sisters aren't down with puny."

Dexter shook his head. Searching for his keys, he locked up the apartment, then headed for Stamford.

6

Dropping her bags to the floor, Marguerite sank into the depths of the old lounge chair. She sighed heavily. Sweet smells wafted from the kitchen, clouding the room with their pungent aroma. From where she sat in the living room, Marguerite could taste the rich, syrupy sweetness of Miss Mae's baked beans lathered in dark Carolina molasses and fatback, with just a hint of brown sugar. Inhaling the deep aroma, she could feel the moist, cakelike texture of freshly baked corn bread dripping with honey-butter easing down her throat, the tender threads of slow-roasted, spiced barbecue gliding past her lips.

In the distance, she could hear Miss Mae humming to herself, an old spiritual bouncing off the kitchen walls as the old woman flitted from pot to pan and back again. Closing her eyes, Marguerite took in the fullness of the woman's strong alto voice.

Pulling off her brown loafers, she stretched her long legs out in front of her, wiggling her toes. The ache in the back of her calves eased slightly as she lifted her feet onto the paisley ottoman. She inhaled deeply, three long breaths of air filling her lungs with the intense, sweet aroma. Her quiet was broken by her grandmother's clear voice calling her name.

Flipping the bright lights on in the living room, Miss Mae studied her granddaughter intently. Her dark eyes scanned the young woman from head to toe, noting that she had changed into a pair of form-fitting jeans and a print blouse tucked neatly into her waistband. Marguerite was lost deeply in her own thoughts, her eyes shut tightly, her face pained. Miss Mae dwelled on her granddaughter's fine features, her chest swelling with pride as she admired the beautiful woman the awkward child had grown into. "My, my my," the elderly woman thought to herself. "My baby would have been so proud of her." Sucking her teeth slightly, she broke the silence.

"Baby Girl, when you get back? How you come in my house, girl, and don't say nothin'?" she asked, finally speaking aloud.

"I'm sorry, Miss Mae. I didn't mean to scare you."

"Girl, you ain't scare me. I just wanna know where dem manners I taught you went to," she responded, flicking a dish towel in Marguerite's direction.

Rising, Marguerite hugged her grandmother warmly. "I really am sorry. I just walked in and I needed a quick moment to myself. I didn't mean to be rude."

"Just as long as you knows betta," her grandmother said, kissing her lightly on her cheek. "Come eat. I'se got plenty of food and it's hot."

Marguerite followed her grandmother into the next room. "Why'd you cook? Aunt Pat offered to wrap up some food for you to bring home."

"Don't none a you girls know how to cook right,"

Miss Mae grunted. "I tried hard to teach all a ya and ain't a one of you any good at it. I made my own dinner."

"I can cook, Mama, and Uncle Clarence cooks good too," Marguerite stated as the woman's robust frame moved easily about the kitchen.

"Dat fancy stuff don't count. I'm talkin' down-home cookin'. Can't none a you do dat right. Clarence comes close, but he still needs to work at it."

Miss Mae shook her head, swatting a towel in Marguerite's direction. Marguerite marveled at her spryness. Miss Mae dashed about gathering glasses and silverware. Pulling two plates from the cabinet, she set the aged china on the table, two red place mats beneath them. Marguerite reached over the old woman's shoulders to pull a third set out of the cupboard.

Miss Mae watched as Marguerite set the table with the silverware she had been handed, adding the third setting. "I missin' somethin'?" she asked as she filled a melange of dishes with the warm food, placing them onto the center of the table.

"No, Mama. I just asked my friend to join us is all. I didn't think you'd mind. He should be here any minute now."

Miss Mae nodded, slightly surprised. She had sensed the girl's anxiousness, and had been per-plexed when she thought Marguerite had been too willing to forgo a second encounter with this man to spend the evening with her. She was pleased to see such was not the case.

"Well, put the food in the oven until he get here then so it don't get cold," she said heading for the living room. Marguerite did as she was told, then followed her grandmother inside. Miss Mae sat comfortably in her easy chair, rocking her body slightly to and fro. Marguerite sat down on the sofa, stretching the length of her legs atop the cushions.

Looking about the room, Marguerite noted that the elderly woman had replaced her summer drapes with her fall set. The peach fabric hung heavy with starch from the high rods, the color having faded harshly from years of being hung, dry-cleaned, packed away, and rehung again. Marguerite made a mental note to purchase the woman a new set the next time she went shopping.

In Marguerite's thirty-five years, the room had not changed, except for the addition of a new family picture here or there. The curtains were always the same, changing only with the seasons. The white and yellow floral set during the spring, the sheer white panels during the heat of the summer, the peach ones for autumn, and right after the Thanksgiving holiday, the plush burgundy velvet drapes, which hung until the first crocus pushed its purple head past the damp, rich earth.

The tweed sofa and love seat, each draped with one of her great-grandmother's quilts, sat against the far walls, the brown tweed now as faded from age as the curtains. One end table and a coffee table carved lovingly by her late grandfather's hands and his paisley easy chair and ottoman, which now sat as a tribute to his memory, completed the furnishings.

Family photos graced the tops of the tables and the walls. Photos as yellow with age as the tweed fabric of the furniture. Marguerite stared lovingly at pictures of kin whom she knew only through Miss Mae's memories. History stared back at her through dark eyes that told stories of hard times and good times and tears and laughter.

Marguerite ran her fingers lightly across the glass frame encasing her great-grandmother's reflection, reveling in how much she took after the woman whose stern gaze belied the softness that epitomized the woman's character. Her favorite photo was that of her grandparents, young and in love, posed stiffly in front of his first car. Miss Mae had been filled with adoration for this tall man who held her firmly clasped within his arms, her affection etched in the smile upon her face.

"So what's da matta wit' you?" Miss Mae asked, breaking the silence.

Marguerite shrugged. "Just tired."

"And dat's it?"

Marguerite shrugged again. "I really don't know, Mama. I just seem to be missing something I guess."

"You needs a husband," Miss Mae stated, still rocking.

Marguerite laughed. "I don't think that's my problem, Miss Mae."

"Now what I say? If you had a man and some babies of your own to look after instead of givin' all your time to that job, you'd be a lot happier."

Marguerite shook her head. "I like my job and well, as far as kids go . . ." She shrugged, not needing to finish her thought.

Miss Mae sucked her teeth. "Foolishness. You like me. You might think bein' a big-time 'secutive is gon' make you happy, but it ain't. You a porch rocker. Just like me, just like my mama was. You need to be rockin' your days away with a baby on your chest, shellin' peas to put in your husband's belly."

Marguerite rolled her eyes at her grandmother. "If that's so, why did you spend all that money for me to go to college? You could have just married me off and been done with it."

"Sure coulda, but you needed to have options. Everybody needs options. Now you just needs a man."

"Easier said than done," said Marguerite.

"Well, if you didn't waste so much a your time on dem pretty mens you keep going out wit', you wouldn't have dat problem."

Marguerite chuckled again.

"What about Mr. Munson's boy Arthur? Now he a good boy for you."

"Mama, please," Marguerite responded. "If I ever have to settle for a pathetic excuse like Arthur Munson, then just shoot me and put me out of my misery."

"Ain't nothin' wrong with Arthur. He just ain't pretty like dem men you keeps wastin' yo' time wit'. Now what about dis boy you got comin' tonight?"

Marguerite sighed. "I don't know. I like him, but I'm worried that our going out might jeopardize our business relationship."

"Chile, please. It's a bit late for dat, don't you think? Besides, a good black man is too hard to find for you to be worryin' about yo' bizzness relationship. Now my Sharon done found herself a good man, and I hopes to see both of you married with at least two babies befo' I die, so you betta gets ta work on it."

"You like Randy?" Marguerite asked, referring to her best friend's current love interest.

"He a good boy. Too skinny, but he a good decent boy."

"You only like him because he's always kissing up to you whenever he's around."

"It don't hurt him to show me some respect."

"Well, sometimes I think Sharon can do better than Randy, even if I did fix them up with each other."

"'Cuz you ain't got no man."

Before Marguerite could comment, the doorbell rang. They both jumped, startled from where they sat.

As Marguerite reached the door to let Dexter in, Miss Mae came to her feet to stand politely.

Marguerite held the door open for Dexter, and as he swept into the room he stopped to kiss her gently on the cheek, squeezing her shoulder lightly as he did. Marguerite smiled warmly.

"Hi, beautiful," he murmured into her ear, conscious of the older woman's presence.

"Hi, please come in." Taking him by the elbow, Marguerite led him into the center of the room to stand before Miss Mae's scrutinizing gaze. "Miss Mae, this is Dexter Williams. Dexter, this is my grandmother, Mae Cole," Marguerite said, completing the formal introductions.

"Good evening, Mrs. Cole. I hope I'm not intruding this evening."

"No, no, not at all," Miss Mae said, losing her hand within Dexter's massive grasp. "It's a pleasure to meet you and please, call me Mae," she said primly.

"Thank you. It's a pleasure meeting you also."

"I hope you're hungry," Marguerite said as she

took Dexter's coat. "Miss Mae cooked and we were just about to sit down to eat a little something. I set an extra plate for you just in case."

"I am," Dexter responded, "and it smells wonderful."

Dexter and Marguerite followed as Miss Mae led the way into the kitchen. Gesturing for him to take the seat at the head of the table, Miss Mae filled three tall glasses with iced tea tinted lightly with lemon as Marguerite set the food back onto the table. Settling herself in a chair beside Marguerite, Miss Mae gestured in Dexter's direction. "Dexter, would you bless the table, please?"

Bowing her head in prayer, her parched lips mouthing absolutely nothing, she waited only for Dexter's prayer, not wanting any other response. Marguerite smiled at her friend, then followed suit, dropping her chin to her chest. Dexter did likewise, then with a quiet grace, gave thanks for the meal before them, asking that the food and they all be touched by God's blessings.

"Amen," Miss Mae said aloud, reaching for the bowl of beans. Filling her plate, she then passed the bowl to Dexter. "So," Miss Mae said, "you come from Connecticut, Dexter?"

"No, ma'am. I was born in Chicago, but I was raised in Arizona, in Tucson."

Miss Mae nodded. "I ain't never been to Arizona. You ever been there, Marguerite?"

"Last year, on business, Mama."

Under the table, Dexter's leg brushed lightly against Marguerite's. Out of the corner of her eye she saw him smile, could feel him teasing her as he continued to make conversation with her grandmother, the marble of his voice like a thick, dark fluid flowing eagerly.

As they ate freely, biting into thick slices of corn bread, dabbing at their plates to absorb the rich juices, he talked of his travels, and his family, his friends, and his ambitions, and with each sentence that fell from his full lips, Miss Mae studied him, debated with him, and understood what Marguerite saw in him. Marguerite knew the look in her grandmother's eye, and as Dexter made Miss Mae laugh, at one point bringing her to wipe faint tears from their corners, Marguerite imagined the words upon the woman's lips that etiquette would not allow her to utter until he was hours away. "Too pretty. Too smooth. Too . . . too . . . too . . ."

Marguerite swallowed the food in her mouth, rinsing the last bite down with a large gulp of tea. "We'll clean up the dishes, Miss Mae. You need to get some rest," she said, sweeping the empty plates into the sink.

Miss Mae sighed heavily before responding. "You right, Baby Girl. It been a long day." Rising from the table, she extended a wrinkled hand toward Dexter. "Dexter, please come by again. It was real nice meetin' you."

"Thank you," he responded, rising to his feet. "Everything was delicious, Miss Mae. Thank you for having me."

As the woman eased herself out of the room, she called back over her shoulder.

"Marguerite, do me a favor and run by da liquor store and play my numbers for me tomorrow, okay?"

"You said you weren't playing the numbers anymore."

"I ain't. I just had a dream this afternoon that Jesus was walkin' wit me down Route 106 headin' fo' heaven. I know it's a sign, so I want you to go play it fo' me is all."

"Then you're still playing the numbers," Marguerite stated matter-of-factly, the tips of her fingers starting to wrinkle in the water. She could feel her grandmother's reproachful glance piercing her back. Shaking her head in exasperation, Marguerite reached for a cotton dishcloth to dry the dampness from her hands. "A dollar straight and a dollar boxed?"

"Yes, and tell Mr. Munson and his son I said hello."

As Miss Mae mounted the stairs, Dexter wrapped his arms lovingly around Marguerite, kissing her warmly. Marguerite allowed her hands to roam freely along his back, resting just above the curve of his derriere.

"So, how'd I do?" he asked.

"I fell for it, but she's a hard lady, Miss Mae is. Only time will tell."

Dexter laughed, kissing her again.

Pushing him away, she passed him the dish towel. "You dry."

Side by side, they stood doing the dishes, the low hum of the refrigerator echoing about the room. Rinsing the soap from each dish, Marguerite shook her head laughing as Dexter spun story after story of his exploits. With all the dishes dried and placed back on the shelves where they belonged, Dexter tossed the damp dishcloth across the countertop and guided her back into the living room. Upstairs, they could hear Miss Mae humming loudly to herself as she settled down for the night.

Dexter pulled her down onto the love seat beside him, hugging her tightly. Wrapping his lips around hers, he played with her emotions, rousing light moans of pleasure as he stroked the length of her body.

"You need to stop," she sputtered when he finally allowed her to come up for air.

"Only if you really want me to," he whispered, his hands still roaming.

He smiled widely, the white of his teeth gleaming brightly. At that moment, she felt as if he could read every perverse thought that crossed her mind.

"Why are you here?" she asked, wanting to know what motivated him.

"I wanted to be with you," he responded, pulling her closer.

"For the sex?"

Dexter stared at her, his expression questioning. "Is that what you think?"

"I don't know what to think. It all seems to be happening too fast."

He nodded slowly, his thoughts flooding the warmth of his face like ice water atop hot coals. Rising to his feet, he reached for his coat.

"Thank you. I had a nice time tonight," he said politely, squeezing her hand beneath his.

"I'm sorry. Did I say something wrong?" Marguerite asked, suddenly confused.

Dexter took a deep breath before shaking his head. He kissed her on the lips, barely brushing the surface of her mouth with his own. "I'm flying to New Orleans tomorrow. We're interviewing new reps for the Southern region this week. I'll call you during the week and maybe we can make plans for the weekend, okay?"

Marguerite nodded, conscious of the wall of tension that had risen between them.

Dexter pulled her close again, nuzzling his face into her hair, then walked to the door. Pausing, his hand on the knob, he turned to face her one last time, studying the lines of her face intensely.

"How long have we known each other?" he asked her.

"It's been over nine months at least."

"How many times have we gone to lunch on those lunch dates that weren't real dates?"

Marguerite shrugged, biting at her bottom lip. "Too many times to count them."

"And how long have I been trying to get you to make this relationship more personal?"

Marguerite hesitated, thinking back to how he had pursued her, encouraging her to let go of her reservations, to express what she was feeling but refused to share. Her eyes met his pensive stare, then fell.

Dexter cupped his hand beneath her chin and lifted her gaze to meet his. "It isn't and has never been about sex, Marguerite. Yes, we made love last night, and it was the most incredible experience. I have never felt about any woman the way I feel about you. And even if I hadn't been intimate with you, I would still feel the same way. You are going to have to learn to trust me. And more than that, you've got to learn to trust yourself." Kissing her one last time, he stroked her cheek, his caress soothing. "I will call you."

Marguerite clung to the front door as Dexter

made his way down the walkway to his vehicle. As he climbed inside and started the ignition, she could feel the threat of tears rising to her eyes. She inhaled deeply, her hand still clutched tightly around the doorknob. It was only after he'd driven off and she could no longer see the reflection of his taillights that she could move herself to close the door and lock it securely behind her.

As Dexter pulled his car onto the Merritt Parkway, he shook his head. His thoughts were preoccupied with Marguerite, and he was angry that the first time he wanted, no, needed, a woman to trust his sincerity, she didn't. Had it been any other woman, she would have been right. He would probably have only been there for the sex, but not with Marguerite. Although the sex was exceptional and he found his excitement rising just standing next to her, it was not at all what he sought from her. He wanted more, needed more, and he wondered what he would have to do to prove it.

7

Marguerite tapped her foot anxiously as she waited for her uncle to pick up the telephone. Upstairs, Miss Mae slept peacefully, her robust body wrapped in a large down comforter, liniment rubbed into her chest, her hair pinned in neat plaits.

Clarence answered the phone, sleep tinting the edge of his voice. "Hello?"

"I'm sorry, Uncle Clarence. I didn't mean to wake you."

"It's okay, Baby Girl. What's wrong? Mama okay?"

"Miss Mae's fine. She upstairs sound asleep."

"What time is it?"

"Not quite eleven-thirty."

"It's late. I didn't realize I'd fallen asleep. I still have to finish packing."

"What time's your flight?"

"Nine-thirty. My limousine should be here around seven."

Marguerite tightened her grip on the receiver. "Uncle Clarence. I need your advice."

"Must be serious. Who is he?"

"The guy I went out with last night."

"The one you spent the night with, you mean?"

Marguerite nodded, oblivious to the fact that her

uncle could not see her through the telephone. "Yeah."

"He must be very special."

"He's a great guy. Almost too great, and I think I really messed up."

"What in the world did you do?"

Marguerite paused, suddenly embarrassed. "I asked him a stupid question. I asked him if he was only with me for the sex, and I think I offended him. Now I don't know what to do."

"You don't do anything. If you're right and it is only for the sex, he probably won't call back, and even if he does, he'll just expect you to put out again. If you were wrong, he'll call and he'll go out of his way not to have sex with you just to prove you were wrong."

"You think so?"

"Baby Girl, trust me. Your Uncle Clarence has been with enough men to know what I'm talking about. And you aren't stupid. You know if he really cares about you or not."

"I guess."

"Are you sure it wasn't you who was just in this for the sex? It has been a long time, if I recall."

"No, and it hasn't been that long. Well, maybe it's been a while."

"Just use some common sense and you'll be okay."

Marguerite nodded. "So who's the guy you're going off with tomorrow? Anyone I know?"

Clarence laughed. "Not yet. Just someone I've known for a while who's decided to stop hiding in the closet. If it's going anywhere, I promise you'll be the first to meet him. At the moment we're just very good friends."

Marguerite laughed back. "I love you, Uncle Clarence, and thank you. You have a nice trip."

"I love you too, Baby Girl. Stay sweet and I'll call you when I get back."

As Marguerite hung up the phone, she smiled broadly. Even when he had no clue what he was talking about, Clarence always made her feel better. Rising, she checked the lock on the front door, shut off all the lights, and headed up the stairs.

Peeking into her grandmother's room, she watched as the elderly matron slept comfortably, a peaceful expression gracing her face. Leaning down to kiss the woman's forehead, Marguerite tucked the covers neatly around her. Miss Mae's breathing was even and steady, and as Marguerite watched the rhythmic rise and fall of the matriarch's chest, she was comforted. Miss Mae's presence always brought her comfort. As she turned to exit, pausing momentarily to take one last look, she thought better of it and instead curled up on the other side of the bed, curving her body around the old woman's, and drifted off to sleep.

As Dexter pulled his car into his parking space, he noticed Shepard's SUV parked across the way. As he stepped from behind the driver's seat, his brother exited from his own vehicle. Dexter could see him smiling shyly in the distance.

"Hey, you," Dexter called out, extending his large hand. "How long have you been waiting?"

Shepard Williams shook his younger brother's hand, wrapping him in a quick hug as he did. "Not long. How are you doing?"

Dexter nodded his head. "Doing really well."

"You're home early. I actually wasn't expecting to see you tonight. Figured you had a hot date."

Dexter laughed. "Well, it was an interesting one, but let's go inside. It's cold out here."

Shepard followed behind him.

As Dexter flipped on the lights, he noticed the anxiety gracing Shepard's face. He immediately sensed that this was not one of his brother's casual just-dropped-by-to-say-hello calls.

"So, what's up?"

Shepard dropped onto the living room sofa, twisting his hands nervously. "Well, I'm going away for a few days and I wanted to speak with you before I left."

"Everything okay?"

Shepard nodded. "Yeah, fine, sort of."

Dexter sat alongside him. "So talk. What's eating you?"

Shepard rose, pacing the room. Dexter studied him anxiously, the distress pasted across his brother's brow unnerving. Shepard was exactly twelve years older than Dexter was, and Dexter was usually the one going to cry on Shepard's shoulder. In fact, Shepard had been privy to the Marguerite saga since the day Dexter had met her. He was not use to their roles being reversed.

Their parents, Charles and Olivia Williams, had been killed in a car accident the week before Dexter's twentieth birthday, leaving the two of them alone to support each other. They had no other family. Shepard had been married briefly when Dexter was still in high school, but that had not lasted long. Neither of them had ever had any children, although Dexter had experienced his share of close calls. They were the Williams boys, and they had always stuck together like glue through everything.

"You're starting to scare me," Dexter said. "Are you okay?"

Shepard nodded. "I'm sorry. I've been practicing this all day and now I feel really . . ." He shrugged his broad shoulders, not finishing his thought.

Dexter lifted his hand, gesturing for him to continue.

Shepard sat back down next to his brother, inhaling deeply. "I've met someone and we're going away together. I wanted to let you know where you could reach me, just in case."

Dexter laughed, his eyes darting back and forth. "Is that it? You were nervous about telling me you're going away to get laid. What's it been? Twenty years since you gave up the dirty deed, big brother? You forget what to do and need to ask for some pointers? Need to borrow some condoms?"

Shepard shook his head. "Don't joke. This is serious. And it's not like that. We're just good friends."

Dexter slapped his brother's leg. "Has my big brother fallen in love? Who is she? Do I know her?"

Shepard rose again, crossing to the other side of the room. He stuffed his hands deep into his pockets. "I've met a man, Dexter. A man I think I've fallen in love with."

Dexter looked up stunned. He could not comprehend what his brother was trying to tell him. Shepard continued to talk. "I've known ever since I was real young that I was gay. I've tried to deny it. I've gone to counseling, gone to the Church, but nothing has ever changed. Mom knew, but of course there was no way we could have ever let Dad know."

Shepard exhaled. "I didn't know how to tell you, Dex. I didn't know how you'd react, but I'm tired of pretending. I'm too old to keep pretending. I want to be happy. I want to share my life with someone. I need to have someone love me."

Shepard took a deep breath, waiting for Dexter to say something. Dexter sat, his mind racing. This was too much for him to have to deal with. There was no way possible for him to understand what his brother was trying to tell him. He rose from where he sat.

"Where are you staying?"

"I'm flying to London. I'll be at the Britannia Hotel." Shepard reached into the pocket of his wool blazer and pulled out a small scrap of paper. "I've written all my flight information and the telephone numbers here." He dropped the paper onto the coffee table.

Dexter nodded. "Well, I shouldn't have any problems, but I'll call if anything comes up."

Shepard reached out to rub his brother's shoulder. "We can talk more when I get back, okay?"

"Yeah, yeah. Okay," Dexter said, pulling away from the embrace. "When you get back."

Shepard headed for the door, looking back over his shoulder quickly. Dexter had not moved from where he stood, his expression stunned. Instinctively, Shepard knew that he had not taken the news well and he himself had yet to experience the fallout. He sighed heavily, then closed the door behind him.

The stewardess leaned across the first-class seat, shaking Dexter lightly. "Mr. Williams, the plane is about to land. If you'd please return your seat to the upright position and put on your seat belt."

Dexter looked up into her smiling face, stunned that he had fallen asleep and had slept so deeply. He nodded, wiped the line of drool from his mouth, then returned her broad smile with a weak bending of his own lips. She grinned again, squeezing his arm gently before continuing up the aisle.

As Dexter stared out the window to the land rising toward him, he thought of Shepard, wondering if his brother's journey was more eventful than his. Wondering who it was that sat at his brother's side, companion and not a stranger.

How could he be thirty-nine years old and not know his fifty-one-year-old brother was gay? It made no sense. Shepard had always been macho in his mannerisms. There had never been anything feminine in his nature to indicate such a predilection. If you disregarded his obsession with his hair or the loss there of, there was nothing in his demeanor that would make one suspect he was queer.

Dexter sighed heavily. Queer. He had just labeled his brother queer. Something was not right about that, and he was suddenly ashamed of himself. But wasn't that what his brother was? Others would certainly paste the tag on him and even worse. Dexter slapped his fist against his thigh. How was he supposed to handle this, and why had Shepard waited until now to tell him?

As the plane touched down, Dexter's thoughts were still with his brother. He had so many questions to ask, and now he regretted having thrown Shepard's telephone number into the trash. Once settled into his hotel room, Dexter grabbed the telephone and dialed quickly. As he waited anxiously for the other end to pick up, he found himself biting uneasily on his nails. "I'm losing it," he thought to himself, pulling his fingers from his mouth. "I'm really losing it."

Marguerite finally picked up on the other end. "Hello?"

"Hi."

"Hi, yourself. Where are you?"

"New Orleans. I just got in."

"How was your flight?"

"Okay. Look," Dexter asked anxiously, "would you be interested in flying down here this weekend and joining me? My treat."

Marguerite hesitated.

"Please. I need to be with you. I'll even spring for a second room if that will make you more comfortable."

The pause was brief. "I'd love to and two rooms isn't necessary. Twin beds will do."

Dexter sighed.

"You were supposed to laugh. I meant that as a joke."

"Ha ha ha," he replied unenthusiastically.

"Are you okay?" Marguerite asked, suddenly concerned, his anxiety evident in his crisp voice.

"No. I just need you. I just found out . . ." Dexter dropped to the edge of the bed, lowering his head in his hands. Inhaling deeply, he caught his breath, fighting not to display any emotion he would not be able to handle. "I'll have my secretary call you with all your flight arrangements. Can you leave on Thursday?"

"If you really need me to I will, but Friday morning would be better. I'm supposed to give a presentation on Thursday."

Dexter nodded. "How about Thursday afternoon, late but not too late?"

"I think I can swing that."

"Are you sure?"

"Yes. But if you need me before then you call, okay?"

"I promise," Dexter responded, then paused momentarily. "Marguerite?"

"Yes?"

"I . . . nothing. I'll see you soon."

Hanging up the telephone, Marguerite stared off into the distance. There was an edge to his voice that she had never heard before, and she found it unsettling, wondering what had him so upset.

Crossing to the other side of the room, she switched on the stereo, pulling off her navy business suit and dropping it across the back of the wing chair. It had been an overly long day and she was tired, exhaustion pressing at her temples. What she needed was a hot shower, she thought, heading into the bathroom, stopping just long enough to drop in an Aretha Franklin CD and turn the music up loud.

8

Someone had gone to great pains to make the sterile room more personable. A delicate floral arrangement had been painted in watercolors across the ceiling and down one stark white wall. As Marguerite stretched her body across the reclined table, she found the flowers calming, the serene colors intensely soothing. She closed her eyes, inhaling deeply. The starched green medical gown, left open in the front, was suddenly irritating, and she attempted to pull the garment closer around her. She felt very self-conscious about being so exposed. A visit to the gynecologist hadn't been a part of this month's plan, but her involvement with Dexter had made it a necessity.

Dexter. Just the mere thought of him brought a smile to Marguerite's face. She could feel his touch even when he wasn't present, the sensation of his hands having burned an imprint against her flesh. When she sat still enough, it was as if he were sitting beside her blowing warm breath against her neck, over her shoulders, and down the length of her arms. She felt possessed, as though her whole person was under the spell of something not quite natural. The man had awakened sensations that she hadn't known she possessed, and the emotions that rode shotgun frightened her. A warm rush flooded her body, almost orgasmic in nature. Dr. Quentin Smith's entrance intruded upon her thoughts, and Marguerite felt herself blushing.

"Marguerite Cole, good morning." The balding black man smiled, flipping through the chart he'd taken from a holder on the door.

"Hi, Dr. Smith. How are you?" Marguerite asked, raising to a sitting position, her hands clutching the gown closed.

"I'm well, thank you. So what brings you here today?" Dr. Smith asked, taking a seat at the foot of the table.

Marguerite inhaled deeply. "Well, I figured it would be a good idea to get a checkup. I need to go back on the pill and thought it would be smart to make sure everything is okay."

The doctor nodded, making some notations on her chart. Marguerite studied him as she always did. He'd been her doctor since she'd been eighteen and Miss Mae had insisted she go see him. His crisp, clean-cut features and staunch demeanor reminded her of Sidney Poitier in the movie *To Sir with Love.* She'd always thought him to be attractive, and he had a wonderful bedside manner that instantly calmed her. All the women in her family had made regular visits to his office in their lifetime, so he was definitely no stranger to her. She and Sharon jokingly called him the "beaver-ologist," an expression her grandmother had not found particularly humorous. Marguerite giggled out loud. Dr. Smith looked up at her and smiled.

"Is it that funny?"

"I'm sorry. That was rude. I was just thinking that you must be glad I'm the last of the Cole women."

Dr. Smith smiled again. "Oh. I thought perhaps you and Miss Sharon had come up with another clever nickname for me. Wasn't I some animal or something the last time I saw you?"

Marguerite blushed. Either Miss Mae had told their secret, or Sharon had been talking out of turn again. Marguerite guessed it to be Miss Mae. "I can't believe my grandmother told you. I am so embarrassed. But Sharon was the one who made it up, not me." Marguerite pouted slightly. The only thing missing to complete her school-brat look was the hands resting defiantly on the hips. But she was still clutching the medical gown closed, reluctant to let go. Unable to resist, she laughed again, loudly, the sound bouncing off the walls.

Dr. Smith laughed with her, shaking his head. "And no," he said, regaining his composure. "I definitely have not gotten my fill of the Cole women. You're one of my favorite families. No one makes a sweet-potato pie like your grandmother does. Besides, I was hoping to still be around to welcome a daughter of yours into the troops."

Marguerite rolled her eyes. "I don't think so. That's why I'm here, remember?"

The man nodded, smiling. "So are you sexually active, or are you just planning to be?"

The young woman blushed ever so slightly. "Active, and I have to be honest and tell you I had a recent encounter where I was unprotected. My cycle came right on schedule, so I'm not pregnant, but I figured I should get an HIV test just to be safe."

Dr. Smith nodded, his expression never changing. "So you think you may have reason to be concerned?"

Without hesitation, Marguerite shook her head. "My partner has been tested and he's negative, but I just want to make sure all is still well with me and with him."

"Smart girl. It's always best to be safe these days, Marguerite. We'll do an exam and take those tests. I want to give you a pregnancy test also. Just to be sure. Then you and I should probably sit down and talk in my office to discuss all the possibilities and what your options are. Okay?"

Nodding, Marguerite lay back down against the table. "Sounds like a plan, Dr. Smith. Sounds like a plan."

9

Sharon watched her as she dropped mounds of raw dough into a pot of hot cooking oil. The sweet smell of frying doughnuts quickly filled the room. Marguerite's best friend smiled slyly, shaking her head.

"It must be love," she said, shaking powdered sugar over the crisp confections as Marguerite lifted the warm pastry onto a clean plate.

"Please."

"Well, it must be something. It's got you cooking."

Marguerite laughed. "I just wanted to try the recipe. It doesn't mean a thing."

"Uh-huh."

"He called last night from New Orleans. He wants me to fly down tomorrow and spend the weekend with him."

"Well, are you going?"

"My flight's at three."

"You are too much for me, girl. I get to go to Randy's mother's house for the weekend and you get to go to New Orleans."

"How is his mother?"

"Fine. Spends all her time babying him, though."

"Don't complain. At least *you* don't have to do it."

Sharon laughed. "Yeah, I guess it could be worse."

Turning off the flame under the pot, Marguerite pulled the last of the fried fritters from the pan. She and Sharon sat comfortably at the table over the warm platter, consuming the hot doughnuts eagerly.

"If I keep eating like this, my butt is going to be as wide as a house," Marguerite said, filling her mouth.

"Your butt is already wide as a house."

"Thank you."

"You're welcome. So tell me more about Dexter."

"Girlfriend, the brother has got my nose wide open. I can't breathe when I'm with him. It is just too good to be true."

"Doesn't sound healthy to me."

"It's not. I can't believe I actually slept with him like I did. No protection. No nothing. I have never done anything like that, not even when I was in school," Marguerite said, shaking her head in disbelief.

"Well, don't look at me. I've only done it once, and we both know where that got me. Brother turned out to be a major waste. He was cheap, tacky, and had the sexual skills of a beached whale."

They both laughed.

"Well, Dexter's not tacky. I don't think he's cheap, and he's got good, real good, too, too good sexual skills."

They laughed again.

"Seriously, Marguerite," Sharon said, the smile on her face falling into a broken line of concern. "Go slow with this. You don't know much about him. Make sure you're doing this for the right reasons, please. I know it's been a long time since you last had a man, but don't get yourself so wrapped up in how good he makes you feel that you're blind to when he doesn't make you feel good. You don't need to waste your time making any mistakes. Don't forget that last fiasco with Anthony What's-his-name."

Marguerite pushed herself away from the table, rising to go stand by the sink. Sharon rose from her seat in the kitchen, doughnut plate in hand, and headed into the living room, plopping down onto the sofa.

"I don't know what's happening yet with me and Dexter, but I don't plan to make any mistakes if I can avoid it. Anthony has long been laid to rest, so I don't know why you even brought his name up. And please, don't tell your mother I'm going to New Orleans with Dexter. I don't want the old people to know yet."

Sharon shrugged. "I don't know a thing. I'll be in Springfield, so you are on your own. Just please be careful. I mean, just because he wears a suit and tie and carries a briefcase—three very important elements in my book, of course—doesn't mean he isn't a psychopath."

Stacking the dishes into the dishwasher, Marguerite wiped the counters clean, clearing away the mess she'd made. Heading into the living room, she dropped her body onto the sofa beside Sharon. Engrossed in a pro basketball game on TV, the two women sat together for some time eating doughnuts. As they got into the excitement of the game, they'd spring from their seats, bouncing about the room. Their energy filled the air.

"Did you see that pass? What was Chris Childs doing?" Marguerite asked.

"Playing ball. It's not his fault no one on that team can catch."

"Please." Marguerite rolled her eyes. "Did you see the game between Orlando and Houston last night?"

"Caught the end of it. I had a meeting down at the Board of Ed. The new superintendent was telling more lies about what he's not planning to do for our minority students."

Marguerite shook her head. "Do you remember those old Nike commercials with the little Penny doll?"

"The little what?"

"The little Penny doll. Penny Hardaway?"

"Don't say it." Sharon grinned.

"I wish I had me one of those Penny dolls. It was too cute. They haven't had any good commercials since then."

Sharon laughed. "You ain't got no sense."

Marguerite laughed with her. "Check it out. You know you want you a little Penny doll too."

"Might want me a big Penny doll."

"For what? Brother ain't got no meat on his bones. You'd hurt him."

"I'd like to. You would too if you could."

"Not my type. I had my eye on Rodman before he took off."

Sharon laughed hysterically. "To do what with? Give him some makeup tips or lend him a dress? Besides, brother got him a white woman now."

Marguerite swatted her hand at Sharon. "I want to ride on the back of his bike. I'd wrap my arms around his waist, maybe run my hands up his thighs at a stoplight and just give him a taste of what this sister could do for him."

"Go right on. Personally, I think you should just

give his wife a 'Thank You for Saving a Sister' T-shirt. That is one brother who scares me. I wouldn't remember what to do if I found myself locked in a room with him. Would probably die on the spot."

"Yeah, but I'd bet you'd die happy."

Their laughter rang through the room.

"So what's up with you and the Orlando Magic?" Sharon asked. "I thought your heart belonged to the Knicks."

"I'm still loyal. I had to go through some major withdrawal when they traded Charles Smith, though. That's been how long now, and I still haven't gotten over it. Then they turn around and lose Patrick Ewing. I don't know about you, but I haven't gotten any major warm and fuzzy over all the new guys. Since that strike fiasco and then Jordan leaving Chicago, the game hasn't been the same."

Sharon shrugged her shoulders, taking a quick sip from her glass. "Well, I'm still a Knicks fan. The rest of them just don't measure up. Never have, never will."

"Yeah, that and you still have a thing for Chris Childs."

"Don't talk about my Childs. The man takes my breath away. Not like Patrick, though. I bet five minutes with Patrick Ewing and a woman would change religions. Shaquille too, for that matter. I bet that other brother, what's his name . . . Barkley, Charles Barkley, got it goin' on too. Religion-changin' men." Sharon nodded vigorously.

Marguerite giggled loudly. "How would you know?"

"I've heard about big men like them," Sharon said, still nodding. "Big man like that would have you praying like you have never prayed before. In fact, you told me. You always manage to find them big brothers. Now a man like Shawn Kemp is more my speed."

"Shawn's too fertile for my blood. Besides, for all you know he might be a bigger man than Ewing and Shaq put together."

Sharon paused. "That's a thought. I could work with that."

They slapped hands, roaring in unison. "Give me some syrup so I can eat 'em like a biscuit."

The laughter was pervasive, sweeping through them both. Marguerite wiped the tears from her eyes, gasping for air. "I know we have lost it now."

Sharon continued to giggle, her head still bobbing up and down. "I need to get out of here," she said finally, stretching during a commercial break. "I'm never going to make work tomorrow if I don't get home to get some sleep."

"I hear that. I told them I'd come in for half a day, then I needed to take some personal time off."

"You still having a hard time with your new boss?"

"Not really. I can read her like a book now, so I just play her games better than she does. Besides, she's too busy trying to get the chairman to take her to bed to care about what I'm doing."

"That is one tacky office you work in."

"It pays the mortgage and until I can get enough freelance work to pay the bills, it'll have to do. Besides, at least when I do leave, my resume will read Vice President of Creative Development. That will take me a lot farther than Director."

"Well, I just hope it's all worth it."

Marguerite shrugged, wrapping her arms about her chest. She yawned widely. "Excuse me."

"I can take a hint," Sharon said.

"No hint. Sleep in the guest room if you want."

"Please. I'm surprised Helen hasn't called looking for me yet. You know how my mother is. Randy will call first, and then she'll call to tell me he called."

Marguerite laughed. "Your mother is not that bad."

"No, she's not, but he is. He asked me to marry him, you know," Sharon stated uneventfully.

"What?" Marguerite responded, surprised. "When?"

"Last week. I haven't given him an answer yet, though."

"Why didn't you tell me?" Marguerite exclaimed.

Sharon shrugged, contorting her face in a mock grimace. "Nothing to tell yet."

"Well, are you going to tell him yes or what?" Marguerite asked. "And you say I'm difficult," she said, throwing her hands up in exasperation.

Sharon smiled, draining the last drop of cool chocolate from her mug. "I don't know. I keep thinking that we're just at two different levels of commitment, you know? He's soaring way up here," she said, gesturing at the ceiling, "and I'm still crawling along down here. I don't know if I'm ready to marry him."

"Well, don't tell my grandmother that. She thinks you should be barefoot and pregnant with your fifth child by now. Personally, I went to see Dr. Smith yesterday for some extra-strong birth control."

Sharon nodded.

"Do you love him?" Marguerite asked.

"Yes, but . . ."

"Enough said. If there's a but, then something's not right. What is it?"

"Girl, I wish I knew. I'm beginning to think there's something wrong with me. But just like you think what you're feeling for Dexter is happening too fast, it's almost like my emotions for Randy are moving too slow. Does that make sense?"

Marguerite nodded. "Don't do it if it doesn't feel right, Sharon. Life is too short to settle for less than you deserve."

Her friend nodded in agreement, heading for the door. "It's after midnight. I've got to get home. Give me a call when you get back. I'll be home early on Sunday."

Marguerite waved as Sharon made her way down the steps of her town house toward the parking lot. Once Sharon flashed her headlights to indicate that she was safely inside the vehicle, Marguerite closed the door and secured the lock, checking the double bolt.

In the kitchen, she filled the dishwasher with the balance of the dirty dishes, then turned the unit on. As the loud rumble of water swirled deep within the cavity of the appliance, she quickly straightened up the living room, turned off the television, then headed upstairs for bed. She muttered out loud, "I wish my problem was whether someone wanted to marry me or not."

Closing the bedroom door behind her, she tossed her clothes over a chair and went into the bathroom. Staring at herself in the vanity mirror, she sighed heavily, then splashed a handful of cold water across her face. After brushing the sugary film from her teeth, she twisted her braids up into a bun, then wrapped a silk scarf around her head. Back in the bedroom, she cut off the lights and crawled easily into bed. Time clicked slowly by, her eyes focusing on the dark shadows about the room.

Marguerite shifted uncomfortably in bed, crushing the pillows beneath her. Why was she doing this to herself? she thought, cursing at the faint light peeping beneath the window blinds. As tired as she had been, she hated the thought of another sleepless night wasted on memories of every man who'd ridden out of her life faster than he'd ridden in.

She wiped at her eyes. Pulling her legs into her chest, Marguerite inhaled deeply. No matter how often she analyzed her relationships, she had no understanding of what it was about the men she loved that moved her so. They could make her feel both strong and weak at the same time, and no matter how in control she was with all other aspects of her life, she was most out of control when it came to a man who'd captured her heart.

Anthony had been the last. They'd met at work. He'd been one of the leading salesmen at Braedman Marketing Services when she'd joined the firm as their manager of marketing development. Their first contact had been a two-line scribbling across company letterhead welcoming her aboard. His kind words, written out of sheer politeness, had possessed her.

Anthony quickly became her lifeline to an outside world of sales presentations and promotional offerings. Marguerite enjoyed his tales of soft pitches, hard sells, and competitive monopolies. His notes had come frequently, pleasant ramblings praising each of her major accomplishments. Marguerite had found the affirmations of his appreciation, always printed boldly in his trademark green ink, both obnoxious and endearing. Their conversations were always comfortable, peppered with laughter. Anthony had been a man who truly enjoyed life and how he was living it, and Marguerite had found his enthusiasm infectious. His straightforward demeanor had been intriguing, and the more she discovered about him, the more she wanted to know.

The first time they'd met face-to-face had been at a national sales and marketing meeting. Anthony had stood off in a corner engaged in an intense conversation with his counterpart from the West Coast. He'd been tall and imposing, his features neatly molded in white ice. His dark curls had been flaked with snow, and a full beard and mustache had flattered the fine curves of his dimpled cheeks. Marguerite had found him intoxicating.

Their friendship intensified as daily conversations found them sharing secret intimacies. Marguerite began to envy any woman he dated, wondering if the other woman appreciated the beauty in the man who slept beside them each night. She began to imagine herself being able to wake up beside him, to plan his meals, fold his clothes, and kiss his children each day.

Their second sales and marketing meeting was held on the sunny shores of Miami, the hotel deep in the elbow of the Biscayne Bay. The sun had kissed the brown of Marguerite's skin the moment she'd stepped off the airplane. Basking in the fiery orb, the crisp ocean air foretold many a tale to come, whispering the secrets of lovers in the warm breeze. Marguerite was like a young girl with her first crush, puppy love dripping from the faucet of her being.

Once the meetings were over, they'd found themselves behind closed doors, sharing a mutual dislike of heights as they looked cautiously over the rail of his balcony down into the pool below. Marguerite had walked into his arms willingly, offering all of her womanhood up to him. In the months that followed, their meetings were frequent, passionate reunions that made up for the times he spent away and Marguerite spent alone.

She'd fallen hopelessly in love with this man, choosing to ignore everything that was contrary to what she believed in. Marguerite disregarded the obvious, their racial difference, the variance in their ages, her family's opinion, shutting out everything that would have distracted her from the dream she'd wrapped them in.

The last time they'd been together he'd been reserved, concerned about the direction his life was headed in. Marguerite had reached out to comfort him, wanting to drive the thoughts from his spirit, and when he'd rolled above her, pushing into her timidly, his erection had melted into limpness. Muttering a faint apology, he'd rolled to the other side of the bed and out of her life.

The silence that followed was the most devastating. Calls were not returned and dates were broken. He continued to send letters, writing only of business, and their conversations became laced with formality. Marguerite had no clue about who or what to blame, so she blamed herself. She had eased into the silence with a valley of tears and a mountain of anger. Somewhere during all of it, the essence of her being had been rocked.

Never again, she promised herself, would any man have that effect on her. Never again would she make such a complete and total fool out of herself for the sake of love. Poor Dexter would be made to suffer the consequences of every man who had ever treated her badly as she struggled to insure it never happened again.

Easing herself back into bed, Marguerite closed her eyes tightly. She rolled onto her side, and sleep finally embraced her, its delicate hug blissful, and as she gave into its warming caress, she dreamt of Dexter, knowing that tomorrow he'd be waiting for her.

10

A limousine had been at the airport waiting to pick her up when her plane landed. The flight had been long, but uneventful. Marguerite was looking forward to the quiet of the hotel. As the car dipped down a steep hill, she wondered if Dexter would be waiting for her.

Entering the Hotel Inter-Continental New Orleans, she inquired at the front desk about his whereabouts. The desk clerk passed her a sealed envelope and the key to Suite 797. "The bellman will take your luggage for you, Mrs. Williams." Smiling weakly at the tanned man, she raised her eyebrows only slightly before tearing the envelope open.

Dexter's dark handwriting, sprawled on hotel letterhead, greeted her: "M. My last meeting's at six-thirty. Just make yourself comfortable and I'll see you real soon. Love, D."

As she followed the bellman into the elevator, she folded the note neatly and placed it in the pocket of her coat. The suite she was led to surpassed anything that she could have ever imagined. The vast room, enveloped in glass, looked down upon the lights of the city. As Marguerite looked out at the setting sun shimmering against the bright sky, she was suddenly excited about being there, her apprehension replaced with a childlike anticipation of what was to come.

Once she was alone, she hung her clothes in the closet next to Dexter's, brushing her hand along the fabric of his dark suits. Three suits and five shirts hung in plastic cleaner bags, pressed crisply with light starch, and a pair of brown shoes and a pair of sneakers were lined neatly on the floor.

In the larger of the two bathrooms, she filled the massive tub with hot water and bath beads, melting easily into the warmth of the scented fluid. Lying back against the head of the porcelain pool, she dozed lightly as the water cooled slowly around her. When her muscles had relaxed into limpness and the strain of the trip no longer pressed at her forehead, she rose, drying her body with the plush white towels, then wrapping herself in an oversized bathrobe, the hotel emblem embroidered boldly in blue.

Returning to the bedroom, she found Dexter relaxing on the king-sized bed waiting for her. "Hi," she said, surprised by his presence. "I didn't hear you come in."

"Hi, yourself. I just thought I'd give you some time alone. It's a long flight from New York, and I knew you probably wanted to relax a bit. I just changed in the other bathroom and figured I'd wait until you came out."

Marguerite smiled. "You could have joined me."

He smiled back. "Trust me, I thought about it."

Easing over to sit beside him, Marguerite eagerly pressed her lips to his. Dexter kissed her hungrily, easing his hands beneath the terry robe to press his palm against the bare skin of her back.

"I'm glad you came," he whispered, easing himself beneath her.

"Me too," she responded as she pressed herself closely against him. They lay together for some time just holding each other tightly, his hands moving lightly across her spine, hers pressed against his chest. Their kisses were light and easy, like faint whispers blowing sweetly throughout the room.

Her tongue searched out his, darting eagerly past his lips, playing an erotic game of hide-and-seek. Easing her hands past the elastic of his boxer shorts, she pushed the silk fabric past his hips as he lifted his pelvis up to meet her. Trapping him between the warmth of her legs, she held him tightly, still caressing his lips with her own.

Encircling his arms above his head, he lay motionless as she fondled him, stroking the taut muscles of his abdomen against her belly, caressing his thighs with her own. He leaned into the crevice of her breasts, inhaling the perfume upon her skin. He laughed lightly, pleasure etched upon his face.

"You want me, don't you," he whispered into her ear, plunging his tongue into her ear as he reached toward the nightstand for a condom.

She could only nod as he rolled the prophylactic over his taut member. Her throat was dry, the words caught deep within her chest. Rolling her onto her back, he plunged deeply within her, his hands burning against her flesh, the sensation of him drawing the breath from her body. He continued to play with her, arousing every nerve ending in her body, until she could no longer refrain from shouting out his name as he spilled himself deep within her.

It was dark when they awoke. Blackness had finally

swallowed the setting sun, edging the night in the stark white of a luminous moon. Dexter kissed her lightly on the forehead, then patted her rear end. "Get up, lazy. It's time to go play."

"Hmmm. Why can't we just play right here?" she asked, stretching.

"Get up," he said with a laugh, pulling her to her feet.

It was not long before they were dancing down Bourbon Street, both intoxicated by the crowd. People were laughing and singing, many guided by the constant flow of alcohol. From balconies above, couples looked down upon them, cheering the antics of the more extroverted, everyone enveloped within the excitement of the city.

They strolled arm in arm, giggling like teenagers away from home for the first time, finally settling down in a dark, quiet corner of The Jazz Room. Four ebony musicians, aged by bad gin and good music, whispered a cool lilt of blues out of shining, brass instruments. Marguerite laid her head easily on Dexter's shoulder, settling into the comfort of his solid arms wrapped possessively around her. The music surged through her, two-stepping with her spirit. When the lights came on signaling last call, and Dexter rose, guiding her back to the hotel, she was only slightly disappointed.

11

There was no breeze. The heat rose in large swells, suffocating. Marguerite and Dexter sat staring out over the dense water of the Mississippi and sipping lazily on two cups partially filled with lukewarm piña coladas watered down by melting ice. It was too hot to carry on a conversation. Short jaunts through the mall and a leisurely stroll through the Aquarium had provided brief reprieves from the warmth, but there was no stifling the fever of the blistering sun.

Marguerite relished the intense heat as she brushed the moisture from the cup's surface against her skin. It never got too hot for her. She was odd that way, preferring the intense warmth of a summer day to anything else. On the other hand, Dexter's discomfort was obvious as the salty sweat dripped off his brow.

"There's much to be said for anonymity," he said suddenly, breaking the silence.

"Excuse me?"

"Anonymity. There's much to be said for it. People keep looking at us like we're crazy, but as long as they don't have a clue as to who we are, it doesn't make much difference," he answered, brushing the back of his hand against his forehead. "Are you ready to go back to the hotel yet?"

Marguerite sighed heavily. "No," she stated, eyeing him playfully. "I could stay here forever."

He shook his head. "Woman, you're crazy. Let's go," he said, rising to his feet. "I can't take this heat anymore."

Clasping her hand within his own, he pulled her alongside him, guiding her down the stone-paved walkway, back toward the center of town.

"Do you remember the first time I laid eyes on you?" he asked.

Marguerite smiled. "Yes."

"You were complaining about it being cold. It was close to seventy-five degrees in that office. You had on two sweaters and a jacket and you were complaining that you were cold. I should have known then that I was dealing with a crazy woman."

"I am not crazy. I just like it hot is all. I don't like cold."

He kissed the back of her hand. "I swear, you must be from another planet or something. You cannot convince me that you like this kind of intense heat and be human. I'm not buying it."

Marguerite rolled her eyes at him, swatting him lightly on his behind.

"So tell me, Mr. Williams. What 'unnatural' things do you like, sir?"

Dexter thought for a moment. "Nothing 'unnatural.' I'm pretty normal for the most part."

"Uh-huh."

"I am. I believe in the basics. Love, trust, family, honesty . . . I consider myself to be very down-to-earth for the most part."

Marguerite nodded.

"What about you? Although we already know you're a little bizarre."

"I prefer unique, thank you. I'm not sure what I believe in, to be honest with you. I mean, I ascribe to your basics, but I'm also consumed by something more. It's difficult to explain."

"Try."

Marguerite hesitated. "Well . . . I'm sometimes overwhelmed by my feelings. I thrive on the intensity of my own emotions. I'm a very physical person, so I need to really 'experience' my emotions to truly feel them, if that makes any sense."

Dexter shook his head. "I'm not sure that it does."

She sighed. "I don't really understand it myself. I just know that basic emotions and experiences for me must be intensely tactile for me to truly 'feel' them. For example, my friend Sharon says I equate sex with love, but for me, I can't equate love with anything if I cannot feel the passion and the lust."

"What about the love for a parent or a child?"

"It's the same. To feel it exists, I have to 'feel' it, and that doesn't necessarily mean it has to be sexual. Don't misunderstand. With my grandmother, I feel the love between us in the way she would cuddle me as a child, or how she'd comb my hair or wash my face. With Sharon, who is my dearest friend, it's how we interact, how we disagree or laugh together or cry together. I am just a very physical person. If I distance myself from you, then I am also distancing my emotions. It's just how I am."

Dexter shook his head pensively, inhaling deeply. "I'm still not sure it makes sense, but knowing you, I think I kind of understand."

Marguerite smiled slightly. "Like I said, it doesn't make a whole lot of sense to me most times either."

As they entered the lobby of the hotel, he wrapped his arm about her shoulder, the action almost possessive. It was his silent announcement that the black beauty whose brown gleamed under the light coat of perspiration against her skin belonged only to him.

In the elevator, she kissed his neck, caressing his earlobe lightly with her tongue. "You ever make love in an elevator?" she whispered seductively, raking her long nails lightly along his bare leg at the edge of his denim shorts.

"I can't say that I have," he responded, gently pushing her away from him. "I guess I'd be afraid of getting caught."

"Half the thrill," she said, pressing against him once more as the small enclosure came to a stop.

As the doors opened, he laughed lightly, disengaging himself from her. "Let's go," he said with a laugh, as she smiled broadly at him, the wickedness dancing across her face. "I don't know what I'm going to do with you."

Marguerite followed like an obedient child, walking eagerly behind him. Inside the room, Dexter turned the air-conditioning up high, the cold air blowing briskly from the vent in the ceiling. Marguerite watched as Dexter stripped out of his clothes and headed into the bathroom. "I need a shower," he said over his shoulder, his briefs falling down to his ankles.

Turning on the radio, Marguerite swayed to the music, a sultry blues selection seeping into the sun-draped room. Slipping her crimson sundress over her head, she headed into the other bathroom to wash the salty sweat away in a warm bath. Lazing in a tub of water, she dozed lightly until Dexter's full hand cupped her right breast, his fingers heavy against her nipple. A faint moan eased past her lips as she reached her arm around his neck to pull his lips down upon hers. His kiss was warm, searching, the fullness of his lips fitting snugly around hers, his tongue exploring her mouth easily.

Pulling her up and out of the water, Dexter dabbed a plush towel against her body, swiping at the heavy moisture against her skin. As he gently caressed and patted every crevice, Marguerite was awed by the beauty of him, his own flesh glistening under the bright lights. Dropping the towel to the floor, Dexter pulled her close, pressing his naked-ness against hers. Marguerite wrapped her arms around his back, reveling in the body warmth against her palms. Taking her by the hand, Dexter guided her back to the bedroom, easing her slowly onto the bed, then dropped his own frame down beside her. Their kisses were light, and Marguerite was warmed by the brush of his cheek against hers, their bodies gliding one over the other. They made love slowly, languishing in the heat of each other's touch, and somewhere in the back of her mind, Marguerite momentarily thought she heard him whisper that he loved her.

12

Seated under a striped green-and-white canopy at the Cafe du Monde, Dexter and Marguerite quickly devoured a plate of sugar-coated beignets and two cups of dark, rich coffee. The morning was slipping away quickly, leaving them willingly behind.

Marguerite finally broke the silence that hovered over their table. "I could stay here forever."

Dexter smiled, leaning over to kiss the sugar from her lips. "Me too." He sighed, a heaviness crossing his face.

"Dexter, what's the matter? There has been something on your mind since you called me to come down here with you. What is it? What's bothering you?"

Dexter shrugged. "Family problems. Nothing for you to concern yourself with."

Marguerite bit her lip. "Okay, if you want it like that."

"I'm sorry. I didn't mean to offend you. It's just that I don't know how to handle this. I don't know what to do."

"Handle what? I want to help, but I can't if you won't talk to me."

Dexter took a deep breath. "The night before I

left, my older brother told me he was gay. He met some guy he was going away with and he told me he thought he was falling in love with him." Dexter cringed, the movement unconscious.

Marguerite nodded slowly. "So what's the problem?"

Dexter cut his eyes at her. "My big brother's a faggot. That is the problem."

Marguerite leaned her elbows against the table, clasping her hands in front of her. "No. Your brother is homosexual. He's attracted to men. I personally don't like the word 'faggot.'"

"Well, you can have a cavalier attitude about this. He's not your brother."

"No, he's not, but yours isn't the first family to have someone in it who's gay, and it sure won't be the last."

Dexter leaned back in his seat, his mouth pushed into a pout. "You don't understand."

"I understand you're homophobic."

"I am not. I just. . . ." He shrugged.

"I told you about my family, my aunts and my uncle."

Dexter nodded.

"Well, my uncle is gay, so I do understand."

Dexter leaned closer. "When did you find out about your uncle?"

Marguerite smiled. "I was eight years old when he told me. I'd asked him why he didn't have a wife. He answered that he didn't like girls." Marguerite chuckled softly. "My feelings were hurt because I thought it meant that he didn't like me or my grandmother. I asked him why he didn't like us and if it meant he wouldn't love us anymore, and he told me that he would always love me. He said he just didn't like big girls who weren't family.

"I guess I was about fourteen or fifteen when I really understood. He'd brought a friend home to visit and they'd slept together in the spare bedroom. I remember my aunts whispering about it and my grandmother yelling at both of them to grow up."

"Did it ever bother you?"

Marguerite shook her head. "No, but then for me it has always been a part of who he is. He never tried to be anything other than himself. I love the man. He's one of my best friends and I want him to be happy. If another man can do that, then so be it."

Dexter sighed. "I don't know what to do."

"Well, first you need to talk to your brother. His being gay has nothing whatsoever to do with you and the relationship you two share. He's still your brother and you still love him no matter what. He's going to need to know that."

"I guess."

"Guess nothing. Don't worry about what he's doing in his bed. Just worry about what's going on in yours." Marguerite kissed him, reaching to stroke his leg beneath the table.

Dexter laughed, moving her hand away. "Okay."

Marguerite rose from her seat. "Come on. Let's go buy some T-shirts." She rubbed her hand against Dexter's shoulders.

"It's going to be all right, really," she said, her voice comforting. "I doubt that your brother is going to start wearing dresses or think about having a sex change. If you're just now finding out, I think you can be fairly sure he's not going to be flamboyant about it, if that's got you worried. And even if he does, it doesn't change who and what he is to you."

Dexter laughed. "I guess that *did* worry me. I guess I really don't know what I expect."

"That's why you need to talk to him. Just listen and don't pass judgment. Be honest with him about your feelings, but let him know you support him."

Dexter nodded, then wrapped his arms around her shoulders. "T-shirts, huh? Why don't we buy those matching his and her numbers to wear home?"

Marguerite laughed. "Let's not and just say we did."

13

Marguerite dropped her luggage on the floor, tossed her clothes over the small armchair in the corner, then reached for the telephone. As it rang on the other end, she tapped her fingers impatiently.

"Hello?"

"Sharon, it's me."

"Hey, girl! How was N'Orleans? When did you get back?"

"Just this minute. I don't think this is going to work."

"What?"

"Me and Dexter. It is definitely not going to work."

"What happened?"

Marguerite inhaled deeply. "Nothing. I had a great time. Too great. He's too good to be true, and I'm not going to wait around for him to turn into Mr. Hyde. How was Springfield?"

"The usual, so don't change the subject. What are you going to do?"

"That's what I called you for. Catch up."

"So now I get attitude?"

"Don't be bitchy. It's so unbecoming."

"Hmmm, I see where this is going. I'm coming over. You need to be slapped back into reality and I can't do that over the phone. You got any food in the house?"

"I guess."

"Don't guess. If you don't, I can stop by the store and pick something up, but you get to cook it."

"No sweat."

"Okay then. I'll see you in a few minutes," Sharon finished, disconnecting the call.

Marguerite held the phone waiting for a dial tone, then dialed her grandmother.

"Hey, Miss Mae."

"Hey, Baby Girl. Where are you?"

"I just got home. You okay?"

"I'm fine. Clarence been here wit' me all day. He done fixed that leak in the toilet for me like I been askin'."

"That's good. I just wanted to let you know that I was back and to make sure you were okay."

"Uh-huh. How's that pretty Dexter boy? You still messin' wit' him?"

"Miss Mae, I'm not messing with Dexter. He's just a very good friend."

"What kind a good friend?"

"Good-bye, Miss Mae. I'll call you tomorrow, okay?"

"Don't think we ain't gon' finish this conversation, Miss Freshy. Here, say hello to Clarence before you hang up." Miss Mae shouted into the other room. "Clarence, come take the phone. It's Marguerite."

Marguerite inhaled deeply, shaking her head.

"Hey, darling."

"Hi, Uncle Clarence. How are you?"

"Glad she's got someone else to yell at besides me."

Marguerite giggled. "She's definitely on a roll."

"Are you okay? Mama said you were away on business."

"Yeah, monkey business, but don't tell her."

Clarence laughed. "I won't, but don't think anything gets past her. She's got a sixth sense about these things. "

"Don't I know it."

"Well, you be good and come see me sometime this week. I've got to catch you up on my trip. London was kickin' it."

"Ohh. I am too jealous, and what about this new man of yours?"

"Well he was good while he lasted."

"That doesn't sound good. Are you okay?"

Clarence was silent for a brief moment. "Yeah, nothing I won't get over, Baby Girl."

"I'll come by tomorrow so we can talk. Tell Miss Mae I said good-bye."

"Not a problem. Bye, darling."

Hanging up the telephone, Marguerite kicked her shoes under the bed, then headed for the shower. An hour later, when she opened the door for Sharon, she'd finally relaxed, feeling more in control of herself.

Sharon flew into the town house, dropping the brown bags where she stood, the groceries spilling to the floor.

"I hate shopping. Do you know what this stuff cost me?"

Marguerite laughed as she stooped down to pick up the food rolling about their feet. "Girl, you kill me. What's this?" she asked, staring at two metal cans that had lost their labels.

"Who cares. For twenty-five cents a can, we're going to call it gourmet surprise."

Marguerite shook her head, making her way into the kitchen to put the pots on the stove.

Reaching into the refrigerator, Sharon pulled out a bottle of chilled white wine and poured herself a glass.

"So, girlfriend. What is going on with you?" she asked, sipping slowly from a crystal goblet. "Here you just come back from spending what I think was a great weekend with this fine black stallion, and now you're wondering whether or not you should be breaking up with him. Have you lost your mind?"

Taking a seat at the table beside her, Marguerite filled her own glass, twirling the cool crystal slowly between the palms of her hands. "It's not like that. I just had such a good time I got scared."

"You mean got stupid. Why you playing my brother wrong like this? Here you got him thinking something's going on between the two of you, and you here crying over what you should do."

"Dexter's great and it's not like that. I am not playing him. It's not like he's put a ring on my finger."

Sharon rose to go stand by her side. Wrapping her arms about Marguerite's shoulders, she hugged her warmly. "You got to let it go. If there's going to be anything between you and Dexter, you have got to let go of what happened between you and Anthony and between you and whoever else is haunting you."

Marguerite nodded, tears welling in her eyes. "I know, but I just can't shake the feeling that I'm going to get burned again. I'll be damned if I'm going to let another man stomp my emotions like Anthony did."

Sharon flipped a hand in her direction. "Girl-friend, if you cry one more tear over that pathetic piece of trash, I'm going to slap the black off a you."

Marguerite laughed, wiping at her eyes. "Thank you. I'd really appreciate that."

"So tell me about your trip."

"We had a great time. New Orleans was terrific. You and I need to go by ourselves some time."

"Just say when. I need me some play time, especially after my weekend."

Marguerite sat back down at the table with Sharon. "How was Springfield?"

"It was great until I told Randy I wanted a prenuptial agreement."

Marguerite laughed. "You did what?"

"That's right. I told him the only way I'd marry him was if we had a prenuptial agreement. I will not risk everything I have worked my butt off for just to marry him. He could get half if this doesn't work out. Half of my hard-earned stuff."

"I can just imagine what he said."

"Brother started poutin' and actin' like I'd asked him to donate his mother's kidney to me. He says if we need to start our marriage off distrusting each other, then we don't need to be married."

"I kind of agree with him."

Sharon rolled her eyes. "You would, but if you marry Dexter, you better make sure you have one too just to make sure you get your fair share and he doesn't get more than his."

Marguerite shook her head as she headed back to the stove. Stirring the pots, she flipped off the flames, and grabbed two plates from the dish rack.

"So what happens now?"

"He suddenly thinks we should just live with each other to see if things work out. Changed his tune real quick. But I have no intentions of living with any man I'm not married to."

Marguerite raised her eyebrows. "Why not?"

"Why should I pay half the bills living with him, when I can just keep on living with my folks for free? Until my mother tells me to get my behind out, I'm not going anywhere."

Dipping spaghetti and sauce into serving dishes, Marguerite grinned at her best friend. "Well, I guess I shouldn't start planning a shower anytime soon."

"Nope." Sharon spooned a forkful of food into her mouth. "This is good," she hummed, smacking her lips. "And that's another reason I'm not moving in with him. Brother can't cook and neither can I. We'd starve to death if KFC ever closed."

It was well after midnight and Marguerite could not sleep. She'd been tossing and turning since she'd laid her head on the pillow, and sleep seemed to be eluding her. She sighed heavily. Raising her body off the bed, she pulled herself into a sitting position, leaning back against the headboard of the mahogany sleigh bed. After tucking the covers tightly around her body, she reached for the telephone.

Her hand shook ever so slightly as she dialed his telephone number and pulled the receiver to her ear. Sinking back low against the pillows, she waited anxiously for him to answer.

"Hello?" His voice was low and throaty, his tone indicative of a man who'd been awakened from a deep sleep. Marguerite instantly regretted having called.

"Hi. I'm sorry. I didn't mean to wake you."

"It's okay, baby. Is something wrong?"

"No. I just couldn't sleep."

Dexter nodded into the telephone, a drowsy nod that could have easily dropped him back into a state of slumber. Fighting the sensation, he pulled himself upward and back against the headboard. "What's got you so wired up?"

Marguerite wanted to say, "You," but didn't. She shrugged, snuggled closer to the pillows behind her, and instead said, "I don't know. Overtired I guess."

"So, what do you want to talk about?" Dexter asked, stretching the length of his legs out against the mattress, kicking the blankets tangled about his feet.

"Nothing in particular. I was just thinking about New Orleans and being with you and I suddenly wanted to hear your voice."

Dexter shook his head, trying to shake the grogginess that clouded his senses. "I had a good time. I'm glad you could come. It meant a lot to me to have you there with me."

Marguerite smiled into the receiver. "It meant a lot to me too. It was very special. Thank you for making it happen."

"I hope you and I have a lot of special times together like that. I really care about you, Marguerite. You are very special to me."

Marguerite's smile flooded the room as the warmth of his words flooded her body. "Hey, you need to go back to sleep. I really am sorry that I woke you."

Dexter yawned. "Yeah. I've got a long day tomorrow. I'll be thinking about you, though. I'll call you during the day to say hello, okay? Maybe we can make plans for dinner."

"Okay. Good night."

"Good night, baby. I love you."

Marguerite hung up slowly, the words he'd just whispered still resonating from the receiver. The faint light reflecting against the bed was teasing, and Marguerite's mind was running rampant with thoughts of Dexter. It felt too good to be true. He couldn't possibly love her, but he'd just said so again. Marguerite pulled a hand to her breast, the vibration of her speeding heart pulsating against her palm.

Marguerite couldn't deny that something was happening between her and Dexter. It was out of her control and she wasn't ready for it. It felt like being on a speeding train that was ready to crash headfirst into a brick wall and being unable to get off. She pulled her legs close into her chest, rolling into a fetal position against the mattress. Panic was starting to set in.

14

Dexter saw the car parked in front of his door as he rounded the corner into the parking lot. He thought about turning around, not sure if he was ready for any type of confrontation with Shepard. He could feel the muscles along his chest tightening. Swinging his long legs out of the car, he smiled weakly as Shepard ambled over to his side. Extending his arm, Dexter shook the man's hand.

"Hey, there," Dexter said.

"How are you?"

Dexter nodded his head. "Okay. I've been trying to catch up. Just got back the other day from a business trip, so I'm a little tired."

"I thought we should talk."

Dexter exhaled, nodding. "Yeah. I guess we should. Why don't you come on in."

Shepard stood nervously behind him, his hands stuffed deep into his pockets as Dexter struggled to get a silver key into the door lock. Pushing the door open, he gestured for his brother to enter, then closed and locked the door behind them.

"So where did you go off to?" Shepard asked.

"New Orleans. Had to do some interviewing."

Shepard sat down on the sofa, twisting his hands

in front of him. "Did you get a chance to do any sight-seeing?"

As he dropped his coat onto the back of a chair and pulled a seat out from the dining room, Dexter smiled. "Yeah. Marguerite flew down to meet me. We spent the weekend together."

"I can't wait to meet this lady. Sounds like you two are really getting serious."

Dexter nodded. "Yeah. She means a lot to me."

Dexter turned his head to stare out over the dining room table. The moment was awkward as Shepard sat silent, neither of them speaking. Meeting his brother's eye, Dexter knew he had to be the first to say something. He instinctively knew that if he did not open the door and let Shepard know he was welcome, their relationship would never again be the same.

He took a deep breath, then rose from where he sat to go sit beside Shepard. He grinned stupidly as they both sat twisting their hands.

"So how was London?"

Shepard watched him out of the corner of his eye. "It was nice. Very nice."

"So, you and your . . . umm . . . friend had a good time then?"

With tears in his eyes, Shepard dropped his head into the palm of his hands. Then clearing his throat, he turned to look Dexter square in the eye.

"My friend . . ." He paused, searching for the words. "Dex, I have spent the better part of my life pretending to be something I'm not because I was afraid to face rejection. I was too worried about what everybody else thought. In London, I realized that I could enjoy a relationship with someone who cared about me. I discovered that I was worthy of being loved. Then I stepped off the airplane in New York and I threw it all away."

Tears were streaming down his face. "My friend is more than that to me. I love him and I hurt him and I lost him because I couldn't stop being a coward. I can't believe I could be such a fool." Shepard's tears had turned to a quiet sob as he sat hunched over. Dexter's own eyes welled up at seeing his brother's tears spill slowly past his dark lashes. Reaching out to hug his brother, he pulled the man close to him and let him sob on his shoulder.

When John opened the front door to let himself in, the two men were still huddled shoulder to shoulder. Meeting his friend's eyes, John nodded with understanding and backed quietly out of the room. As he turned an about-face, closing the door behind him, Dexter pulled Shepard closer, hugging him warmly. His brother's tears had slowed to a thin flow, and his own eyes burned red from crying. Reaching toward the end table, Dexter passed him a tissue, then wiped one across his own nose.

"First things first," Dexter said, rising from where he sat. Strolling over to the bar, he poured them both stiff drinks, then sat back down.

"Have you spoken to this guy since you got back?" Shepard shook his head.

"Why not?"

Shrugging, Shepard took a sip from the glass. "Afraid to. Didn't think it would change anything."

"Does he want to be with you?"

"I don't know anymore. I know that he wants to be open about whatever is going on with us, and I don't think I'm ready for that."

Dexter nodded. "You know, this is virgin territory for me, but if you love him, then you shouldn't be ashamed of that."

Shepard eyed him curiously as Dexter continued. "Hey, man, love is too important to throw away because of what other people might think. I know it's not going to be easy for you, in fact it might well be downright difficult, but if you two are willing to face it together, then I don't see what the problem is."

"You don't?"

Dexter shrugged.

"You who wouldn't answer my calls and who pulled back from me when I told you I was homosexual? You don't see what the problem is?"

"Hey, it was a shock to me. I didn't expect you to tell me you had a thing for men."

"Didn't you ever wonder? I never ever talked about being with women. You knew things hadn't been good for me and Rochelle when we divorced. Didn't you ever give it a thought?"

"No. Why would I think you were gay? It's not like you swished around or anything. You seemed normal."

Shepard chuckled, shaking his head. "Normal?"

"You know what I mean."

"Yeah, and that's why I've always kept it a secret. People mean well, but that's not how it ever comes out."

Dexter bit his bottom lip. "What did Mom have to say about it?"

Shepard leaned back against the sofa. "She sent me to Confession. She thought if I prayed hard enough I'd be able to change my ways. And she swore me to never tell Dad. She figured it would kill him."

"Does anyone else know?"

Shepard shook his head, biting at the skin along his thumbnail.

"So where do you go from here?"

"I don't know. I don't know what I'm going to do."

Dexter reached out to squeeze his brother's hand. "Well, whatever you decide to do, big brother, I'm right here for you. I may not understand it, I don't even know if I'm accepting of it, but I sure will be here for you if you need me."

Shepard smiled, nodding.

Dexter sat back against the sofa, lifting his legs onto the coffee table. "Can I ask you a stupid question?"

Shepard nodded, making himself comfortable in the sofa's corner.

"What's it like? I mean, what do you get out of being with a man?"

Shepard thought for a brief moment. "I get the same things that you get from being with women. It's not much different. The problem most people have is when they think of a gay couple or a lesbian couple, they automatically think about the sexual aspects. What is he doing to him in bed? It's about more than sex. I feel more comfortable and my emotional attachment feels more secure when it's with another man. I don't get that from being with a woman.

"And if you want to know about the sexual aspect of it, it's just like you being with your girl. She brings you pleasure. You enjoy bringing her pleasure. She feels and looks the way you need for her to. I don't want a woman's softness. I don't feel right being with a woman."

The expression on Dexter's face was pensive as he mulled over his brother's comments. He took a deep breath. "Do you remember George Winston, the guy I roomed with for a year back in college?"

"The real militant brother, changed his named to Mohammed Something-or-other, right?"

Dexter nodded. "Yeah. Well, he use to preach about how homosexuality was unnatural and how we as black people should be unaccepting of it because when the Europeans and Spaniards bought us over on the slave ships, they forced their perversions on us. I mean, some of his rhetoric was a lot of bull, but I got to tell you, man, I kind of believed some of the stuff he use to spout. I mean . . ." Dexter paused. "At least I thought I did."

Shepard shook his head slowly, leaning his elbows against his thighs and his chin into his palms. "Do you believe your sexuality was learned?"

Dexter shrugged.

"Really, do you think your desires and your urges were gained by outside instruction or influences?"

"No. I believe it was inherent."

"Then if heterosexuality is inherent, why would homosexuality not be?"

"I know the arguments, Shepard, but it just seems unnatural."

"Because it's not who you are. It does not directly influence your persona. Because it's not a part of what you are and what you believe doesn't mean it's wrong."

"What about what the Church taught us?"

"Who says the Church is right about everything?

When did any one religion corner the monopoly on perfection, with a totally perfect congregation? My God says to love my neighbor, not love him only if he's heterosexual, or only if he's white or rich or whatever else someone thinks he should be." Shepard slapped his hand against his leg, the veins bulging along his neck.

Dexter nodded. "Look, if I say or do anything stupid, don't take it personally. This came right out of left field and I'm going to have to get used to the idea. I can't make you any promise other than I'll try my best to deal with it. All right?"

"Deal."

Dexter stood, crossing over to the other side of the room. Reaching over the counter, he picked up the telephone receiver and passed it over to his brother. "I'm going to go take a shower. Make that call. If you end it, end it because you just don't want to be in it. If you love him"—he swallowed hard—"tell him and work it out."

15

Marguerite sat at her uncle's kitchen table sipping on a glass of freshly squeezed orange juice. Clarence was busy stirring a pan of vegetables and beef. Their chatter filled the room, warming the stark white kitchen.

"Baby Girl, I don't know how I manage to do it, but I always find myself hungry for these uptight brothers who aren't sure whether they're coming or going. Now I've actually gone and fallen head over heels for a man who wants to be cured like he's got some kind of illness." Clarence slammed his spoon down onto the stove top.

Marguerite shook her head, her look sympathetic. "Are you going to call him?"

"No," Clarence stated emphatically. "I will not be the first one to pick up the telephone. I refuse."

"He wasn't home, was he."

"He was, but I hung up when he answered the telephone." Clarence grinned at his niece, shrugging.

"How can you be so hard on him when you've been in his shoes before?"

"When? I have always been open about being gay. I've never had to hide from folks."

Marguerite raised her eyebrows. "Oh, no?"

Clarence met her glance, sucking his teeth. "Okay, so maybe I did for a real brief period in the very, very beginning, and that was only because I was dating Tyler. My boy was more comfortable in drag than anything else. He was a pretty queen and passed as a woman most of the time."

Marguerite laughed out loud as Clarence plopped down into the seat beside her. She reached out to pat her uncle's hand.

"You'll get through this, Uncle Clarence. You're going to have to talk to him before you can work it out, though."

Clarence nodded. "So how are things with you and your new guy? We gon' have us a wedding or not?"

Marguerite rolled her eyes. "Well, if he were to ask, I might actually say yes." She giggled. "I really care about him, Uncle Clarence. He's . . ." She smiled, her focus drifting.

"Say no more. Baby Girl's got it really bad. You tell Miss Mae yet?"

"I haven't said anything to anyone except Sharon. I'm afraid it's just too good to be true. You know my track record. It's only a matter of time before it blows up on me."

Clarence scrunched up his face, the expression exaggerated. "Please. Now who needs to be talking to who? Have you even told him how you feel?"

"Nope."

"No wonder you're sitting here eating dinner with your uncle when you could be dining with this wonderful man of yours."

Marguerite smiled. "No, I'm eating dinner with my dear uncle because I enjoy his company," she said as Clarence spooned food onto two plates.

Just then the telephone rang. The look on Clarence's face was all-revealing as he pressed the receiver against his ear. His voice dropped to a low whisper as Marguerite excused herself from the room. Although her uncle waved her to stay, she knew that he needed a private moment alone to digest whatever was being said on the other end. She just hoped that the conversation would not be too painful for him.

In his office, she sat down behind the glistening black marble desk that had been specially designed by Clarence's college roommate, Darwin Harris. The two men had been friends for as long as Marguerite could remember. For a very brief period they'd been lovers, which Marguerite had thought to be quite hypocritical of Darwin since Clarence had been best man at his wedding and was godfather to Darwin's eldest son. As she'd said to her uncle, she was glad she wasn't Darwin's wife.

As Marguerite looked around the room, she took particular notice of all the artifacts and trinkets bequeathed to Clarence over the years. His collection of black art was especially intriguing, with many of the paintings and lithographs signed or numbered. His collection was quite impressive.

As she ran her hand over the cold desktop, the cool sensation felt soothing against her palm. She could remember lying across it when she was little and pretending to make a snow angel like they did in the winter months. She laughed quietly to herself. Glancing briefly at her watch, she wondered if the conversation was going well. At that moment her uncle appeared in the doorway, his expression blank.

"Everything okay?"

He nodded. "Your dinner's getting cold."

Marguerite rolled her eyes. "What did he say?"

"He's coming over later so that we can talk."

"And?"

"And your dinner is getting cold, young lady."

Rising, Marguerite laughed. "You kill me. I don't know how you can be so calm and collected about this."

Clarence shrugged. "Nobody's said anything for me to get excited about yet."

"Doesn't it ever bother you, Uncle Clarence? Does it ever get to you, the way some people behave and treat you because you're gay?"

Clarence dropped to the office sofa. Marguerite took the seat beside him. "Baby Girl, Miss Mae use to tell us when we were growing up that we had to work harder and be better than everybody else because we were black and we were poor and because Pat, Leah, and your mama were girls. She also use to tell us to let those things work for us in life, not against us, because if we let them get in our way, it would give others permission to knock us down.

"My being homosexual worked the same way. I've let it work for me and I've never allowed anyone to use it against me to put me down. People react to what they don't understand or what they're afraid of. Ignorance perpetuates their fear. If I can educate them and help them to understand who I am and what I'm about, fine. If I can't, then it's their loss, because I'm one heck of a great guy."

Marguerite smiled.

"I can't let other people bother me, Marguerite. I have never belittled another person for what they

think or believe or feel, and I will not allow someone else to draw my world and color in the picture
for me."

His niece nodded. "My dinner is getting cold."

"Well, you're going to have to take it with you and
heat it up at home. I need to get ready. Can't be
looking shabby when I get my apology."

Arm in arm, the two giggled out the door, and
Marguerite marveled at how Clarence made the
most difficult seem so easy.

16

At precisely six-thirty, Marguerite lit the candles on her dining room table just as Dexter rang the bell at her front door. Taking one quick glance in the mirror, she pulled the door open and pulled him inside, into her arms.

"Hey, you."

"Hey, yourself." He kissed her slowly, his lips flowing from hers down the side of her cheek to her neck. "You look beautiful," he said, admiring the silk dress that graced her voluptuous frame, the rich color, a deep blue, delightful against her skin.

Marguerite giggled as she pushed him away. "Hungry?"

Dexter nodded. "What smells so good?"

"We're eating Italian tonight. I made lasagna."

"Homemade?"

"Yes, sir. Is there any other kind?"

"Well, I know some women who'll cook some Chef Boyardee and try to fool you."

Marguerite swatted at him. "Not this woman. I even made the pasta myself."

Dexter raised an eyebrow. "Where'd you learn to make homemade pasta?"

The woman laughed. "Sixteen weeks of Italian

cooking classes. Miss Mae even bought me my own pasta maker for Christmas last year. Want to see it?"

Wrapping his arms around her waist, he pulled her close. "I'm scared a you, woman. A man would be a fool to let you get away from him. Fine as wine and you can cook too."

Marguerite giggled like a little kid as she extracted herself from his grip. "Yes, he would. But sit down, the food's ready."

Marguerite had adorned a formal table in her dining room. Dexter took his seat and admired her handiwork. The flames from white candles, in varying heights, danced around an expansive arrangement of white and yellow roses. The floral composition cascading down the length of the table was a dramatic backdrop for her fine china and expensive crystal. Laying a cloth napkin against his lap, he smiled as she fixed him a plate and set the food in front of him. The aroma was taunting as the sweet scent of fresh tomatoes, basil, oregano, and cheese flooded one over the other. Dexter inhaled deeply, the aroma coating his tastebuds.

After Marguerite served herself and had taken her seat, Dexter blessed the table. "Heavenly Father, thank you for the food we are about to receive. Bless the hands that prepared it, bless the hands that brought it from the fields. Bless it that it may nourish our bodies and strengthen our souls. Amen."

Marguerite smiled, nodding ever so slightly.

"So, how was your day?" she asked, poking at her meal with her fork.

"Pretty good. I got a lot accomplished. This morning I made offers to two of the men I interviewed in New Orleans, and I spent the afternoon going over expansion proposals from my marketing people."

"That sounds exciting."

Dexter paused, resting his own fork against the edge of his plate.

"It is," he answered, excitement mounting in his voice. He rested his elbows against the table, his chin atop his clasped hands. "I have always imagined what my life would be like when I got to this point and I've got to tell you, Marguerite, it has surpassed my wildest imagination. I could never have dreamt about being so blessed." He beamed, the pensive expression across his face highlighted by an energy of self-satisfaction and confidence.

Marguerite returned his smile. "I'm so happy for you."

"You have a lot to do with it, you know."

"How so?" she questioned, sipping slowly from her glass of red wine.

Dexter inhaled deeply before continuing. "You being in my life gives me someone to share my success with. Having someone by your side who's interested in what you do and how well you do makes even the smallest success more meaningful. It's also a great motivator. I find myself wanting to do more, not only for me but for you too. I want to do it for us and what I want us to have together."

Marguerite's eyes dropped to the table as she took in his words.

"Are you blushing?" Dexter's smile widened.

Even as she rolled her eyes, Marguerite could feel the color rising to her cheeks. "So, how's the lasagna?" she questioned, changing the subject.

Dexter resumed eating. "Very good. I am very impressed."

"Well, save room. I made tiramasu for dessert."

Dexter chuckled. "That sounds decadent."

"Yes. I was hoping for decadent," she said, heading into the kitchen to get dessert ready for serving.

The rest of the conversation was casual as they finished their meal. When they were done, they retreated into the kitchen and Dexter helped her load the dirty dishes into the dishwasher. Laughter rang between them as they straightened up the kitchen.

After blowing out the lit candles on the dining room table, they settled down in front of the fireplace and a freshly lit fire. Dexter poked cautiously at the burning embers, savoring a glass of sherry. Settling down beside him, Marguerite made herself comfortable. Music played softly in the background.

"This brings back memories." She smiled.

Dexter chuckled, a deep rumble that rose from his midsection. "Yes, very nice memories."

Marguerite blushed ever so slightly as she leaned up to kiss Dexter's cheek.

Time passed quickly, the minutes racing by. The pair sat contently, comfortable with the surroundings and each other. The music was soothing, and both could feel the stress of their respective business days melting away into oblivion.

"I could sit here with you forever," Dexter said, breaking the silence.

Smiling, Marguerite leaned up to kiss him again, lightly brushing his lips with her own. Dexter responded by hugging her closer against him. It did feel good, Marguerite thought to herself. It felt incredible to feel so close to a man who seemingly felt the same way she did. As she brushed her palm against his chest, fingering the buttons of his starched white shirt, she couldn't help wondering how long it would be before it would end. As if sensing her fear, Dexter took her hand into his own, planted a light kiss against her palm, held it closed beneath his own, and pulled it tightly against his heart.

"Forever baby. Forever," he whispered gently.

Marguerite nodded slowly, a faint smile gracing her face. She sighed softly.

"Do you want children?" Dexter asked suddenly, turning to stare into her eyes.

"I do. Family has always been very important to me. I want at least two children."

"Me too. I've always imagined myself with two daughters."

"Just daughters?" Marguerite smiled.

Nodding, Dexter grinned. "I like spoiling the women in my life. I have always seen myself catering to my little girls."

"And what if you have sons?"

"That'll work too. I can do Little League, Scouts, all of it. I just know I want to be a father."

Marguerite dropped her head ever so slightly. "It's rare to find a man of thirty-nine who's never been married and who doesn't have any kids. Most of the men I've encountered over the past few years were all dealing with some type of baby-mama drama."

"I've been very careful, for the most part. I've had a few scares, but I thank God that they were just that, scares. I don't want to ever be a part-time father. It's important to me to be in a committed relationship with a woman who wants the same things I do. I want my children to know they were planned and wanted and that together their mother and I would sacrifice everything for their happiness."

Marguerite leaned back, reflecting on what he'd just said. Together, they sat staring into the burning flames.

"Would you have my baby?" Dexter asked her, reaching to rub her hand beneath his.

Marguerite turned her head slightly, raising her eyes to look into his.

"I can see us together, Marguerite, raising a family, loving each other and them. I want that with you someday."

She smiled, nodding slowly. "Maybe someday," she responded, reaching up to kiss him lightly on the lips.

Neither moved as the flames died slowly away. Exchanging gentle caresses between them, they were absorbed in the moment, the contentment all-consuming. As the last of the fire finally flickered away, Dexter heaved a heavy sigh.

"I guess I should be heading home. It's late."

Marguerite lifted her body and turned to face him. "You know you can stay if you want. I don't want you driving if you're too tired."

He smiled, reaching out a hand to stroke the side of her face. "I know, but if I stay, I doubt either one of us is going to get any rest."

Marguerite smiled, resting her hand atop his. "Call me when you get home to let me know you're okay."

Dexter rose, pulling Marguerite up beside him. "I will. I'm going to miss you."

"I'm going to miss you too."

His kiss good-bye was a sweet caress that flowed from the surface of her mouth throughout her entire body. He held her close, pressing his body into hers, their two frames curving one into the other. She was tempted to tell him to stay. She didn't want him to leave, wanting him to caress the rest of her body with his lips. He finally pulled away, planting delicate kisses against her cheeks, the tip of her nose, her closed eyes, then wrapped her hand within his own as he pulled her behind him toward the door.

Marguerite watched as he made his way to the car, and as he pulled his vehicle onto the main road and out of sight, she whispered into the darkness. "I'm falling in love with you, Dexter Williams. I'm falling in love."

17

Miss Mae stared out the back window, watching as Marguerite wrestled the iron patio furniture into place on the deck. The sun shone brightly, hurting her eyes, and she squinted through narrow slits to see. "What dat chile gon' do when I'm gone, Lord?" she prayed silently. "How she gon' make it wit'out me, Heavenly Father? She still a baby. Still just learnin' to walk. Walk wit' her, dear Lord. Let her lean on you when dey ain't no one else for her to lean on. Please. Amen."

Going back to her dishes, Miss Mae hummed quietly, rocking her body from side to side. When Marguerite finally entered the back door, Miss Mae had placed the last clean dish back into the cabinet and was sitting over a warm cup of tea. "Come sit for a spell," she said, gesturing for Marguerite to take the seat beside her. Marguerite first washed her hands in the sink, wiping them dry on a checkered towel hanging across the drip tray.

"How are your feeling today, Mama?"

Miss Mae nodded. "Today's a good day. I can feel the Good Lord holding onto me. It feels real good," she finished, rocking in her seat. "But tell me, how you doin'? You ain't said much to me lately. What's goin' on wit' you?"

Marguerite shrugged. "Nothing really to tell, Miss Mae. I've had a lot of work to do this past week."

"And how's dat pretty Dexter boy?"

Marguerite raised her eyebrows slightly. "Fine, I guess. I had lunch with him Tuesday and he was okay."

Miss Mae nodded again. "Seems like a nice boy. Too pretty, a course, but you like dem real pretty mens."

Marguerite smiled, rolling her eyes back. "So you approve?"

"Didn't say all dat. Just said he seems like a nice boy. You two serious?"

"Mama, we're just friends. We're taking it slow for now, so don't start."

"Seems to me you takin' it too fast. Don't come up here pregnant or nothing, you hear me," she said, staring Marguerite down.

Marguerite met her grandmother's intense gaze, then dropped her eyes to her lap. "Trust me. That won't happen."

Miss Mae nodded, rising to refill her cup with hot water. Marguerite watched as she lifted the kettle off the stove, her hands quivering slightly with arthritis.

Miss Mae sat back down, warming her hands against the cup. "I worry about you, Baby Girl," she started, drawing her chair up closer to Marguerite's. "Let me tell you somethin'." Miss Mae paused momentarily.

"I was younger than you when I met yo' Aunt Patricia's daddy. I won't but fourteen, fifteen years old.

His name was Joe Green. Sweet Joe Green, dey use ta call him. Sweet Joe Green." Miss Mae stared off into the distance as she continued. "He was a pretty man and won't nothin' good about him. Nothin'. He use ta run around chasin' all da girls, and one day he chased me. I thought I had won the big prize at da state fair.

"My mama tole me then dat Joe Green won't no good for me, but I swore I knew betta than she did, so I let him get to my suga spot. He got to it real good too." Miss Mae smiled lightly.

"Joe Green made me all kinda promises. Tole me I was da best thing ever happen to him. Tole me he loved me, and when my belly got real big wit' Pat, Joe Green took his pretty self and went chasin' afta someone else. Just like dat I was nothin' to him." Miss Mae sipped from her cup, pausing momentarily.

"For a long time I kept chasin' Sweet Joe Green. Now I didn't go runnin' behind him in the streets or nothin' like dat, 'cuz I had a baby to look afta and my mama would a slapped the life outta me, but I kept chasin' him in my heart. I kept thinkin' in my head dat he just didn't know what it was he wanted, but as long as I kept waitin', he'd figure it out and come back to me, but dat ain't never happen'.

"My mama tole me back then dat what I had was just a yearnin'. I was hungry for him 'cuz he knew somethin' 'bout me I didn't know 'bout myself. He knew dat I was betta off wit'out him. He knew dat I could do and be betta wit'out him. It took me a long time ta figure dat out.

"Now I'm tellin' you dis 'cuz I can see it in yo' eyes. I can hear it in yo' voice. You yearnin' fo' somethin' that you ain't yet learned 'bout yo'self. Dis Dexter boy might be what you yearnin' for and he might not be."

Miss Mae pushed her cup away, rising to wrap her arms around Marguerite. "Wantin' can leave you empty most times, Baby Girl. Yearnin' afta the wrong things can lead to no good. Yo' yearnin's like an itch you need scratched. Some boy might can scratch it, but da problem is it keeps comin' back like a bad rash. You need ta get dat itch scratched for good so it don't come back no more."

Miss Mae continued. "You done found a nice black boy who likes to show you off on his arm. He want ta be part a you. He want ta know yo' people. And you weren't shame to bring him home. If dat don't tell me somethin', it should show 'nuf tell you.

"I knew when Papa came into my life dat yearnin' for Joe Green won't gone bring me da happiness yo' papa cud. That's when I let yo' papa scratch my itch. I can't make you see your own, you gots ta learn it fo' yo'self. Just don't wait until it's too late."

Miss Mae went to sit back down in her seat, tears in her eyes. Marguerite cupped her hand around the older woman's clenched fist, biting her own lower lip to keep from crying.

"Mama, I really don't know what I feel." She shrugged before going on. "I really care about Dexter. I enjoy being with him. But I'm not sure he and I together is right. I'm not sure it feels right."

Miss Mae inhaled deeply, wiping at her cheek with the back of her hand. "Why you so 'fraid to love Dexter? Why you so 'fraid to try lovin' him? He make you feel good 'nuf to be spreadin' yo' legs for him. I knows you doin' that. So why you so 'fraid to spread yo' heart open for him?"

Marguerite shrugged, a rush of crimson rising to her cheeks. "I don't know."

"Well, you best figure it out before dey ain't no more man there for you to try wit'. Black man ain't gon' wait but so long for no woman who don't want him."

"How did you know with Papa? What made you give him a chance to change what Joe Green did to you?"

"Any man put up wit' yo' garbage and still say he love you is a good man. Papa put up wit' a lot a garbage from me and he kept right on lovin' me. I couldn't help but love him back.

"Baby Girl, I just wants ta see you happy. I think this Dexter boy can make you happy, and if he can't then somebody else can. You just need ta start lookin' fo' him. But ya need to find him soon 'cuz I can't go to my grave worryin' 'bout ya."

Falling to her knees, Marguerite laid her head in her grandmother's lap. "I'm scared, Miss Mae. I don't want to lose Dexter, but I'm terrified he might hurt me."

Miss Mae stroked her brow. "You can't lose what you ain't tryin' to hold onto. I raised you smarter than dis. You knows betta."

Marguerite nodded. "I guess I need to figure out just what it is I'm yearning for, huh?"

Miss Mae smiled, a thin turning of her lips, heightened by the brightness in her dark eyes. "Uh-huh," she whispered, nodding. "All you needs do is look inside yo'self, chile. Just look inside you.

"Now, tell me what you know bouts dis boy yo' Uncle Clarence thinks I don't know abouts. . . ."

18

The day had not gone well. Marguerite had gone from one meeting to another, each more explosive than the first. She sighed. All would have been okay if Anthony had not popped into the conference center's meeting room to say hello and to ask if she were interested in sharing a drink with him.

Marguerite shuddered. It never ceased to amaze her how some men figured no matter what they might have done to you, that you would forget about it like it never happened. He had actually had the audacity to tell her how much he missed their getting together. She had endured twenty minutes of hearing how therapy had helped him see his way clear out of his bad habits, and how he'd met a woman who moved him in ways he'd not thought possible. They were engaged to be married, and he hoped that Marguerite could be happy for him. He'd even suggested they try to be friends.

Sharon would have been proud of her. She'd smiled sweetly, slipped on her Nipon blazer, picked up her briefcase and purse, and had told him what he could do for himself as she eased out the door.

In the lobby, Marguerite headed for the telephone. She dialed frantically, charging the call on her local calling card. As it rang, she shook, the waves of frustration rocking her entire body.

"Hello?"

"Hey, there. What are you doing?" she asked, whispering into the receiver.

"Hey, baby. Trying to find you. I've been calling all day. Where are you?"

"I was out of town all day. I just got out of my last meeting and wanted to know if you wanted to go dancing. I've got a lot of energy to burn."

Dexter laughed. "Sounds like fun. I can be dressed and out the door in thirty minutes. Where are you?"

"Manhattan. I took the train."

"I'll tell you what," he responded, his mind racing. "If you don't mind hanging out for another hour, I can meet you over at The Savoy. You can take a taxi over and wait there for me. Okay?"

Marguerite fought to keep her voice normal. "Okay."

"Hey, are you all right?"

"Fine, I'm just missing you is all," she said, clasping the telephone tightly, her eyes clenched shut.

"Well if you get to The Savoy before I do, you make sure the brothers know you're waiting for your man. I don't want to have to hurt anyone tonight, and if I see some guy pushing up on you I may get crazy."

Marguerite giggled, grateful for his jealousy. "Don't worry. Just hurry up."

As she replaced the phone onto its hook, she turned to find Anthony at the lobby door, watching her. Pushing past him, she ignored his attempts at further conversation, exited the building, then hailed a cab. As it drove off, she watched him standing alone on the sidewalk, waving good-bye behind her.

By the time Dexter entered the smoke-filled club, Marguerite had already downed two gin and tonics and was working on her third. The music was consuming as she rocked alone atop her seat at the bar. Hearing her name, she turned to watch him walk toward her.

The Armani suit, a charcoal-gray silk, flattered the brown of his complexion. He looked good and as she stood to greet him, he smiled. Pulling her close, he kissed her hard, his hands roaming the length of her back. When neither of them could breathe, he pushed her away.

"What's wrong?" she asked.

"I think I should be asking what's wrong with you."

Marguerite returned to her bar stool, sipping her drink. "Nothing."

Dexter nodded, unconvinced. "You look incredible," he said, eyeing her curiously. "Who'd you get all dressed up for?"

"Thank you, and I got dressed up for me, no one else."

Gesturing for the bartender, Dexter ordered himself a drink. "So who did you spend the day meeting with? Anyone I know?"

Marguerite smiled guided by the alcohol. "No, and what's with the twenty questions?"

"Just making sure there isn't some other brother I need to be concerned with."

"Don't worry. I'm going home with you tonight and that's all that matters."

Dexter studied her. There was a sadness in her eyes he'd not seen before. She looked wounded, and he was suddenly paranoid with thoughts of who could have painted her with so much hurt. He shook his head, draining his newly acquired glass quickly, the scotch burning the length of his throat. Clasping her under the chin, he lifted her face, meeting her gaze with his own. "We will talk about this later. There's something you're not telling me and I will find out."

Marguerite wrapped her hand around his, pulling his palm to her lips, sliding her mouth along the length of his fingers. "Dance with me," she said, rising. "I need to dance." Pulling her close, he nodded. Marvin Gaye's *Let's Get It On* was playing, and the room was packed with couples groping each other. She leaned on Dexter heavily as he guided her to an empty spot in the crowd, brushing her cheek alongside his.

Dancing a slow grind, Marguerite lost herself in the warmth of him, giving into the music. Hours later, when he'd finally persuaded her to take a break, she was sober again and exhausted, and she welcomed the long ride back to Danbury.

Pretending to sleep, she was grateful that Dexter wasn't pushing her for conversation. She desperately needed to think about what was going on in the back of her mind. "What is wrong with me?" she cried to herself, fighting back the tears under her eyelids. "Here I am sitting beside a man who wants me and I'm crying over how he might turn into Mr. Hyde on me like Anthony did." In the back of her mind she could hear Miss Mae whispering to her.

"Take it to the Lord when it's too heavy for you to handle, chile. Take it to the Lord."

Marguerite tried to pray, tried to form the words she thought she should say, but her mind was numb. No God would want to hear the frivolous cries of a woman who had walked into this mess with her eyes open. No. She could not bring herself to take it to God or anyone else.

Back in the warmth of Dexter's condo, she delighted in not having to spend the night in the emptiness of her own home. Behind the privacy of his bedroom door, she stripped naked, wrapping herself around his long limbs. He cuddled her close, his hands clasped tightly around her shoulders, their bodies rocking easily atop the watery mattress. The radio played quietly above their heads, Anita Baker stroking them both with a melody.

When Dexter finally spoke, she wished him away, not wanting to confront her pain with him by her side.

"What is it, Marguerite? What in the world has you so upset? Is there someone you're not telling me about?"

"Don't, Dexter. It wasn't like that. It's just been a very long day. I had to spend most of my time pacifying salesmen and I'm tired. No more, no less."

Dexter stared out into the darkness, sensing an untruth falling from her lips. "I don't want to come across like the jealous fool I can be, but I am worried about you. You don't talk to me. I don't know what you're thinking or feeling, and I don't like that. I get the feeling you're hiding something from me and I . . . don't . . . want to . . . lose you," he finally stammered.

Rising above him, Marguerite kissed him, lightly brushing her breasts against his chest. "Don't do this to yourself. You don't need to," she muttered. "Everything is okay. I'm here with you and that's all that you should care about."

Lying back down beside him, she brushed her hand lightly across his chest.

"The family's all gathering at Miss Mae's tomorrow for dinner. I would really like you to come and meet everyone," she said, her voice pleading mildly.

"Meet the family? Sounds serious."

She laughed. "Yeah. I think you need to experience all the Cole women firsthand. I also want you to meet my uncle. I think the two of you will really hit it off."

"Hey, I won you over and I know Miss Mae's falling for me. The others will be a piece of cake."

She giggled again. "I wouldn't be so sure of that if I were you."

Pulling her closer, Dexter pressed his face into her hair, inhaling the sweet scent of coconut coating her braids. "I'm sure. You're the one that's worried."

19

When he walked through the door, Patricia, Delores, Sharon, and Marguerite were trying to teach Miss Mae the new Electric Slide. Marguerite grinned widely as he made his way into the room.

Laughing, Miss Mae brought them all to a stop, extending her hand out to Dexter. "Hello there, Dexter. How you doin' today?"

"Just fine, thank you," he said as she hugged him warmly.

"Come on in here, boy, and let me introduce you to all my chilen." Still grinning, Marguerite swayed to the music as Miss Mae took control. Dexter met her eyes, bemusement across his face.

"Everybody, dis here's Marguerite's new boyfriend, Dexter." Marguerite winced as Sharon giggled quietly behind her.

"Dexter, these here's my daughta's Leah and Patricia. And over there is my cousin Minny and her daughter Delores. And who else?" Miss Mae said, spinning herself around. "Oh, yes, behind Miss Freshy over der' is my other baby girl Sharon." Sharon waved hello, then hit Marguerite on the shoulder.

"And somewhere in the kitchen is Sharon's beau

Randy, my son Clarence, and his friend . . . what dat nice boy's name again, Beagle, Boxer . . . ?"

"Shepard," Pat responded, extending her hand out to Dexter. "Hi, Dexter, it's nice meeting you."

"The pleasure's mine," he said, shaking first her hand, then Leah's. His eyebrows raised, he looked over at Marguerite curiously. Had Miss Mae said Shepard?

"Where da rest a dem men folks?" Miss Mae asked. "Well, never you mind, Dexter, you'll meet da rest a dem soon enough. Dey probably out on the porch smokin' dem nasty cigars. I don't 'low no smokin' in my house, so dey takes it out back."

Dexter nodded politely, then made his way over to Marguerite, kissing her boldly. "Hey, there," he whispered, his bright smile meeting that of Sharon, who was standing behind them.

"Hey, yourself," Marguerite said. "Didn't know what you were in for, did you?"

Dexter laughed, shaking his head no. "Did I hear Miss Mae say . . ." he started to whisper before being interrupted.

"Come rest yo'self down, Dexter. My girls was just tryin' to teach me da 'Lectric Slide. You know dat dance, boy?" Miss Mae asked, patting the seat beside her.

Dexter nodded. "Yes'm, I do, but I'm not very good at it."

"Me neither, but my girls keep tryin'. I likes the Macarena best." Miss Mae nodded. "Are you hungry? Get him some food," she commanded in one big breath. "Fix him a plate, Marguerite."

"Thank you," Dexter said, settling himself com-

fortably on the cushion beside Miss Mae, "but nothing for me just yet."

"So, Dexter, where are you from?" Leah asked
primly.

"Arizona. My parents were originally from Chicago,
though."

"You work?" Delores asked rudely, sitting on the
arm of the sofa beside him.

Dexter nodded. "Yes. I own my own company.
Doing quite well, as a matter of fact."

"You women need to stop," Clarence interjected,
entering the room. "Hi, I'm Clarence, Marguerite's
uncle," he said, extending a hand toward Dexter. "I
see they've got you cornered. They're like a pack of
wolves these women are." Dexter chuckled as the
two men shook hands like old friends.

Miss Mae sucked her teeth. "Don't you start, boy.
We was just makin' conversation."

Marguerite laughed, hugging her uncle. "Save
him, Uncle Clarence, or he won't be any good for
me by the time they all get through with him."

Clarence laughed with her. "Come on, Dexter, let
me introduce you to the rest of this crew. Can I get
you a beer?"

Dexter rose to his feet still smiling. "Thanks. A
beer sounds real good right about now. Excuse
me," he said, smiling at Marguerite's aunts and
grandmother.

Brushing past her, Dexter squeezed her hand,
then disappeared behind Clarence.

"My, my, my," Sharon sputtered. "Brother is
kickin' it. You said he was cute, but you didn't say
he was this fine."

Marguerite rolled her eyes.

"What's wrong wit' him?" Delores asked, picking something from between her teeth.

"I beg your pardon?"

"Well, any man that fine and his age who doesn't have a woman must have something wrong with him," she said, her whiny voice irritating.

Sharon busted out laughing. "Oh, no, she didn't!"

Marguerite flipped her hand at Delores. "He's got a woman, thank you, and there is nothing wrong with him. He beats those pathetic excuses you keep dating."

Delores rolled her eyes, going to stand by her mother. "Mom, what you think?"

Miss Minny smiled a toothless grin. "Look like dat pretty boy Mae use to go wit', don't he, Mae? What dat boy name was?"

"I ain't never waste my time wit' no pretty mens. You mus' be talkin' 'bout yo'self."

Miss Minny grunted. "I know who I talkin' 'bout. Don't you tell me . . ."

Patricia interrupted. "He seems very nice. So are you two serious, Baby Girl?"

Marguerite shrugged. "We'll see."

Sharon grinned. "Let's see if he can survive you old women first."

"Humph. Don't know who you callin' ole," Miss Mae said.

In the kitchen, Dexter smiled warmly as Clarence introduced him around. As he stepped out on to the back porch, he instantly recognized the dark figure, with his back to the door, who stood as tall as he did, their builds similar. When Shepard spun around, meeting his brother's eyes, they both

smiled hesitantly, then laughed nervously. Clarence
stood off to the side visibly confused.

"You two know each other?"

Shepard nodded. "Clarence Cole, I'd like you to
meet my baby brother Dexter. Dexter, this is my
friend Clarence."

Dexter shook his head. "I don't know what to say.
I had no idea. . . ."

They all laughed again.

"Mmmm. Does Marguerite know?" Clarence
asked.

Dexter shook his head. "I don't think so. I
haven't had an opportunity to introduce her to
Shepard yet. Obviously you've met, though."

Shepard nodded. "Briefly, a few minutes ago, but
neither one of us put it together."

Clarence laughed again. "Well, I always said my
darling niece and I definitely had good taste when it
came to men." Shepard laughed nervously with him.

"Well, let's get you that beer," Clarence said,
pushing Dexter toward the door. "I think we could
all use a drink right about now."

When Marguerite entered the kitchen, Dexter sat
at the table across from Randy, between her Uncle
Martin and Uncle William, debating the merits of
Deion Saunders. Marguerite grimaced as she entered. Basketball she could handle. Football, on the
other hand, bored her to death. This was definitely
not the conversation she wanted to join in on. Behind him, her Uncle Clarence was piling fried
chicken and macaroni and cheese onto a plate.
Shepard stood off to the side. As she entered,
Clarence gave her the thumbs-up sign and smiled
broadly.

THE "THANK YOU" GIFT INCLUDES:

- 4 books absolutely FREE (plus $1.99 for shipping and handling).
- A FREE newsletter, *Arabesque Romance News*, filled with author interviews, book previews, special offers, and more!
- No risks or obligations. You're free to cancel whenever you wish with no questions asked.

INTRODUCTORY OFFER CERTIFICATE

Yes! Please send me 4 FREE Arabesque novels (plus $1.99 for shipping & handling). I understand I am under no obligation to purchase any books, as explained on the back of this card. Send my free tote bag after my first regular paid shipment.

NAME _____

ADDRESS _____ APT. _____

CITY _____ STATE _____ ZIP _____

TELEPHONE ( ) _____

E-MAIL _____

SIGNATURE _____

Thank You!

AN123A

Accepting the four introductory books for FREE (plus $1.99 to offset the cost of shipping & handling) places you under no obligation to buy anything. You may keep the books and return the shipping statement marked "cancelled". If you do not cancel, about a month later we will send 4 additional Arabesque novels, and you will be billed the preferred subscriber's price of just $4.00 per title. That's $16.00* for all 4 books for a savings of almost 40% off the cover price (Plus $1.99 for shipping and handling). You may cancel at any time, but if you choose to continue, every month we'll send you 4 more books, which you may either purchase at the preferred discount price. . . or return to us and cancel your subscription.

* PRICES SUBJECT TO CHANGE

THE ARABESQUE ROMANCE BOOK CLUB
P.O. BOX 5214
CLIFTON NJ 07015-5214

PLACE
STAMP
HERE

"Do you want some collard greens, Dexter?" Clarence asked.

"Please, thank you," Dexter responded. "I can get that myself if you want."

"No problem. If I don't take care of you, my niece over there will never let me hear the end of it," he said, gesturing in Marguerite's direction.

"Leave me out of this," she said, smiling, going to stand beside Dexter. "You okay?" she asked, brushing her hand across his shoulders, the cotton shirt warm against her palm.

Nodding, Dexter grabbed her hand within his own. "Why didn't you tell me my brother was going to be here?"

"Your brother?" Marguerite looked around confused.

Dexter pointed in Shepard's direction. "Marguerite, this is my older brother, Shepard. Shepard, this is the gorgeous woman I've been telling you about."

Shepard smiled. "Small world, huh?"

Marguerite shook her head in disbelief. "You mean . . . ?"

Clarence laughed, hugging her tightly. "Sure do, Baby Girl."

Marguerite wrapped her arms about Dexter's shoulders, hugging him warmly. "I'm speechless."

Dexter nodded. "I think we all are."

"So what you think about that last game with San Francisco?" William asked, changing the subject back to football.

Exiting gracefully, Marguerite didn't wait to hear Dexter's answer. Looking back over her shoulder, she saw all the men were talking as Dexter pulled a warm piece of meat into his mouth.

Back in the living room, Delores was bemoaning her last weekend away with three friends from work.

"Well, I told her if she and Angela wanted to waste money at some restaurant, then that was their business, but she had better respect any food I put in the refrigerator. Now does it make any sense to you to be wastin' money when we could have all just pitched in and cooked?"

Sharon was shaking her head laughing. "Ohhh, Delores. Girlfriend, you are too cheap. Here you are supposed to be on vacation and you worrying about spending two extra cents to eat out. I can't believe you really expected them to waste what little time they had cooking just because you wanted to save a dime."

Delores sucked her teeth. "I work hard for my money, thank you."

Miss Minny shook her head. "Delores, you's cheap, honey. Gots it from yo' daddy. Ain't nothin' to be shamed of, though."

Miss Mae laughed, a deep cackle that shook the brown of her skin like a warm breeze across raspberry Jell-O. "Yes, Lord, dat Otis was cheap. Minny couldn't a spent a nickel wit'out him checkin' to see if he could a got the same thing for a penny." She laughed again. "We wents to dis nice restaurant once and he must a eat twice as much as da rest a us did, but sho' 'nuf wanted us to split da check fifty-fifty. He 'n Papa almos' come to blows."

"Now don't be speakin' ill a da dead. My Otis had his faults, but yo' Clarence won't no perfect angel neither!"

They both laughed. "But dey sho' 'nuf was a good time," both women cackled simultaneously.

The other women joined in as Delores went off to sulk in a corner.

Marguerite sat down at her grandmother's feet, resting her head against the woman's leg. Miss Mae brushed her crinkled fingers alongside Marguerite's brow. "Dexter all right in there?"

Marguerite nodded. "He's talking with the men and his brother, Shepard."

Sharon leapt from her seat. "His what?"

Marguerite nodded. "Brother. Uncle Clarence's friend is Dexter's older brother."

The women each jumped in with a question, their chatter flooding the small room. Miss Mae put up her hand to quiet them all down. "Now you girls know better. Don't be embarrassin' yo'selves none this afternoon when we's got company. Now, did you feed him? You knows you got to keep your man fed."

"Mama, a man today can feed himself if he's hungry, but yes, he got himself something to eat. Uncle Clarence fixed him a plate."

"Is he any good in bed?" Delores asked suddenly. "'Cause Clarence said being wit' Shepard was like headin' for heaven."

"Delores, chile, what got into you?" Miss Minny asked, turning around to glare at her daughter. "Nice girls don't be worryin' 'bout whether no man good in da bed and talkin' dat nastiness. And I know Clarence ain't said no foolishness like dat. He knows betta. Sinful is what it is. Sinful."

Pat laughed, dropping her head onto Leah's shoulder.

"Miss Minny," Leah said, giggling herself. "These days, young girls find out right away whether or not a man is any good. Don't want to waste too much time if a man doesn't know what he's doing."

Miss Minny clasped her hand to her chest. "Lord, I swear . . . "

"When Minny and I was girls you didn't talk about nothin' like dat," Miss Mae said. "Wud a got yo' mouth washed out wit' soap if our mamas caught us talkin' 'bout some boy and his privates. But we use to whispa' about it when dey wasn't listenin', didn't we, Minny?"

"You was fas' an' easy, Mae, but I was a good girl," Miss Minny professed.

"You a lie," Miss Mae said. "I knows full well Otis got into yo' suga spot before you was married, and you a lie if you say he didn't."

Miss Minny wrinkled her face. "Otis da only one got my suga' spot, you ole' evil sight you, but we knows Clarence wasn't da only one got yo's, now don't we?"

Patricia was laughing hysterically. Gasping for air, she wiped tears from her eyes. "Mama . . . do . . . you . . . know for years, I had no idea what my 'suga spot' was. You were always yelling at me not to let the boys get my 'suga spot,' and I had no idea what the heck you were talking about."

Miss Mae flicked her hand at Pat. "I didn't have to worry 'bout you. Now Leah and Greer were da ones I had to keep my eye on."

Leah raised her eyebrows, her stomach aching from laughing with Pat. "Not me, Mama. Greer was the fast one. I couldn't keep up with her."

Miss Mae nodded. "Yes, Lord. Marguerite, yo'

mama was fast. I was always beatin' some rusty-behind boy outta my house, an' da more I beat 'em, da more dey kep' comin'.'"

"Until she met your daddy," Leah said, sighing heavily. "When she met him, she didn't have time for anyone else." She smiled remembering.

"Humph. He got her suga spot, and den we couldn't get rid a him neither. Boy was like root rot da way he kept comin' roun' my house." Miss Mae shook her head.

Sharon fell to the floor beside Marguerite. "I cannot believe we are here talking about sex with these old women."

"Ole peoples like sex too," Miss Minny chimed in. "At least dat what dey say over at da Civic Center. Had a class on it didn't dey, Mae?"

"Surely did. 'Sex over Seventy.' Problem was most a da mens couldn't barely remember where dey thing was, let 'lone know where to puts it." Miss Mae and Miss Minny burst into laughter. "Lord, I think I hurt myself," Miss Mae said, grabbing her chest.

"You okay, Mama?" Leah asked, a touch of concern rising in her voice. Marguerite twisted around to look up at her grandmother.

"Are you okay, Miss Mae?"

"Ain't nothin' wrong wit's me. Now don't yall start no fussin', dat ain't necessary. Girl, go check and see if dat boy okay in there. I don't hear nothin'."

"He's okay, Mama. And he's a grown man, not a boy. He's going to have to deal with you folks all on his own."

"Hello," Sharon piped in.

"Humph," Miss Mae grunted, rising to her feet. "I swear, Minny, you try to teach these girls somethin' 'bout men folks and dey think dey knows everythin'. I will go check on him myself," she finished, heading toward the kitchen.

As she disappeared out of hearing range, Pat leaned down toward the two women on the floor. "I don't know, Baby Girl. Looks like Miss Mae might be a little sweet on Dexter herself." She chuckled.

Leah shook her head, still laughing. "I wouldn't worry about Miss Mae if I were you, but I thought you might have had a problem the way that brother of ours sure lit up when he saw Dexter. I can't believe you and Clarence are dating brothers."

"I don't believe you two," Marguerite said with a laugh, as Sharon fell out hysterical.

"So," Pat continued. "Is he any good in bed?"

Leah hit her sister playfully. "Now Pat, you aren't that old yet. All you have to do is look at the way he walks to know he's good. Shepard too, for that matter. Now that sho' 'nuff is a waste of good man."

"Sinful," Miss Minny chastised. "All a you's is just sinful."

"I think it's time we changed the subject," Marguerite said, giggling with the rest of them.

They were interrupted by Miss Mae calling out to them. "Anybody want dessert? Me an' Dexter an' Shepard gon' cut dis here chocolate cake, and I'se got 'tata pie and pineapple cake too."

Marguerite shook her head. "I swear, he is such a kiss-up. Cutting chocolate cake with Miss Mae." She rolled her eyes.

Sharon smiled, helping Marguerite to her feet. "Hang onto him. Brother definitely ain't stupid. He knows who to kiss up to."

Heading into the kitchen, the group of women

continued to laugh and giggle among themselves, joining the others who sat comfortably around Miss Mae's kitchen table, plates piled high with sweet confections.

Dexter smiled, pulling Marguerite down onto his lap. "Your grandmother says if I marry you I'll have to send you back to cooking school because you can't cook soul food. Said you didn't know a turnip green from a collard."

"No, she didn't," Marguerite laughed.

"Yes, she did," Clarence said, leaning down to kiss her cheek. "Dexter said that's okay, though. He's still going to marry you anyway." He walked to go stand by Shepard's side, rubbing his hand along the man's broad back.

Marguerite dropped her head into her hands, a rise of red flitting across her cheeks.

Dexter kissed her other cheek, hugging her tightly, meeting his brother's eye.

"Ummm," Sharon muttered behind her as Miss Mae rested her hands lightly upon both of their shoulders, a wide grin gracing her face.

20

The three couples squeezed comfortably into a cushioned booth as the waitress rushed over to assist them. Sharon and Randy, Marguerite and Dexter, and Clarence and Shepard were laughing quietly among themselves.

"What can I get you?" the thin blond girl asked, a wad of bubble gum filling the cup of her cheek. "We've still got some blueberry pie left, and the carrot cake is to die for."

"Carrot cake sounds good to me," Clarence quipped. "I'll have a cup of coffee too."

"You didn't get enough cake at Miss Mae's, Uncle Clarence?" Sharon asked, shaking her head.

"Child, I never get enough sweets."

"Actually, it sounds pretty good to me too," Randy piped in, reaching out to squeeze Sharon's hand. "I'll take the same."

"Me three," said Shepard.

Dexter laughed. "I can't pass it up either."

"Mmmm," Marguerite hummed. "Well, I'll just have coffee."

The two women exchanged a look between them. Sharon giggled. "I guess that'll be a round of coffee for everyone and carrot cake for the four little pigs."

Marguerite laughed loudly as Clarence tossed a napkin at Sharon's head.

The waitress headed toward the kitchen. Within minutes a pot of coffee and four slices of cake sat on the table.

"So what is it you do, Dexter?" Randy asked, cupping his hands atop the table.

"I own a computer technology firm. We do high-scale network installations and programming for smaller organizations. And we've recently expanded our Web development division, providing Web design and services."

Randy nodded. "I've been seriously thinking about how I can better utilize the Web for my business. Everyone's starting to live by computers now, and since investment is always a hot commodity, I need to consider how I can better tie them together."

"You're an investment broker, correct?"

Randy nodded.

"Yes," Clarence said, "and a very good one. There aren't too many people I'd trust with my money, and Randy has proven himself to be the cream of the crop. I've got quite a portfolio since he and I started to do business."

"Me too," Sharon smiled. "I'll be able to retire comfortably thanks to Randy."

Randy blushed.

"You two should talk," Marguerite said to Dexter. "It might be a profitable venture."

"I'd like that," Dexter responded.

"You have my card," said Randy. "Call me and we can schedule some time to meet."

"I can remember when the only thing my brother wanted to do was play stickball down in Watson's field," Shepard said with a laugh. "Now he's talking computers, and the only thing I know about a mouse is that it's a nasty little rodent."

The table laughed.

"I've tried to give you a crash course, but you're one of those persons who's totally computer illiterate," Dexter said with a smile.

"And proud of it," his brother responded.

Clarence high-fived Shepard. "Don't let it bother you. I only know how to get my e-mails and how to send one when I have to."

Marguerite chuckled. "You're killing me."

Sharon laughed with her. "That's okay. I don't know anything about computers and even less about investing. That's why I keep Randy around, and you too Dexter will come in quite handy."

Randy raised his eyebrows. "I'm glad I can be of some service to you."

Sharon leaned to kiss his cheek. "I'll let you know when I can't use you anymore, honey."

"So," Marguerite said, "will we be hearing wedding bells soon?"

Both Sharon and Randy glared in her direction.

"Yes," Shepard responded, turning to his brother and Marguerite. "Will we be hearing double wedding bells soon?"

Dexter laughed as Marguerite blushed profusely.

"You need to talk to your friend Marguerite," Randy said.

"No she doesn't," Sharon responded, her tone short.

"Someone needs to talk to you," Randy said to her

before turning his attention back to Marguerite. "Did she tell you she wants a prenuptial?"

Dexter laughed. "She's only protecting your interests, right?"

Randy laughed with him. "Yeah, and she has no intentions of ever spending a dime of my money."

Both Marguerite and Sharon took attitude. "What are you tryin' to say?" Marguerite asked.

"Yeah, Dexter, you think all we want from a man is his money?" quipped Sharon.

"Hello, girlfriend," Clarence said, snapping his fingers. "I'm glad us mens don't have that problem."

"I take offense," Sharon said. "Where'd you say you found this man Marguerite? Send his behind right back."

Dexter smiled. "My baby can have a prenuptial if she wants one. I don't mind."

"Well, I do," Randy said. "Where's the trust?"

"The second page, fifth paragraph," Sharon quipped. "I'm gon' trust that I keep mine and you gon' trust that you keep yours. Better safe than sorry, I say."

Dexter and Marguerite laughed. "If you couldn't tell," she said, wrapping her arms around him, "this is a sensitive subject for these two."

Shepard sighed. "I'm glad we don't have that problem."

Clarence agreed. "Me too, baby. It's not worth all the drama."

Sharon sucked her teeth. "Humph. You two had better think about some type of contractual agreement too. I don't know why all you people think all these love stories have fairy-tale endings."

Dexter reached over to embrace the woman

warmly. "Sharon, my love, the ending is what you make it."

Sharon rolled her eyes. "Well, make it so I don't have to worry and I'll marry the man tomorrow."

Randy smiled, reaching to pull her out of Dexter's arms. "I love you too, honey."

Later that night, Marguerite lay by Dexter's side, his arm curled comfortably over her breasts, his face nuzzled in her hair. He'd drifted off to sleep quickly, laughing over the feminine assault of her relatives. He'd won them over just like he said he would, and they truly liked him, Miss Mae in particular. Marguerite could see it in her eyes.

She was glad that they'd gone and had coffee before heading home. It was important to her that he get to know Sharon and Clarence. Marguerite was delighted to see him warming up to his brother's relationship. Though she knew it was still not easy for him to accept, she was proud of how hard he was working at it for his brother's sake. They'd all laughed at the coincidence, and Marguerite had been thrilled to see her uncle so happy.

Rolling close to Dexter, she wrapped her legs about his, pressing her body as near to him as she could manage. She marveled at his blackness, his complexion complementing hers. Brushing her hand along his chest, she enjoyed the feel of him against her, enjoyed the fit of him within her. She suddenly felt as though he deserved more than she would ever be able to offer, and the coldness of that thought hit her broadside, knocking the breath from her lungs.

She inhaled deeply, drawing his scent deep into her nostrils. He smelled sweet, like warm cake cooling, a mixture of light vanilla and honey. She shuddered lightly, the aroma of him addicting, a sweet fix she found herself craving. As she stroked his chest and back, she could feel him hardening against her thigh, his organ quivering with a mind of its own. She stroked the dark length, kneading the growing fullness within her hand, the muscle straining to be possessed.

Running her lips along his chest, she suckled lightly on his nipple, tasting the sweetness that rose to her nostrils. A light moan eased past his lips as he shifted closer against her. Their loving was easy, a slow grind against freshly washed bedsheets. His hands burned against her skin, her breasts melting beneath his palms.

"Whoa, baby," he whispered against her ear, his breath hot. "Oh, my sweet Marguerite . . ."

Her wanting hurt. A delicious pain flooding every crevice of her being. She pressed against him straining to get closer, wanting her insides to fuse with his. Clutching him hungrily, she could hear herself moaning, muffled cries shouted into his shoulder. When he could get no closer, when their bodies were more one than two, she could find no air and she gasped, struggling to breathe, her tears washing warmly over them.

Spent, they lay side by side, neither wanting to be the first to move. Dexter kissed her, brushing his lips across her nose, her eyes, brushing his tongue against her lips, wiping the moisture from her cheeks. Marguerite still clutched him tightly, not wanting to let go, wanting only to enjoy the solace found where she now lay.

21

On Saturday, the seventh of June, Marguerite dressed carefully, easing her firm body into a designer dress, the elegant knit tank falling in a classic line down the length of her torso, past her hips, and resting just at the edge of her ankles. Its color was a deep lavender, a rich, vibrant purple that was warm and alluring against her complexion. A delicate sandal dyed to match the dress's fabric adorned her feet, her manicured toes a complementing shade of pale pink. Her braids had been swept up into an elegant bun, single wisps of thin braids falling along the length of her face to her shoulder. Marguerite had adorned the hairdo with a comb of lavender flowers. Her makeup was light, faint enough to appear nonexistent, yet strong enough to warm the coloring of her face.

Checking her reflection in the mirror one last time before heading toward Greenwich, she wanted to insure that Dexter would be pleased when he saw her. It was John's wedding day. Dexter's invitation to join him at his best friend's wedding, though expected, had still come as somewhat of a surprise to Marguerite. Although she could not deny that Dexter had become an important part of her life, she still had trouble reconciling to the fact that they were a couple. Today he wanted her to meet his friends and his employees, and Marguerite did not want him to be disappointed.

As she stepped into the church, Marguerite was conscious of her surroundings, the Catholic church steeped in history, its congregation and neighborhood one of great wealth. Very white wealth. She was prepared to put on her formal face, the one needed for certain business encounters and social events. She wore this face well, as did many sisters when such was necessary.

An usher, a lanky boy of sixteen or seventeen, lifted an arm to escort her to a seat. His dusty blond hair was tousled into place, the acne raging against his pale complexion. He introduced himself as Jason, the bride's brother, then sat her on the groom's side, rushing to seat other arrivals.

Only moments passed before the organ sounded and John and Dexter appeared from a back room to take their places at the altar. The two looked elegant in their dark tuxedos, the traditional black jackets and bow ties meticulously fitted. Dexter caught her eye and smiled brightly. Marguerite smiled back.

It was a beautiful ceremony, steeped in Catholic tradition. The tantalizing scent of white roses adorned the church, the bridal and attendant bouquets white and yellow roses interspersed with a faint touch of orange. The bridesmaids wore a pale shade of tangerine, the maid of honor a darker melon. Debbie, the bride, was a long-legged redhead, her curvy frame a dazzling complement alongside John's tall, lean structure. She'd been modeling internationally for a number of years, and together the duo was a striking pair. Her gown was a form-fitting design of antique lace, the ivory fabric showing off the warmth of the woman's complexion. As the couple said their I-do's and the priest blessed their union, Marguerite could not help but imagine the day when she and Dexter might be exchanging vows. The thought brought a smile to her face and as she caught herself in the daydream, Marguerite could not help but blush.

Dexter rushed to her side as soon as the ceremony had ended, sweeping her up into his arms. "You look exquisite," he gushed, kissing her mouth easily.

"Thank you. You look quite dapper yourself."

"Almost makes you think we should be on top of a wedding cake ourselves, doesn't it?"

Marguerite smiled. "The wedding was beautiful."

Dexter nodded in agreement. "It was. John has wanted this for a long time. I'm really happy for him."

"Are you riding to the reception in the limousine?"

"No. I was hoping to ride with you, if that's okay?"

Marguerite nodded. "No pictures?"

"We're done. We took most of them earlier, so I'm ready when you are."

The reception was held at the family's private country club. The large estate looked out over an elaborate golf course and the expanse of the Long Island Sound. Marguerite was duly impressed. The event was a whirlwind as Dexter swept her from one table to another, introducing her to his associates and friends. She met his secretary, Carol Pelt, the matronly figure who often mothered her over the telephone, his key staff members, David Listen and Mark Campbell, both vice presidents, plus an array of installers and technical gurus. After the formality of the event ended, Marguerite and Dexter swept across the dance floor, moving with the beat of the live band. An hour later, they came face-to face with the bride and groom.

"May I have this dance?" Dexter asked, extending a hand toward Debbie. The woman smiled in response, reaching over to kiss her new husband before leaning into Dexter's arms. As Dexter swept the bride across the floor, John wrapped his own hands around Marguerite's waist, leading her in a stiff two-step.

"You have to forgive me," he said.

"Why?" Marguerite asked, obvious confusion crossing her face.

"I don't have any rhythm." John laughed. "Debbie says I'm an embarrassment."

Marguerite laughed with him. "Don't worry about it. You're doing just fine."

"Liar."

Marguerite smiled. "Congratulations. I hope you two will be very happy."

"Thank you. So, when are you and my buddy going to tie the knot?"

The color rushed to Marguerite's face as she stammered for an answer.

John was laughing at her. "It's okay. Dexter used to get tongue-tied when I would ask him that question too. At least he did before he met you. Now he always has an answer and if he has his way, it will be very soon. He loves you a lot. I hope you know that."

Marguerite nodded politely. "He's very special to me also."

John continued to drag her about the dance floor.

"I want you to know that he's my best friend. I'd die for him and I'm jealous as hell."

"Why?"

"Brother can dance."

Marguerite laughed again as the pair came to stand beside Debbie and Dexter.

John grabbed his bride and kissed her warmly, then turned to formally introduce the two women.

"It was a beautiful wedding." Marguerite smiled. "Thank you for having me."

"Thank you for coming." Debbie beamed. "I'm so glad to finally meet you. Dexter talks about you all the time."

Marguerite blushed as Dexter leaned to kiss her cheek.

"We all need to get together once you two get back from your honeymoon and get settled," said Marguerite.

Debbie nodded, the vivid color of her hair reflecting against her face. "Great. And you and I will make all the arrangements. I don't trust these two."

John grabbed her, lifting her off her feet.

"See? He doesn't do anything but play, and when they're together it's worse."

Marguerite rolled her eyes as Dexter stuck his tongue out at Debbie.

"Excuse us," he said, pulling Marguerite close. "They're playing our song."

Debbie and John waved them off, turning their attention to their other guests. Marguerite smiled warmly, nuzzling her face against Dexter's chest, falling into a daydream about her own wedding and dancing alongside this man who thought he loved her.

* * *

When the telephone rang, it startled them both from the warmth of their thoughts. Marguerite lay propped up against the pillows, the Sunday paper sprawled out in front of her. A lukewarm cup of coffee sat on the nightstand by her side. Dexter lay beside her, his backside curved warmly against her long limbs. He walked in and out of sleep, waking every now and then to cuddle Marguerite closer, scan a headline, or to flip the television on to see what he might be missing. It was a lazy Sunday for them, and after dancing most of the night, neither had the energy or the motivation to move.

Marguerite reached across the small end table to pull the receiver to her ear.

"Hello?"

"Marguerite, it's Pat."

"Hey, Aunt Pat. What's up?"

"Miss Mae's in the hospital again, Baby Girl."

"What happened?"

"You should come as soon as you can. Is Dexter with you?"

"Yes, ma'am."

"Good. I don't want you driving yourself."

"Is she okay?"

"She's in serious condition and they're going to have to perform surgery. Her heart's not holding out. We're just waiting for the surgeon to get here now."

"Oh, no," Marguerite whined, tears forming at the edge of her eyes. Dexter sat up beside her, concern pushing the sleep out of his eyes.

"You need to stay strong, Baby Girl. She needs us now. Let me speak to Dexter."

Marguerite passed the receiver to Dexter, wiping at her tears with the back of her hand. Standing, she wrapped her arms around her body, folding herself in a deep embrace. Now seated on the side of the bed, Dexter kept repeating, "Yes," "Yes, ma'am," into the telephone as her aunt filled him in and gave him a list of instructions. When he finally hung up the receiver, she turned to face him, hurt dripping over her spirit.

"Pat said she and Clarence have called everyone," he said. "She needs us to stop by Miss Mae's house to get her emergency file. She says you know where that is."

Marguerite nodded, barely feeling her head move against her shoulders.

Dexter rose, replacing her arms with his own. The embrace felt good, a necessity Marguerite had grown comfortable with.

"Get dressed, baby."

Marguerite nodded, heading for the bathroom. Fifteen minutes later, she was pacing the kitchen floor in a blue cotton jogging suit and sneakers. Dexter appeared ten minutes after that in a pair of worn blue jeans and a t-shirt. As soon as she saw him, the tears spilled over her cheeks and she rushed into his arms to be held. Dexter let her cry, cuddling her close against his chest, and when she didn't have another tear to shed, he wiped her face clean, cupped his hand beneath her chin, and looked deeply into her eyes.

"We are going to get through this. I'm going to

be right here with you. Miss Mae is going to be fine. You've got to have faith."

Marguerite nodded, her braids pulled back into a ponytail that spilled down her back. Locking the door behind them, they headed first to Miss Mae's house, where Marguerite ran inside to grab the file her aunt had requested. Dexter made one other stop at the local Dunkin' Donuts.

They drove in silence, the local gospel station playing softly on the radio. Marguerite flipped briefly through the file, viewing the papers she'd seen so many times before: Miss Mae's power of attorney, a copy of the woman's living will, her medical records, emergency telephone numbers and addresses of distant relatives, and an assortment of other information she had deemed important should something ever happen to her. Marguerite sighed heavily, willing her tears not to drop, as Dexter reached out to hold tightly to her hand.

22

Marguerite entered the Cardiac ICU, waving to the nurses at the desk. Since Pat's call six weeks ago, she had spent every free moment she could find in the hospital helping with her grandmother. Night after night she would sit with Miss Mae, being consoled more than consoling, their conversations peppered with hysteria and laughter and tears and bickering. Tonight would be no exception.

Surgery after surgery to erase the turpitude that had invaded the old woman's body had sapped the last of her strength. Miss Mae wanted only to cross over to the other side where eternal promises awaited her, but she refused to go until she felt comfortable that Marguerite would abide by all her wishes and would promise to fulfill all her dreams.

As Marguerite walked into the room, Miss Mae sat propped awkwardly in bed, fussing at no one about everything.

"What's wrong, Mama?" Marguerite asked, tossing her coat onto the empty chair.

"Nothin'. Jus' tired a dis hospital. How you doin', baby? You look tired."

"I'm fine. You're the one we need to worry about."

Miss Mae flipped her hand at her. "You still seeing that pretty Dexter boy?" she asked.

"Yes, Miss Mae."

"He might seem like a nice boy. Too sometimey, though. All dem pretty ones like dat."

"Miss Mae, Dexter is not sometimey. He's a good man."

Miss Mae grunted. "One day, girl, you gonna listen to me. I told you when you was in love with that big baldheaded Negro that he won't no good for you. And what happened? He went and broke your heart. Then you went chasin' after that white boy, old enuf to be your granddaddy. Where did that get you? You need to stop chasin' dem pretty men. Ain't none of em no good. What you need is an ugly man like Papa. An ugly man'll take good care of ya."

"Papa wasn't ugly, Miss Mae."

"He sure won't pretty." She chuckled, the pain of laughing etched in her brow. "Remember dat boy Arsenio Hall had him a TV show? Him and that baldheaded John B. William what use to do da poetry? Now he da kind of ugly man you need."

"Arsenio or John B.?" Marguerite asked. "And what in the world made you remember them two, Miss Mae?"

Miss Mae ignored her question. "Make me a promise, Marguerite."

"Yes, Miss Mae?"

"At my funeral don't let them put no red lipstick on me. I don't care what dem girls picks out for me to wear, just don't let them put no red lipstick on me. Red lipstick just don't look good on me and I wanna look my best when I go to kiss the Sweet Lord's hand.

And you need ta take some of that makeup off a yo' face. You got too pretty a face to be hidin' under all a dat powder."

Marguerite laughed loudly, the thick sound punctuating the silence of the hospital. "I promise, Mama. But you won't need to worry about that for some time."

Her grandmother reached out to her. "No, it's time, Baby Girl. I'm tired. I ain't got no more to give. Besides, I'm ready to see your grandfather's ugly face again."

Laying her head in her grandmother's lap, Marguerite sighed heavily, whispering lightly. "Papa wasn't ugly, Miss Mae."

For some time she sat quietly with her grandmother before she rose to leave. The woman's breathing had been heavy and labored, and the vast network of monitors hooked to what was left of her body hummed, beeped, and pulsated in synchrony. Starched soldiers came and went adjusting tubes and dials, and with each coming Miss Mae would smile up at them, wink, then lift her frail hand to shoo them away.

As Marguerite finally pulled on her London Fog trench coat, she saw the gleam flicker in Miss Mae's eyes.

"Marguerite Cole, don't you be afraid of your tears. Remember, Baby Girl, when you cry you's shedding one tear for somethin' you've lost and two tears for somethin' you've gained. You just have to search your heart to know which is which."

She nodded.

"And Baby Girl," Miss Mae said, her voice trailing. "Yes, Mama?"

"If that pretty Dexter boy do you wrong, go find yourself an ugly man like Papa."

Marguerite smiled.

The smell of sickness, hiding behind the heavy fumes of antiseptic and disinfectant, rose heavy in Dexter's nostrils. As he made his way through the hospital, he felt a faint threat of queasiness rising in his midsection. He swallowed hard, pushing the bile back down. He had made a brief stop in the over-sized cafeteria before heading the three flights up in the elevator to see Miss Mae. Sitting alone in a back corner, he'd rehearsed the speech he wanted to recite. He knew the older woman's health was fragile, and he didn't want to risk tiring her out with too many unnecessary words.

As he entered the brightly lit room, he was taken aback by how small Miss Mae appeared. She'd been robust and vibrant the last time they'd been able to talk, and was now a mere shell of her former self. The tubes were gone from her throat so that she could communicate, and Dexter welcomed the opportunity to speak with her. Catching his eye, she winked hello, her gregarious smile reaching out to ease his nervousness.

"Dexter. Come on in."

"Hi," Dexter said faintly, smiling back. "I hope I'm not disturbing you."

"No. Not much I can do layin' here in dis bed. I looks forward to my company."

"I won't stay long. I know you need your rest."

Miss Mae nodded. "Come sit and talk to me,

boy," she said, tapping lightly against the bedside. "Come sit right here."

Dexter dropped his overcoat into the chair beside the bed, rested a vase of fresh flowers on the bed table, and sat down lightly on the bed beside Miss Mae. He reached out to take her fragile hand in his.

"How are you feeling?"

"Been better. Done seen me some better days, but I'll get by. But don't talk about me. What's happen' wit' you?"

Dexter shrugged. "Not much. Work keeps me busy. Marguerite keeps me happy."

Miss Mae nodded. "Does she now?"

"Yes, ma'am. Marguerite makes me a very happy man."

"I done tole' Marguerite that a pretty man like you ain't no good fo' her. Pretty mens is too sometimey."

Dexter laughed. "I'm not that good-looking, Miss Mae."

Miss Mae chuckled. "Boy, you knows you too pretty. I don't need to tell you that. But that's okay. You loves my Baby Girl, don't you?"

"Yes, ma'am. I love her very much. That's the reason I came to see you." Dexter hesitated.

"Go on, boy."

"Miss Mae, I would like to spend the rest of my life with Marguerite. I love her very much. I didn't think it was right for me to ask her to marry me, though, until I'd spoken to you and got your blessing." Dexter inhaled deeply. "Do you have any objections to my marrying your granddaughter?"

Dexter could feel the woman's hand quiver beneath his own. Tears rose lightly to her eyes.

"My Baby Girl loves you too. It scares her, though. Scares her so much she don't know what to do wit' herself."

Dexter nodded lightly.

"Has you accepted God in yo' life, Dexter?"

"Yes, ma'am. I have great faith in God."

Miss Mae nodded slowly, the motion almost exhausting for her. "You and Marguerite will need him when times get rough fo' you. Just ask him for help and it'll all be fine."

Dexter nodded in response.

"You promise me you gon' take good care of her, Dexter. Even when she makes it hard for you to do, and trust me when I tell you Marguerite will make it hard for you to do."

Dexter smiled. "I promise."

"Then you have my blessin', and I want me at least two great-grandbabies, you hear me?"

"Thank you, Miss Mae, and I promise you we will give you as many grandbabies as we can."

Miss Mae smiled warmly, then patted Dexter's hand with her own. "God will take care a you," she said as she drifted off to sleep.

An hour passed quietly by as Dexter sat at the old woman's side. He'd not even realized that time had ticked away until Marguerite eased herself into the room and rested her palm against his shoulder. Next to him Miss Mae still lay sleeping, teardrops dried against her wrinkled skin, her lips pulled into the faintest of smiles.

The call did not come that night, or the next, or even the following week. But when it did come, early in the morning as a crisp breeze blew throughout the house, Marguerite had not been at all prepared. She could not comprehend the doctor's slow words that Miss Mae had passed away quietly in her sleep. She only knew that her grandmother was never coming back home to her and the pain was overwhelming. She knew, though, that there'd been a gentle smile upon Miss Mae's face, her thin lips pursed as though to kiss the Good Lord's hand. Only in this could Marguerite find some comfort.

Marguerite went through the motions of paperwork and funeral plans, allowing her aunts and uncle to make most of the decisions. Dexter had come to stay with her, though she brushed him aside. Even though she desperately wanted to hold him close, to feel him next to her, she couldn't get her arms to reach out to him, feared allowing her heart to touch him. He had stroked her hair, kneaded her back and shoulders, and she had fought desperately to ignore the warmth of his touch, wanting to dwell within the loneliness in her heart.

23

She paused in front of the full-length mirror for one last look. Her firm breasts accentuated the jewel neckline of her dress, the crisp, black linen falling in a smooth line past her hips and rotund behind, the hem ending just above the curve of her thick calves. Matching panty hose and a well-polished set of patent-leather pumps complemented her look.

She wore no makeup, her dark eyes clouded. Staring at her reflection, she saw Miss Mae fifty years earlier, before the weariness of days gone by and dreams attained after backbreaking labor had settled in the fine lines of the woman's ancestry.

Warm tears suddenly pressed anxiously at her eyelids, threatening to flow freely down her cheeks. Turning away from her reflection, she brushed the salty flow away with the back of her hand. Miss Mae had always cried easily, rocking herself gently when she did. Marguerite had always thought crying a sign of weakness, but Miss Mae had never been weak. Miss Mae had said tears were only a celebration and nothing to ever be ashamed of, but Marguerite always fought against crying so freely if Miss Mae were not there to cry with her.

Driving to the church, she was thankful for the

time alone. Her Aunt Leah had been less than pleased when she had called earlier to say she would not be riding over in the family limousine. Enduring Miss Mae's wake, with the steady stream of well-wishers the night before, had been enough. She'd lost count of the lips that had pressed against her cheeks and the hands that had soothingly stroked her shoulders and back. Hushed whispers had echoed loudly in the room as memories of days gone by spilled out of everyone's heart.

Aunt Pat had wept incessantly, bemoaning the loss of her mother and the disregard of a husband, whose own mourning was lost in the bitter fluid of Johnnie Walker Red packed under his jacket. Aunt Leah had greeted everyone as though she were hosting a weekend reunion of old friends, absorbing herself in absolving everyone else's pain, oblivious to her own.

A host of aunts and uncles, nieces and nephews, sisters, brothers, and cousins, whose faces were familiar yet foreign, had grieved openly for this woman who had touched them all with her strength and determination and every so often the back of her hand.

Later that night back at Pat's house, the smell of frying food had clung heavily in the air. The aroma of buttermilk chicken, corn bread, bean soup, sweet potato pudding, and greens had coated Marguerite's emptiness with their richness, the vibrant flavors washing her nostrils and caressing the ache in her stomach.

Babies had cried and cooed as they were passed from one mother to another, while everyone reminisced about family heaven-bound long ago and the sins of kin long lost.

The screams of scolded children, whose memories of Miss Mae were faint lights growing dimmer with each passing minute, and the hollow laughter of elderly brethren with loose flesh clinging to fragile bones reverberated in her soul.

As she had moved from room to room searching for some last piece of Miss Mae, Marguerite strained to grasp pieces of conversations that were about her and had nothing to do with her.

". . . loved me some Eartha Kitt. . . ."

". . . never gonna be another man like Martin . . ."

". . . picked cotton 'till our fingas was blue. . . ."

". . . Saw her runnin' with Joe Willie's boy, Jesse . . ."

". . . up to no good. Boy was always in trouble. . . ."

". . . me 'n Ruby Baines stayed at the Harlem YWCA . . ."

The night had consumed her and had left her empty. Back in the quiet of her own home, she had fallen into her bed alone, yearning for more, yet settling for the blackness that eventually overtook her, drifting off to sleep as Dexter's voice called out to her from the answering machine. And now she relished these few minutes of quiet.

Sharon stood in the door of the church searching for her. The church filled quickly, family and friends straining for final glimpses of Miss Mae outstretched in a white, satin-lined coffin. As Marguerite entered the church, Sharon hugged her in comfort, brushing the flow of warm tears from her eyes. Together they entered the sanctuary of Bethel Baptist Church, easing their way down the aisle to the front pews.

Marguerite had not been able to bring herself to view the body the night before, but now she stood peering longingly at her grandmother. Wisps of cotton framed Mae Cole's serene face. Her bronze complexion, kissed by eighty-six years of sunshine, gleamed like that of a freshly scrubbed child, and Marguerite felt that if she stood there long enough she could will Miss Mae to open her eyes and rise.

She longed to be six years old again so she could cuddle her head in Miss Mae's chest and feel the woman's long fingers twining her hair into neat plaits. Standing over the casket with her shoulders hunched and her head held low, she envisioned Miss Mae chastising her for her posture. *"Stand straight,"* Miss Mae would have told her. *"God gave you them big sturdy legs to stand tall on, so stand up straight."*

She pulled her shoulders back as Miss Mae would have commanded her to. Her tentative hand reached out slowly, shaking ever so slightly. Her palm brushed lightly against Miss Mae's fragile fist clasped around the aged Bible she had carried for as long as Marguerite could remember. Feeling the cold flesh against her own warmth, she knew Miss Mae wasn't going to get up and she would never again be six years old.

As her body began to shake uncontrollably, she suddenly welcomed the comfort of the broad arms that wrapped about her. Dexter pulled her close, supporting her with his solid limbs. As he pressed his lips to her forehead, kissing her gently, she could smell the faint scent of sweet cream on his breath. "It's okay," he whispered faintly into her ear. Leading her to a seat in the first row of freshly polished pews, he sat her beside her Aunt Leah, never lifting his arm from around her shoulders. On the other side of them, Clarence sat holding Shepard's hand, the color drained from his face.

Leah rocked gently from side to side, rising every so often to press her cheek against that of a family friend or distant relative who had come quietly into the church.

Marguerite sighed heavily, leaning her head onto Dexter's shoulder. Sharon sat directly behind her, dabbing lightly at her own eyes with a freshly ironed handkerchief edged in fine lace. As Reverend Hill stepped into the pulpit, tall and regal in his gold-trimmed black robe, Marguerite turned to face her friend, reaching for her hand. Rising, Sharon squeezed her hand gently, leaning to kiss her lightly on the cheek, then made her way out of the pew.

Standing against the backdrop of heavily scented floral arrangements, Sharon lifted her voice from the depths of her soul and accompanied by the Bethel Baptist Choir, sang, filling the church with the very spirit that had driven Miss Mae. With choruses of "I Will Follow Him" ringing in her heart, Marguerite felt the flow of tears cascade from her eyes, and she rejoiced in the tears, her tribute to Miss Mae's love.

24

Dexter lay sprawled across the sofa, absently flicking channels on the television remote in his hand. Marguerite was only half aware of his presence as she packed her grandmother's freshly washed clothes neatly into a box. The funeral had been over weeks ago, and for the first time Marguerite had found the strength within herself to go through the matriarch's possessions. The quiet within her head was suddenly interrupted by her grandmother's last words.

"Miss Mae told me she had reservations about you. She said you were too sometimey," she stated, breaking the silence.

Surprised, Dexter clicked off the television, dropped the remote against the table, and rose, sitting properly on the sofa. He studied Marguerite momentarily, then smiled. "She was right. I can be 'sometimey,' if there is such a thing. But maybe you should get rid of me. She told me I was too pretty."

They stared into each other's eyes, both pensive, before breaking out in simultaneous smiles. "No, I don't think so," Marguerite answered. "She also told me once that you were saintly for tolerating my garbage. And a man who'll put up with your garbage is a good man indeed," Marguerite said, mimicking Miss Mae.

Dexter's smile spread into a grin. "Good, because I wasn't planning on being dumped that easily." Rising, he stood before her, tilting her face up and kissing her lightly on the cheek. "Is there anything I can do?" he asked, squeezing her hand gently.

"Yes, take these boxes to the car so I can drop them off to Goodwill?"

"Sure thing," he said, lifting one of the cardboard containers off the floor. "In fact, I can drop them off now and go pick up some lunch while I'm out. You interested in Chinese?"

Marguerite nodded, coming to her feet. Twisting her braids, she inspected her work, pleased that she'd been able to pack as much as she had.

"Ask for some extra soy sauce," she commanded, pinching him lightly on the behind.

He grinned, pressing himself against her, his lips warm against hers.

Brushing his cheek against hers, he squeezed her gently, then bolted out the door, stopping first to heave a second box high up on his shoulders.

At the window, she watched him drop the large packages into the trunk of his vehicle. Looking back over his shoulder as he entered the driver's seat, he waved his hand lightly in her direction, turned on the ignition, then sped off down the quiet tree-lined street. Marguerite sighed.

Peering out into the empty driveway, she marveled at the solitude. The air was still, having been consumed by the rising midday heat, the deep scent of rose blossoms pungently sweet. Marguerite wished for the cool breezes that were known to blow gently through the windows of the old home, or even more, the dull drone of the air conditioner that Miss Mae had forbidden her to install, and once installed, had forbidden her to turn on. Miss Mae had given it away years ago. Marguerite could barely remember when.

Her aunts had been by many times to take the few items they wanted to keep for remembrance sake, but the bulk of Miss Mae's possessions had been left for her to deal with. Marguerite had taken all the old photos, arranging them neatly in the guest bedroom of her condo. Uncle Clarence had only wanted his mother's cast-iron cooking pots and the gold watch his father had received upon retiring from Machletts Laboratories, where he had worked as a mill runner.

Most of the furniture was too worn to save, and Marguerite had arranged for Goodwill to come pick up the larger pieces at the end of the week. The house itself was to remain in the family, and Marguerite and her aunts had convinced Clarence and Shepard to move into it since they'd been looking for a small home to share together. Clarence had retained an interior designer to refurbish the place once it was empty, and Marguerite knew the two men were anxious to get started.

A large crow clucked loudly on the front stoop, drawing Marguerite out of her solitude. The huge bird with the crisp black feathers stared at her mockingly, almost daring her to shoo him from where he rested. She detested these birds, but Miss Mae had once told her they were just lost souls still roaming the earth, not knowing where their final resting places were supposed to be. As the ugly bird, with its beady eyes, seemingly stared in her direction, she was suddenly overcome with the fear that maybe Miss Mae was still roaming, searching for something she had not been able to find before her passing. It was only a momentary feeling, one that vanished quickly, but Marguerite was shaken nonetheless as a flush of water ran down her cheek. She swore loudly as she brushed her eyes with the back of her hand.

Heading up the stairs, she rushed to begin the last of her packing, determined to tackle the large boxes locked away in the attic. Dexter had pulled them all down for her earlier, and now they sat in the middle of her grandmother's bedroom, years of dust painted against the cardboard. Drawn to one in particular, the corrugated case smaller than the rest, Marguerite peered curiously inside. History spilled out onto the floor as Marguerite sorted through the vast pile of papers. An hour or so later, when Dexter climbed the stairs to find her, she was laughing lightly, a warm smile spread across her face.

"Food's here," he called out, watching her curiously. "What's so funny?"

"My grandfather used to mortgage the mule to get money for seed when he and Miss Mae worked on the farm. In fact, it appears that he mortgaged that mule six times."

Dexter shrugged. "Yeah?"

"Well, each year, the mule was a different color according to all these loan papers, but I know for a fact that they only owned one mule, and it died the second year they had it."

Dexter smiled. "What else you find there?" he asked, sitting down on the floor beside her.

"Letters from my mother," she responded, handing him a pile of yellowed envelopes, neatly bound with an elastic band. "I never knew how much she and I were alike until now. She was so intense about everything. Supporting my father and the revolution were so important to her. I can just imagine how these letters must have driven Miss Mae crazy. My mother was so militant. Everything she did was for the sake of the people, to empower the race. I can just imagine what Miss Mae had to say." Marguerite chuckled lightly.

As Dexter fanned the papers, a photo dropped to the floor in front of him. As he picked it up, he marveled at Marguerite's resemblance to the pretty black woman in the picture who stood smiling, her fist lifted high in salute, her large Afro sitting atop her head like an oversized fur cap. "This is your mother?"

Marguerite nodded. "The man behind her is my father."

"He looks white."

"His father was white. My grandmother said he wasn't proud of the fact, though, which was one reason why he joined the revolution."

"I don't imagine the brothers back then gave him too easy a time because he looks real white even with that Afro."

Shrugging, Marguerite took the photo and letters from Dexter. "I never knew my father. Barely knew his name. Miss Mae would only tell me that he was a man who didn't deserve my wasting my time on. What little I have learned about him and his relationship with my mother I got from my Uncle Clarence."

"I have to admit that I really like your Uncle Clarence. He's been great for Shepard. And your Aunt Pat seems very sweet, but I'm not so sure about your Aunt Leah," Dexter said, shaking his head slightly.

"Aunt Leah can be a bit too critical, but she loves me and I know she likes you. In fact, I forgot to tell you she invited us for dinner tomorrow night. I hope you don't mind."

Helping her to her feet, Dexter hugged her warmly. "I don't mind, especially since we will all be one big family soon enough."

Marguerite raised her eyebrows questioningly. "What does that mean?"

"Just that it's not like I'm going anywhere anytime soon, and it's well past time you and I started thinking about making this arrangement a bit more permanent."

Marguerite rolled her eyes.

"Don't roll your eyes at me, woman. You know you want my fine body to be here for you twenty-four, seven, three hundred and sixty-five days a year."

"Aren't you full of yourself this afternoon!"

Taking her in his arms, Dexter laughed. "No, it's not like that, baby. I'm just full of you is all," he said kissing her warmly. "I am just full of you."

Marguerite shook her head, smiling. Back downstairs, she reached for her purse, slipping the picture of her parents into the photo compartment of the leather binder.

"Let me see." Dexter grinned, pulling the wallet from her hands.

"Don't do that," Marguerite implored, attempting to pull the wallet away from him. "There's nothing in there you want to see."

"Let me be the judge of that. What do we have

here?" He smiled pulling her driver's license out. "My goodness, woman, you were not having a good hair day when you took this picture!"

"I got caught in the rain, thank you very much."

"Uh-huh." Dexter continued to peer through the photos she had lined up neatly behind the plastic frames. "Who's this?" he asked, pulling the photo of her and Anthony from its resting spot.

The laughter in Marguerite's eyes dimmed dramatically. She pulled her braids away from her face, twisting them together at the back of her neck.

Dexter asked her again, eyeing her curiously. "What's wrong, Marguerite?"

Marguerite sat down on the couch. "He was someone I cared about a very long time ago."

Dexter sat down beside her, studying the photo closer. He nodded.

"How come you never told me about him?"

Marguerite shrugged. "I was waiting for the right time, I guess."

"Do you still have feelings for him?"

Marguerite shrugged again, the muscles along her shoulders starting to tighten. "It's not like that. I just forgot that picture was still there is all."

"It's not about the picture, Marguerite. It's about what you feel." Dexter handed the photo and wallet back to her, pressing them between her palms. "Before I say anything, is there anything else you haven't found the right time to tell me about? Any other secrets you're still keeping from me?" His voice was low, and Marguerite found his tone disconcerting. There was nothing cold about his words. In fact, Marguerite sensed his desire to be as comforting as he could possibly be. She just couldn't explain why she found his compassion so unsettling.

She dropped her head into her hands. "It wasn't a secret and I was planning to tell you. I just didn't know how."

"How could you not know how, Marguerite? You just tell me. We've talked about my past. I have asked you time and time again about yours. I don't understand what the problem was." They both could feel the edge starting to rise, the tension beginning to build, a slow waft of bitter air rising between them.

Marguerite chewed against her bottom lip. "Look. You're making too much of this."

Dexter shook his head. "How can I be making too much of this? Supposedly we're in a relationship. We should be able to discuss anything and everything, yet there are still things you haven't told me because you didn't know how. That doesn't make sense, Marguerite." Attitude had gained control as Dexter's posture stiffened.

"Dexter, I am not in the mood to do this right now. Why are you pushing me?" Marguerite felt herself growing defensive.

"Do you love me?" he suddenly questioned, nervously tapping his foot against the floor.

Marguerite looked up at him, trying to read his eyes. His look was questioning, searching deep beneath her for answers that she did not think she had. Hurt lingered just along the edge of his lashes, and Marguerite was suddenly saddened, responsible for having placed it there.

Dexter persisted. "Answer me. Do you love me?"

"Dexter, you know I care about you. Why would

you ask?" she responded as nonchalantly as she could manage.

"Do you love me?" Dexter shouted, suddenly consumed with anger. "Not do you like me. Not do you care about me, but do you *love* me," he finished, pulling her roughly to her feet.

She reached for the front of his sweatshirt, her face expressionless except for the tears rising to her eyes. "Don't do this, Dexter."

"Tell me, Marguerite. Say it. I have never heard you say it. You have never said it. It's three words, Marguerite. Do you love me?"

Marguerite stared at him, tears perched at the edge of her tear ducts ready to fall. She stammered hopelessly, opening and closing her mouth like a fish sucking for air. "Why . . . why are you . . . doing this to me . . . now?"

Dexter pulled her close. "Don't do this to me," he whispered into her ear. "I'm not the man who hurt you. I love you. I want to be with you. I want to make everything right for you. You need to believe in *me* if this is going to work. You need to believe in *us*. Tell me you love me, *please.*"

Marguerite dropped her head, the tears falling onto the front of his shirt.

"Marguerite, we can't make this work if you can't tell me how you feel. And we definitely can't make it work if you don't feel for me what I feel for you. If you don't love me, I have the right to know that. You need to be honest with me about how you feel about me. Do you love me?"

Dexter stared at her for what seemed like an eternity, maintaining the hold he had about her shoulders. When no words passed her lips and he could find no response in her eyes, he let her go, shaking his head. Picking up his jacket, he headed for the door, closing it firmly behind him as Marguerite sank to the floor sobbing.

25

"You really messed up this time," Sharon said, settling herself comfortably on the sofa. "How long are you going to wait before you call him?"

Marguerite shrugged. "I don't know."

"Well, it's already been three weeks. Don't you think you've wasted enough time?"

She shrugged again. "I think it may just be better to leave things as they are. I hurt him. He didn't deserve that and I can't ever take that back."

"No, but you can make up for it. You can tell him how you feel. You can be honest with him."

"That's easier said than done."

"Bull. You know, Marguerite, half the reason you and Anthony didn't make it was because you wouldn't open your mouth and tell him what you felt when you were feeling it. You were so busy trying not to rock the boat that you just managed to drown your own fool self."

"That's not fair."

"No, it isn't, but Miss Mae always said fair was what you made it, not what someone else made it for you. How come you never told him about Anthony? He told you about his ex-relationships. At least if you had, he would have known what he was up against. You had the man fighting a ghost he couldn't see."

Marguerite shrugged, wanting to change the subject. "I need to get these braids out of my head. Will you help me?"

Sharon winced. "I guess, but you know I hate doing other people's hair."

"Well, if you won't help me, then I'm going to have to get Delores to do it and I hate the thought of that more."

Sharon laughed. "Well, only because you look bad, girlfriend. You look real bad."

Marguerite rolled her eyes in her friend's direction.

Sharon laughed again. "So, are you going to be my maid of honor or what?"

"You finally said yes?"

"Yeah, I finally said yes. I figure I'm not getting any younger and Randy ain't gettin' no better-looking. Besides, I've got too much time invested in the relationship to throw it away now. Besides, he finally agreed to a prenup."

"Do you love him?"

"Yeah," Sharon said softly. "I do. He and I are comfortable with each other and I like that." She paused. "I love him a lot, probably as much as I think you love Dexter."

Marguerite stared at her best friend, then dropped her eyes to the floor.

"I know you love him, girlfriend. He's good to you. He makes you feel good about yourself. You've just been so caught up in feeling bad about everything that you don't want to let yourself feel anything else at all."

"Why do you think I keep doing this?"

"I think, because you fell for the wrong men before, it's become an obsession with you. You couldn't let it go, wanting to believe that you were the one who was at fault. In reality, you just deserved better and right now better is only a telephone call away. All you have to do is call Dexter and tell him how you feel."

Marguerite pulled her legs into her chest, resting her chin against her knees. "I miss him. I miss his smell. He always smelled so good."

"Call him."

Marguerite shook her head. "I can't."

"Yes, you can, but maybe you need to hear it from someone else instead of me." Rising, Sharon headed for the door. "Go talk to Miss Mae."

"Now I know you've lost your mind."

Sharon smiled. "No. Miss Mae told me that once a long time ago. When I was trying to work through a problem, she took me for a walk down to you grandfather's grave and told me to talk to him. It seemed crazy back then too, but I go to talk to him a lot now. Miss Mae now too. In fact, she was the one who finally convinced me to marry Randy."

Marguerite shook her head. "Girlfriend, you are not working with a full deck here."

"Really," Sharon said, her bright eyes glistening. "Trust me on this one. Just give it a try," she said, opening the door. "Sometimes it's easier coming from the dead than the living. You need help to heal, Marguerite, and you need to go where you might be able to find that help."

Marguerite nodded as Sharon made her way down to steps toward her car. Sharon was right. She did need to heal, but Marguerite wanted to figure out how to heal herself. She just couldn't. She didn't know how to lift the hurt that cradled her soul. Tears washed over her daily, but did nothing to wash away the yearning and the pain and all the anger that had come. The tears did nothing but nourish the unrest and the anxiety that plagued her. She'd not heard anything from Dexter, nor did she expect to, and she was too embarrassed to make contact herself.

Marguerite stared after her friend as the woman eased herself into her car. Watching Sharon as she pulled out of the driveway, Marguerite wondered if maybe Sharon was right, then thinking better of it, she closed the door and headed back to her seat on the sofa.

Tears clouded the longing that once lingered in her eyes, hanging just at the edge. Wanting no longer peeked from behind the thick black lashes, having been replaced by something she had no words for. Love stories didn't always have fairy-tale endings, she thought while flipping the channels on the television set. Stopping on a rerun of *Jerry Springer*, she curled herself up into a tight ball, clutching a half-empty glass of cabernet to her chest. Jerry was shaking his head in mock concern as two women clawed at each other across the stage. They were clawing over a man who sat back smugly like a paid fight promoter who'd just manipulated his most successful bout. Even Jerry was bright enough to know that by tomorrow, each woman would be letting the arrogant fool lick her wounds, forgiving his lies, ignoring his deceit. Marguerite was embarrassed for both of them, knowing that neither had the good sense to be embarrassed for themselves.

Marguerite clicked her fingernails against the crystal container, noting the chipped polish. She desperately needed a manicure and her hair was a mess. Sharon had been polite when she said Marguerite looked bad. Marguerite knew she was worse than bad. She dreaded the thought of looking into a mirror.

She heaved a heavy sigh as she lifted her slight frame off the crushed burgundy sofa, the delicate fabric beginning to mimic the contours of her body. Putting her glass onto the mahogany coffee table, she rose from where she sat, clicked off the television and the lights behind her and headed for her bed.

Back under the covers, she packed the woolen blankets tightly around her. The stereo played softly in the background. Marvin Gaye was crying *Mercy Mercy Me* into her ear. Like clockwork Marguerite started the ritual she'd performed every night since she and Dexter had parted. Her tears would flow easily as she recited the name and ill deed of every man who'd passed in and out of her heart leaving a scar on her soul. When she called Dexter's name and could think of no ill deed, the tears would fall harder and anger would set in, anger that raged at being so foolish.

When there were no tears left, Marguerite would ease into the loneliness, remembering the warm moments when Dexter would be close to her, a gentle hand brushing lightly against her. She would think of the fullness of his lips, sweet like honey against hers, and the penetrating laughter that resonated deep from the core of his being. What had she done? Why couldn't she commit to this man who'd done nothing but show her such tremendous love? Why couldn't she tell him she loved him? Why did those words catch like heavy weights in her throat each time she wanted to push them past her lips? What was wrong with her?

As she slowly drifted off to sleep, she almost thought she heard Miss Mae singing along with the music. Marguerite inhaled the low drone of Muddy Waters. As the darkness clouded the thoughts in her mind, Miss Mae and Muddy were still crooning in the distance.

26

Dexter sat perched on the edge of the leather recliner, staring at the blank screen of an oversized television. Twisting a half-empty bottle of beer between his large hands, he barely noticed when John entered the room, greeting him loudly. "Hey, friend, what's up?"

Dexter shrugged. "Hey," he responded softly. "What are you doing here?"

"Just came to get the last of my stuff and to return your keys."

Dexter nodded, barely hearing a word his friend had spoken.

John stretched his lean body across the sofa, opening his own bottle of cold Heineken. "So, why don't you call her and get this over with?"

Dexter raised an eyebrow, but didn't respond.

"Okay. Why don't you drive down to Stamford and talk to her face-to-face? Now that you both have had some time to think things through, she might be more willing to discuss whatever's going on with you two."

Dexter leaned back against his chair. "Leave it alone, John."

"Come on, man. You've been moaning around

like a lovesick puppy for the last month. I can't leave it alone. You're my boy, remember?"

"I appreciate you trying to help, but I need to work through this on my own."

John nodded. "You got it bad, don't you. That woman has got your whole heart."

Dexter rose from his seat, putting his drink down on the coffee table. "Yeah," he muttered, making his way to his bedroom. "Yeah."

Behind the closed door, his tears fell easily, washing down the front of his white T-shirt. Crying felt good. Stretching across his bed, he pulled a pillow close to his chest. He had been worried that she did not want him. He had even felt deep within his soul that she did not want him. That had been one thing. To see it in her eyes, even without her spitting the words past her lips with a warm breath, had been something else. It had rubbed salt in the open wound of his spirit. It had driven nails deep into the pit of his soul and had left him unwhole, dismembered like spoiled meat, raw and tainted.

"What happened?" he asked himself, just as he'd asked every day since he'd walked out of Miss Mae's home and away from Marguerite. Where had it all gone wrong? To his advantage, he'd not allowed her to see his tears fall. To do so would have added insult to injury, confirming that the loss of her would be a source of anguish for him. When he'd left, he'd refused to even look in her direction. He hadn't even stopped to toss any of his belongings into a bag. It was only when he was safely out the door, out of her sight, that he even thought to stop and cry.

How could he have been so blind? Had he been so caught up in how good he felt about the woman that he'd not bother to notice she didn't feel the same about him? Had it all been a lie? Had Marguerite played him? Dexter shook his head in bewilderment.

His heart hurt. The pulsating muscle actually ached as though it were ready to split in two, the pain spreading throughout his whole body. His tears were the only thing that brought him some comfort, and even they didn't feel right. He marveled at what love had reduced him to. Love. His mama should have warned him against that four-letter word and not all the others he'd been forbidden to speak as a child.

Was Marguerite thinking about him? he wondered. Had any thoughts of him and how he might be hurting crossed her mind? Was she hurting at all? The pain was starting to throb in his head, beating against the back of his eyes, behind his sinuses, down into his neck and back. Was it really over? Had he pushed too hard? Had he not pushed enough? He sighed deeply, fighting not to sob. Real men didn't cry, he told himself. But what did a real man do when the woman of his dreams had his whole heart and seemingly didn't want any part of it?

27

The two men sat side by side on the sofa across from her. She sighed heavily, hanging her chin low against her chest. Periodically, she would reach to swipe at her tears with a moist tissue. Clarence leaned across the mahogany coffee table to refill her empty glass with a rich cabernet, refilling his own crystal goblet at the same time.

Shepard sloped forward in his seat, his hands clutched tightly together. "I tried to speak with him, but he wasn't ready to discuss it. He's really hurting."

Marguerite nodded. "I'm so sorry for that. I feel horrible."

"So why haven't you called him?" Clarence asked, taking a sip from his own glass. "What are you waiting for?"

She shrugged, glancing up at him briefly. " I'm scared, I guess. Dexter is looking for a commitment that I don't think I can give him. He may never be able to forgive me, and I wouldn't blame him if he didn't."

"Darling, my brother loves you. His pride's been hurt, but he truly does love you."

She nodded again, wiping at her eyes. "I can't believe I'm going through this. I feel so stupid."

"Don't you worry none," Shepard said, rising to go wrap his arms around her shoulders. "I know exactly what you're going through and I'm going to tell you like Dexter told *me*. If you love him, then you need to tell him. Somehow, some way. You can't make things right if you don't talk to each other."

Clarence nodded in agreement. "That's right. Look at the two of us. If Shepard hadn't picked up the telephone and called me, he and I would still be sitting home crying for each other."

Shepard smiled. "I didn't cry."

"Yes, you did. Cried like a baby over me."

They all laughed as Shepard tossed a pillow at Clarence's head.

"You two seem so happy." Marguerite smiled. "I'm glad to see everything working out so well for the both of you."

Shepard went to sit back beside Clarence, reaching to squeeze his hand. "It's not been easy, but your uncle here has been like a rock. I'm blessed to have him to lean on."

Clarence beamed. "Shepard still has some issues to work through, but we're getting there. It'll get even easier once the house is finished and we can settle in together."

"I can't believe I'm actually going to be living with another man in a real, committed relationship. I bet my parents are rolling over in their graves."

Clarence laughed. "Don't worry about it. I bet they've already gotten an earful from my mother."

Marguerite joined in the laughter, thinking about Miss Mae giving Shepard's parents one of her lectures. She sighed. She missed her grandmother. The hurt blew across her face, fading the glimmer in her eyes. She sighed again, a deep upheaval of warm breath.

"Sharon says I should go talk to Miss Mae to help me get through this."

Clarence rolled his eyes. "I bet Miss Mae is trying to tell you the very same thing."

Shepard stood up again. "Now you two are getting a bit too spooky for me."

They all laughed again. "It's his Catholic upbringing." Clarence laughed. "He's never heard of talking to the dead."

Marguerite giggled. "It was a bit much for me to take at first too."

"Didn't Mama ever send you to Papa's grave to talk to him?"

"No!"

"That's probably because she wanted to stay in your business. But she used to send me there all the time."

Shepard chuckled, taking the dirty dishes from the tabletop toward the kitchen sink.

"On that note, I think I better be leaving," she said, reaching for her jacket and purse.

Clarence walked her to the door hugging her closely. "It will work out, Baby Girl. Sooner or later you'll see your way clear and do what you need to do."

She nodded. "Thanks, Uncle Clarence. I really appreciate you and Shepard being here for me. I don't know if I can fix this but either way, I know it'll turn out for the best."

Clarence caught Shepard's eye, nodding. "Why

don't you let us take you to dinner tomorrow. We can talk some more and maybe help you figure out what's keeping you from opening up your heart and opening up to Dexter the way you should."

Marguerite sighed, smiling slightly. "Dinner sounds good. I don't know how much talking I can do, but I would love to spend some more time with you two."

"It's a date then," Clarence said, returning her smile as Shepard came to stand by his side.

"Good night," she said, kissing them both on the cheek. "I'll call you tomorrow so we can make plans."

"Good night," they chorused behind her, filling the door frame with their tall bodies.

"Go with God," Shepard whispered as he clasped his hand in Clarence's. "Let him lead your heart, little girl."

"Amen to that," Clarence said. "Amen to that."

28

The day had been a busy one. Dexter was throwing his whole self into his work, having moved the first phase of his expansion up by a month. His staff was none too thrilled, but Dexter saw it as a necessity. If nothing else, the need to meet some extremely tight deadlines and his propensity for perfection gave him little time to think about Marguerite. He may have been unsuccessful in his personal life, but he would not fail in his professional one. John and Debbie's dinner invitation had come at an inopportune moment, but the woman's whiny insistence and her husband's stubborn persistence gave him no opportunity to back out. He decided to grin and bear it as best he could.

When he and John walked into the restaurant, Dexter was tempted to turn tail and run, but John's hand pressed firmly against his back would not let him. Debbie sat at a rear table engaged in deep conversation with a gorgeous woman whose mere presence took a man's breath away. It was a game of blind-date bingo, and although Dexter had to admit to being mildly intrigued by the beautiful creature at the table, he was still clearly not in the mood to play. John and Debbie, on the other hand, had figured a night out with friends and the convenient introduction of someone new might raise his spirits.

"John, I'm not happy about this," Dexter said as they entered the lobby of La Maisons. In the distance he could see Debbie waving them toward the table.

"Loosen up, my friend. Her name's Laila and she's leaving tomorrow. She lives in Paris and she was only here to do some cover work with Debbie. We couldn't very well let her spend her last night in a hotel room. What kind of hosts would we be?"

Dexter grunted. "I'm going to get you for this."

John laughed as they reached the table and Debbie rose to greet them. After kissing both of them warmly, she made the formal introductions.

"Dexter, I'd like you to meet a good friend of mine. This is Laila Harris. Laila, this is Dexter Williams, John's friend I was telling you about."

Laila extended a meticulously manicured hand. "It's a pleasure, Mr. Williams." Her smile was all-consuming. Dexter felt himself inhale sharply.

"Please call me Dexter, and I'm sure the pleasure is all mine."

The two men took their seats beside the women and ordered a round of drinks. Dexter quietly appraised his dinner companion as Debbie regaled them with the details of the photo shoot she and Laila had just completed. Laila Harris was exquisite, her delicate features like fine porcelain. Her coloring was pale café au lait, weak coffee drowned in an abundance of cream. Her hair was a precision cut that complemented the lines of her face, elongating the length of her neck. Her skin was satin, her eyes large pools of black ice, and her lips were full lines that begged to be kissed. She had an incredible mouth. She smiled as though appreciative of his findings, and Dexter could almost feel himself blush.

"So, Dexter, Debbie tells me that you're quite an accomplished businessman," she said.

He smiled, nodding. "I'm trying hard and not doing too badly, if I may say so myself," he said, clasping his hands together in front of him.

She smiled back. "And John works for you, is that not correct?"

John cleared his throat. "Yes, I work for the big guy here."

"John's my senior vice president and second in charge. He's a partner, not an employee. He and I have been together since the beginning, and there were many times that I couldn't have done it without him. His friendship has been a great source of inspiration."

"It must be nice to have friends who care so much about you."

Dexter nodded. "I am very blessed. These two keep me on my toes," he said, meeting Debbie's eyes as she giggled.

Their chatter continued as a tuxedoed waiter came to take their order. Every so often Dexter took in his surroundings, noting that the room was filling quickly to capacity. It was just after their meals had been served that Debbie directed his attention to a table on the other side of the room.

"Dexter, isn't that your brother over there?"

Dexter turned to where she was pointing as John piped in. "Yes, that's Shepard, and isn't that Marguerite?"

Dexter inhaled swiftly as his eyes rested upon his brother, Clarence, and Marguerite. The threesome had just been seated, and were carefully studying their menus. The knot that he'd been carrying in his stomach suddenly rose to his throat cutting off his airway. It *was* Marguerite. His heart raced. The beating in his chest was tremendous as he gasped for air. Dexter took a quick swig of his drink, his sudden discomfort quite noticeable.

"Is something wrong?" Laila questioned, resting her hand against his.

Dexter found himself staring directly into her eyes. "No, I'm sorry. I guess something got caught in my throat."

The woman nodded, still smiling that incredible smile. "She must be very special to you."

"Who?"

"The woman dining with your brother. The one who got caught in your throat."

John laughed as Dexter blushed profusely.

"She's an old friend," Dexter responded, glaring at the other man.

"We thought they were going to get married at one time, didn't we, John?" Debbie said.

John laughed again, his head bobbing up and down like a loose ball bearing.

"This isn't funny," Dexter said, turning to stare at both of his friends.

"Yes, it is," John said, wiping the moisture from his eyes with the back of his hand.

Dexter ignored him, turning his attention back to his companion. "Please excuse these two. She and I were very close at one time, and then we weren't. This is the first time I've seen her since we broke up.

I hope you'll forgive me if I've been rude, but I didn't expect this. It's taken me by surprise."

Laila glanced over toward where Marguerite sat. "She's beautiful. I am sorry that things did not work out for you."

Dexter turned to stare at Marguerite. Once again, he inhaled too swiftly. Marguerite *was* beautiful, and he suddenly thought of the feel of her, her hands, her touch, the way they fit so neatly together. Laila pulled him back from his thoughts as he pushed the air out of his lungs, acutely aware that he'd been holding his breath. She touched his hand again, entwining his fingers between hers. The words falling out of her mouth were soothing, her tone soft and gentle. "Don't worry. It really is okay and I understand. Just relax, finish your meal, and I'll try to make the rest of this evening as easy for you as I can." She reached out to place her palm against his cheek, and it was just at that moment that Marguerite looked over and realized he was there.

The salad fork in Marguerite's hand fell heavy against the table. Clarence looked up from his food.

"You okay, Baby Girl?"

"No. We've got to leave."

"What's wrong?" Shepard questioned, his eyes meeting Clarence's.

Marguerite pulled her napkin from her lap and pressed it against her lips, her gaze falling to the tabletop.

"I don't feel well is all. I just want to leave."

"Don't be silly, child. What is wrong?"

She inhaled deeply. "Dexter is here with a date." She looked up, gesturing across the room with her eyes.

Shepard and Clarence followed her gaze, their view resting on the elegant woman at Dexter's side who was gently stroking the side of the man's face.

"Mmmm," Clarence hummed. "That brother of yours didn't waste any time, did he?"

Shepard chuckled. "I don't know what to say. Dexter never did let any grass grow under his feet, though."

Marguerite took another deep breath. "Can we leave, please? I don't find this particularly funny."

"I'm sorry," Shepard professed. "I didn't mean to laugh."

"No," Clarence said emphatically. "You will not run and humiliate yourself or embarrass us tonight. Suck it up. Enjoy your dinner, be polite when you have to, and cry about it later, but you're not running."

"Clarence is right, Marguerite. You are going to have to face him at some time. There is no point in running. We'll be right here beside you, so don't you worry. Like your uncle said, just be polite."

Marguerite finally exhaled, then inhaled deeply again, pulling her wineglass to her lips. "Who is she, do you know?" she asked, turning her attention to Shepard.

"No. I don't know her."

"She's quite beautiful, isn't she?" Clarence said.

Marguerite sucked her teeth. "She's okay." Then she added, "If you like that type."

Clarence laughed. "I don't, but I can still appreciate when a woman looks good. And she is definitely an attractive woman."

Shepard nodded, pulling a forkful of salad into his mouth to keep from laughing. He patted Marguerite's hand.

"Just eat, darling. It's going to be okay."

Laughter rang around Dexter's table. He smiled politely and chuckled appropriately, but his thoughts and his gaze kept returning to the woman at the other table. He wondered what she was thinking. What had brought them out for dinner on this particular night? And why to this particular restaurant? Had she seen Laila stroking his face? Had he looked as if he was enjoying it? Did they look like they were having a good time? Did he and Laila look like a couple? Was Marguerite thinking about him? Random thoughts raced through his mind, bursting forth like fireworks on the Fourth of July. When John had paid the check and the last of the coffee had been finished, they all rose to leave.

"Dexter, do you mind taking Laila back to her hotel? Debbie and I aren't headed in that direction."

Dexter caught his friend's eye, his expression one of mild exasperation.

"It's not a problem," Laila interjected. "I can grab a taxi."

"No." Debbie smiled. "We can't have that. Dexter doesn't mind at all. Do you, Dexter?"

"No, not at all," Dexter said, his manners kicking into full swing. "A taxi definitely won't be necessary. It's late and I'd never forgive myself if I didn't make sure you got home safely."

"Thank you," she responded, squeezing his hand. "I really appreciate that."

"Dexter, don't you think you should go say hello? I wouldn't want them to think that we kept you from speaking," Debbie asked, pulling on her jacket. She smiled sweetly, a sugary bend of her mouth that turned Dexter's stomach ever so slightly.

Dexter looked from her to John and then to Laila. All three were smiling like Cheshire cats. "Of course. I was planning on it."

"Sure you were," John said, tapping his friend along his back as he turned to lead the way, pulling Debbie behind him. John and Debbie reached the table first, with Dexter and Laila close behind them.

"Hey, Shepard, how goes it?" John asked, extending his hand.

"Good, John, how are you? Hey there, Debbie."

"Hi, Shepard," Debbie said, leaning down to kiss the man's cheek. She smiled and waved at Clarence, then turned to face Marguerite. "Marguerite, how are you?"

"Fine, Debbie. Thank you for asking. How was the honeymoon?"

"Absolutely wonderful. Bermuda was a beautiful island. Have you ever been?"

"No. I haven't."

"Well, put it on your do list. I highly recommend it. It's a perfect place for lovers."

Marguerite nodded as Dexter and Laila came to stand beside them.

"Hello, Dexter," she said coolly.

"Marguerite. How are you?" he responded politely.

"Fine. Thank you." Marguerite's gaze rested on Laila, who smiled directly at her. The woman was gorgeous, her pencil-thin body draped in a beaded, micro-mini dress the color of dark coffee. The form-fitting garment, which nicely complemented the woman's complexion, barely covered her assets. And everyone in the room had noted that her assets were exceptionally impressive. Marguerite tried desperately to smile back, but could feel her face muscles resisting.

Dexter reached out to shake hands with his brother and Clarence.

"Everyone, this is Laila Harris. Laila, this is my brother Shepard, his friend Clarence Cole, and this is Marguerite Cole."

Both men came to their feet, nodding greetings in Laila's direction as she said hello.

"You have a beautiful accent, Laila. Where are you from?" Clarence asked.

"Thank you. I'm from Paris. I'm here doing a modeling assignment."

A model, Marguerite noted. Figured.

They all nodded. "We were recently in London," Shepard chimed in. "They were highlighting some of the new fashion shows while we were there. Do you do more print work or runway?"

"I do both equally. I prefer runway, though. In fact, I'll be headed back soon to prepare for Oscar de la Renta's new show."

Shepard nodded. "How fascinating."

Laila smiled before responding, brushing a wisp of hair from her face as she did. "My passion is photography, though. One day I hope to be on the other side of the camera."

Marguerite reached for her glass, draining the last of her wine.

"Would you care to join us?" Clarence asked. "I'm sure we can pull up a few more chairs."

Both Marguerite and Dexter cringed, hoping no one noticed.

"Thanks, but no, we just finished and were headed home," John answered.

"Yes," Debbie chimed in. "Dexter and Laila might make a night of it, but us old married folks need to get our rest." She squeezed her husband tightly, wrapping her thin arms about his waist.

Everyone chuckled lightly except for Marguerite, who turned to stare at Dexter. He nodded weakly, smiling as broadly as he could. "Yes, I promised to get Laila home safely. She's got a big day tomorrow."

Laila leaned in closer to Dexter, wrapping her arm around his, clasping his hand between hers. She fixed her gaze on Marguerite. "Yes, Dexter has been very sweet to me. I am glad that he and I have this opportunity to get to know each other better. I am hoping that he and I will get to know each other very well," she cooed seductively, a subtle grin adorning her face as she turned to look up at him. Dexter smiled back, conscious of Marguerite's gaze. A rush of heat flooded his cheeks as he inhaled deeply.

"Well, it was a pleasure meeting you all," the woman said, turning her attention back to the table.

"Nice meeting you," Clarence chimed in.

"Yes, very nice," Marguerite said with little enthusiasm.

As the two couples made their way out of the restaurant, John looked back over his shoulder, he and Shepard exchanging a look. Marguerite's eyes were focused on Dexter as he escorted the tall woman out the front to door to his parked car.

"She was very nice," Clarence said, interrupting her thoughts.

"Yes, she was," Shepard agreed, his gazed locked on Marguerite.

"Yeah. Nice," Marguerite responded, gesturing for the waiter.

"You okay, Baby Girl?"

"Wonderful."

The two men caught each other's eye as Marguerite ordered herself a drink, and Clarence gave a subtle smile that spoke volumes to his partner in crime.

29

Dexter found himself rambling on and on about Marguerite and everything that had happened between them. Laila had asked him one question about the woman, and he'd not been able to stop talking since. His companion didn't appear to mind, though, as she nodded with interest, her smile still full and endearing.

"I'm sorry," he said. "I didn't mean to bore you to death with my problems."

"You didn't. It's obvious that this woman means a great deal to you."

"Thank you for being so understanding. I'm sure this isn't what you'd hoped to get from our date tonight."

"I really had no expectations. Personally, I was just looking forward to an evening of good company, and you have been that. I'm sure you've had your share of blind dates. You just hope the other person has an ounce of common sense and isn't on the verge of a nervous breakdown."

"I've definitely been there before." Dexter chuckled softly. "What was your worst blind date?"

Laila laughed. "He had a glass eye, wore a suit that obviously belonged to his bigger brother, and smelled like sour milk. I was polite, made it through dinner, then he became a nightmare. He called and sent flowers every day for three months. No matter what I did to put him off, I couldn't get rid of him. Drake Colby was his name."

"What happened to him?"

"I eventually had to press harassment charges against him. He kept showing up at my photo shoots and causing some real bad scenes. Seems he had some serious emotional issues, and he ended up going back into the mental institution he'd gotten out of before he met me."

"I hope Debbie wasn't the one who fixed you up with him."

Laila laughed again. "No. Trust me, had she been, you and I would never have met tonight." Her laugh was warm and mildly intoxicating. Dexter found himself enjoying it more than he wanted to.

He smiled, reaching out to pat the top of Laila's hand.

"Do you think you and your Marguerite will ever get back together?"

He shrugged, sighing heavily. "I don't know. I love her, but she doesn't feel the same way."

"That's not the impression I got. From what I saw, I think she loves you very much. I think perhaps she is just frightened. I know she was definitely jealous."

Dexter shrugged again. "Maybe. But we can't work this out if she isn't willing to talk to me about it."

"I understand. Whatever happens, though, I wish you much luck," Laila said as Dexter pulled into a parking space at the Sheraton Hotel. Exiting the vehicle, he strolled to the other side and opened the door for her.

"Can I walk you to your door?"

She responded with that incredible smile. "I'd like that very much."

Dexter rested his palm against the curve of her lower back as he escorted her into the building, up the elevator, and toward Room 412, where she'd be spending the night. He paused nervously as she opened the locked door and beckoned him inside.

"Thank you, but I should be going. I'm sure you need your rest."

"No, please, come in. I can pour you a nightcap."

Laila reached for his hand and pulled him inside, securing the door behind them. Dexter stood awkwardly until she gestured for him to take a seat in one of the upholstered wing chairs. It was a comfortable room with a large king-sized bed, a table and two chairs, a large bureau, and a television set. Nothing elaborate, but definitely comfortable.

"Brandy okay?" she asked, reaching for a bottle from the mini-bar.

"That's fine. Thank you."

Dexter suddenly felt warm, as if the room temperature was steadily rising. He was suddenly aware of how well Laila filled out the dress she wore, the length of her long legs, and the way her face filled with laughter when she spoke to him. The rising heat was making him feel uncomfortable, tension rising in the crotch of his pants. As she passed him a partially filled glass, he was acutely aware of the effect her presence was having on him and he was not at all comfortable with it.

He downed the drink quickly, putting the glass

down on the tabletop. "I should be leaving," he said. "We both have a big day tomorrow." He rose as Laila came to stand directly in front of him.

"You don't have to hurry, you know," she cooed, brushing her fingers lightly against his chest.

"I do," he said, "but thank you again. I had a very nice time."

Laila inched closer, her palms crossing his chest, then rising upwards to wrap around his neck. "I am very attracted to you, Dexter. You are an extremely sexy man. I can make this night nicer if you'll let me. No strings, no commitments, and it can be just our little secret."

Dexter inhaled deeply, closing his eyes as Laila pressed her lips to his. The kiss was heated and inviting and though he found her exciting, evident by the swelling in his groin, he could not will his heart and mind to respond. As he could feel his body betraying him, he suddenly wanted nothing more than to be as far from this woman as he could possibly be.

Grabbing her wrists, he pulled himself away, holding her arms down against her sides. "Laila, I'm sorry. I can't do this."

She shook her head as he loosened his grip on her wrists. Clasping her hands in front of her, she conceded gracefully. "It would have been very nice between us. As I said, I find you extremely sexy. You excite me."

"I'm sure it would probably be incredible, but it's not right, not now, not for me."

"Your Marguerite is a very lucky woman."

Dexter nodded and leaned to kiss her gently on the cheek. "Thank you for understanding."

"I do understand."

"I need to say goodnight. I hope you have a safe trip tomorrow."

"Thank you. And may I offer you a few words of advice before you go?"

Dexter paused as the woman continued.

"If you want to keep this woman, you will need to fight for her. Whatever it is that she is afraid of, you will have to do everything you can to let her know that she can trust you to protect her from it. If she can't move herself past it, then you will just have to move it out of her way. Let her know that you will always be there to take away her hurt. I could see it in her eyes how much she loves you, and you have shown just how much you love her. Don't let that get away from you. Love is too precious a commodity to throw it away out of foolish pride."

Dexter hugged his new friend warmly. "Thank you," he whispered as she pressed her lips to the side of his face. "Thank you so much."

"I will look you up the next time I'm in town, Mr. Williams. Perhaps I can have dinner with you and your Marguerite. I would like to get to know her."

The woman blew him a kiss as he made his way to the elevator. As he heard the door close behind him, Dexter suddenly knew what he had to do. With resolution in his heart, he suddenly felt better. He felt relieved, and the buoyancy in his step was quickly revived.

For the third time Marguerite dialed Dexter's number. When the answering machine picked up, she slammed the phone down again. It was already three o'clock in the morning and he was still not home.

"Damn him," she cursed under her breath. "He's spending the night with that woman."

That woman. Marguerite could not get Laila out of her head. She was haunted by the way the woman wrapped herself so comfortably against Dexter, holding tightly onto his arm. And Dexter. Marguerite fought back the tears. He looked so good. She'd wanted to run into his arms, but he'd already replaced her. He'd barely looked at her, almost ignoring her presence, and if she'd been able to crawl beneath the table she would have.

But it was her fault. Why was she agonizing about Dexter having moved on when she'd been the one to push him away? Wasn't it what she'd wanted? She'd turned her back on his love, he'd not turned his back on her. She'd been the one who'd thrown what was between them away. Dexter had fought tooth and nail to keep them together. This was all her fault. Marguerite fell across the bed in tears.

In Danbury, Dexter sat smugly in his recliner, a hot cup of coffee held between his palms. For the third time, he pulled the telephone receiver to his ear and dialed the call identification code, star-six-nine. He smiled at the operator's voice on the other end.

"The last number to call your line was 203-555-3213. For an additional thirty-five cents we can connect you to this line. Please press one . . ."

Dexter dropped the phone back down and laughed out loud. "Good," he thought. "This serves her right."

He laughed to himself, pleased that Marguerite was anxious to know if he was home. He had no intention of picking up, not yet. Let her sweat it out some. He was just comfortable to know she was still very interested in his whereabouts.

At twenty-five minutes after four, Dexter's phone rang for the fifth time. This time he reached for the receiver and pulled it to his ear. "Hello?"

Silence greeted him.

"Hello? Is anyone there?"

Still getting no response, Dexter dropped the phone back on the cradle, disconnecting the line.

Marguerite pulled the receiver to her chest, the tears beginning to fall one more time. As she replaced the phone on the hook and prepared to finally go to bed, it rang. The unexpected ring startled her and she jumped ever so slightly. She hesitated momentarily before picking it up.

"Hello?" Her voice was low and cautious.

"Why didn't you speak?"

She inhaled sharply. "What are you talking about?"

"When you called me a minute ago, why didn't you speak?"

"I don't have anything to say to you."

"I think you do. I think you have a lot to say to me."

"Look, I'm tired and it's late. I'm not in the mood to do this. Besides, I'm sure you've had a long evening and need to get some rest."

Dexter yawned into the receiver. "You're right. I do need some rest. I'm worn out."

"Did you sleep with her?"

"Her who?"

"Your date."

"Oh, her. Does it matter? Are you jealous?"

"Hardly."

"Let's just say I had a really, really good time." Dexter chuckled. "Girlfriend wore me out. She can do the most amazing things."

Marguerite slammed the phone down, and on the other end Dexter laughed until his sides ached.

It was love. And as Miss Mae had warned him, Marguerite wasn't going to make it easy for him. He'd been a fool to think otherwise. He would rest this night, better than he had rested the last few weeks. Marguerite Cole was going to be his. He could feel it. He wanted it. He wasn't about to let her go.

30

John greeted Dexter at the door of his office, two cups of hot coffee in hand. "Good morning, Romeo."

Dexter smiled a wry smile. "Good morning, yourself. And what did I do to deserve this honor?"

"You took Laila home last night." John pulled a fist into his mouth and bit at his forefinger, pretending to be in pain. "Did it hurt?"

Dexter tossed his briefcase onto the desktop, taking a seat in his leather executive's chair. "Did what hurt?" he asked, picking up the cup and sipping at the warm brew.

"Turning her down."

Dexter laughed. "How do you know I turned her down?"

John made himself comfortable in the oversized chair on the other side of the desk. "I know Laila well enough to know she offered, and I know you well enough to know that Marguerite has got you tied up in such a knot that you couldn't think about being with anyone else but her."

"You got me all figured out, have you?"

John nodded. "I saw how you looked at that woman last night. You were ready to toss Laila aside and throw down with Marguerite right there on the table. Your honey's got you whipped."

Dexter laughed. "Where did you and Debbie find that woman? She was gorgeous," he exclaimed, still chuckling.

"She and Debbie go way back. They started modeling together years ago, and when Debbie goes to Paris she usually stays at Laila's house."

"How come I never met her before?"

"This is the first time she's been here when you've been around. In fact, if I remember correctly, the last time she was in the States you were away in California. I think you two have passed each other two or three times and the timing's always been bad.

"Laila's a love-'em-and-leave-'em kind a girl. She doesn't hang on to any man for any length of time. Debbie always figured it would just be a quick one-nighter with the two of you and that's it."

"So you introduce me to her now?"

"Well, if you had been weak, it wouldn't have amounted to anything. Marguerite would never have had to know and you could have still worked things out with her. Quite a surprise running into them like that, huh?"

Dexter cut an eye at his friend. "Weak?"

"Look, I love Debbie dearly, but Laila gives me an erection over the telephone. She calls and I'm no good just thinking about her. If she ever offered herself to me, I don't know if I'd be able to resist. Can you imagine those legs wrapped around your back? Humph!"

"Speaking of," Dexter said as he pushed the intercom for his secretary.

"Yes, Mr. Williams?" a small voice responded on the other end.

"Carol, come in here for a minute, please."

"Yes, sir."

Carol Pelt sauntered into the office, pad and pencil in hand. Greeting John, she pushed his lean legs off the top of Dexter's desk. "Didn't your mother teach you any manners? This is an office."

John winked at her. "Good morning to you too, Miss Carol."

Carol offered a wry smile, patting the top of his head. "Yes, sir, Mr. Williams?"

"Carol, arrange for three dozen yellow roses to be delivered to Marguerite tomorrow. I need them to be delivered first thing in the morning, preferably just after nine A.M."

"Yes, sir. Yellow roses at nine. Any message for the card?"

"Tell me."

"Excuse me?"

"You heard me, Carol. The message should read, 'Tell me.' Nothing else. Just the words 'Tell me.'"

Carol raised her eyebrows. "Yes, sir."

As she made her way out of the office, John laughed.

"You decided to fight, I see."

"I decided I'm not letting her get away from me. I love her and she loves me. Somehow, some way I'm going to make her realize it."

John nodded. "She knows. She's running from it, but she definitely knows. I saw the expression on her face last night too."

Dexter nodded, thinking about Marguerite. He was suddenly flush with embarrassment as his friend stood grinning at him. "Don't you have some work to do?"

"Yes, sir, Boss." John rose to his feet. "We actually have a meeting in ten minutes with the development team. I'll see you in a few."

As John turned and exited the office, Dexter turned on his computer and contemplated the balance of his day.

Bloomingdale's Department Store was having a one-day sale, and Sharon and Marguerite were muddling through a rack of half-priced dresses on their lunch hour.

"Aren't you a bit old to be playing such childish games?" Sharon asked, holding a red dress up against her torso.

"I know. I didn't expect him to know that it was me calling, though, and I sure didn't expect him to call me back."

"So did you talk to the man?"

"No. He was bragging about his good time and I hung up on him."

Sharon shook her head. "Both of you need to grow up."

Marguerite shrugged. "You should have seen her. She was gorgeous."

"You're gorgeous."

"Not like this. Sharon, this woman was drop-dead beautiful. I felt like an ugly duckling beside her. Dexter didn't even look in my direction. She was holding onto his arm like she'd won the prize at the state fair and she kept grinning at me."

Sharon laughed. "I'm sure it wasn't that bad."

"Trust me, it was." Marguerite heaved a heavy sigh. "I miss him so much. I want him so badly."

"So what's stopping you?"

She shrugged. "I don't know. I'm just so scared that it's not going to work for us. I almost feel like it's just best to leave well enough alone and go about my business so he can go about his."

Sharon paused in her search. "What are you more afraid of, that he will hurt you or that you will hurt him?"

Marguerite stopped abruptly, contemplating her friend's question. "I guess I'm afraid that I won't measure up. I'm afraid that I'll disappoint him, then he won't want me, then we both get hurt."

"So you hurt him first just to get it over with, is that right?"

"Sharon, it's not like . . ."

Sharon interrupted her. "Yes, it is. It's just like that. Grow up, Marguerite."

Tears sprang to Marguerite's eyes although she knew she was all cried out.

"You've found your soulmate," Sharon went on. "You love this man so much that it hurts when you aren't together. When you are together, it's like everything is right with the whole world. Grow up. Stop being little Marguerite who gets left behind or left alone. Dexter is not your mother and he's not your father. He's not Anthony or any of the other Tom, Dick, or Harry who left you. Understand that you have something beautiful and significant to offer this man, or any man for that matter. Accept that this man, Dexter, loves you, faults and all, and you love him. Love him and, damn it, let him love you back." Sharon's voice had risen an octave, and a group of women on the other side of the rack were nodding in agreement, eavesdropping on the conversation. The two friends stared at each other, both silent, oblivious to the stares. Sharon reached out to hug Marguerite, pulling her friend in close.

"Let him love you. I promise you it won't hurt nearly as much as pretending you don't love him does."

Marguerite reached to wipe at her eyes.

"You been to see your grandmother yet?" Sharon asked.

Marguerite shook her head.

"Please do. You are really starting to get on my nerves. If anyone can set you straight, Miss Mae will."

Marguerite pulled a beaded tank dress from its hanger, holding it up to her body. "Do you like this?"

"Hooker-ville. You'll look like you should be on the corner peddling your trade."

Marguerite sucked her teeth, putting the dress back on the rack.

"Sharon."

"What?"

"Thank you."

31

As Marguerite approached the large marble headstone that marked Miss Mae's burial site, she inhaled deeply. It was a beautiful day, the sun shining brightly as it dropped a cloud of warmth over her shoulders. The warmth filled her, overwhelming the mild chill she'd felt moments earlier. Marguerite had never liked cemeteries, but she was suddenly comfortable, a peacefulness filling the air around her. Fresh flowers adorned the base of the headstone, a mixture of spring color in shades of yellow, pink, and orange against the dark gray marble. Marguerite dropped to her knees to add her own collection of white carnations to the bouquet. When she was finished, pleased with the arrangement, she settled herself comfortably against the ground, her palm brushing against the cool stone as she outlined her grandmother's carved name with her fingertip.

"Hi, Mama," she whispered softly, almost fearful of being heard by the neighboring occupants, as if they could hear her. "It's me." Marguerite inhaled deeply, feeling extremely self-conscious. Maybe this wasn't something she could do. Her eyes filled with tears threatening to flow down her cheeks.

Marguerite pushed ahead, forcing herself to continue. "I miss you so much, Miss Mae. I wish you could be here right now to help me fix this mess I've made." Marguerite took another deep breath before telling her tale. "I''ve think I've pushed Dexter away for good this time, Mama. I didn't mean to, but I hurt him."

Intuitively, Marguerite felt as if she could almost hear her grandmother's soft clucking in the wind. In her mind's eye, she imagined the old woman shaking her head at Marguerite as she'd done so many times. Marguerite continued, filling Miss Mae in on all that had happened, all that she had done.

"I know. I know. If I didn't mean it, then why did I do it, right? I guess it was because I was scared, Mama. I was scared that he was going to stop loving me and that I was going to get hurt. I didn't think I could deal with being hurt anymore. Everyone's left me, Mama. First my mommy and daddy, then every man I have ever cared about dumped me. Then you . . ." Marguerite paused. "It hurts, Miss Mae. It hurts when people you love keep leaving, and everyone I've loved has left me."

The wind rustled louder, and in the lull of the leaves Marguerite could hear her grandmother's heart speaking to the throbbing tissue in her own chest.

"Chile, what I'm gon' do wit' you? People gots to go at sometime, Baby Girl. Even you gon' have to leave someone at sometime. Doesn't mean the love's gone, baby. If they loved you, it will always be a part of you. That Dexter boy loves you, and even wit' you leavin' him like you done, you still feelin' his love in your soul. That's why you want

it back so badly, 'cause you know it's there and you know it belongs to you."

Marguerite could feel her heart expand. "Dexter loves me, Mama. And I love him. I love him so much. I don't want to lose him. I need him in my life."

"Then tell him. Tell him you love him. Boy can't love you if you don't let him."

"I've got to tell him. I've got to show him. He can't love me if I don't let him, can he, Miss Mae?"

"Baby Girl, Baby Girl. You gon' be just fine. If you and that Dexter boy don't make it, you can always get you an ugly man like yo' Papa. I keep tellin' you 'bouts them pretty mens."

"If it doesn't work out, I could always just go get me an ugly man, huh?" Marguerite laughed out loud, reaching to trace her fingers along her grandfather's engraved name. "But Papa wasn't ugly, Miss Mae."

Laughter whispered through the trees. *"He sho' won't pretty."*

At five minutes past nine o'clock, the office receptionist entered Marguerite's office with a vase of yellow roses, her favorite flower. The arrangement was delightful, the glass container topped off with a graceful yellow ribbon.

"Look what you just got," she said. "It's not your birthday or anything, is it?"

Marguerite looked up with surprise as the woman rested the large floral arrangement on her desk. "No, it's not."

"Well, there's a card," the other woman said. "Enjoy them. They're beautiful."

As Marguerite reached for the card, pulling it from the envelope, the telephone on her desk rang. Absentmindedly she reached for the receiver.

"Marguerite Cole."

"Well?"

Dexter's voice surprised her. "Well what?"

The words on the card jumped up at her. TELL ME, printed in bold black ink, all the letters capitalized.

"Something you want to say?" Dexter asked.

Marguerite could feel herself smiling. "No. You called me, remember. Is there something you want to tell me?"

Dexter smiled on the other end, noting the enunciation she'd placed on the word tell. "You're having a good day, I hope?"

"It's getting brighter by the minute."

"Brighter is good."

"Thank you for the flowers."

"What flowers?"

Marguerite hesitated momentarily. "I've got to go. Thanks for calling."

Dexter tightened his grip on the telephone. "Call me when you're ready. I'll be waiting to hear what you want to tell me. I want you to understand that I'm going to wait. I'm going to wait," he emphasized. "So you call me, okay?"

Marguerite nodded, then whispered softly, "I will. I promise."

As she hung up the telephone, Marguerite pulled the flowers to her nose, deeply inhaling the fragrant aroma. The door was still open. She heaved a deep sigh of relief. He'd let her know he'd not given up on her. Dexter had shown her clearly that the door was still open. Now she only had to find the steps to walk her way through it. This time when her tears fell, they flowed with joy.

32

Both Shepard and Clarence skittered around the house making last-minute adjustments to the furnishings and decor. The family was due to arrive any moment, and both wanted to insure everything was perfect. Clarence knew how critical his sisters could be, and though their pretentiousness didn't faze him in the least, he didn't want Shepard to be thrown off guard or hurt by it.

Together, with the assistance of a professional designer, they'd converted Miss Mae's home into a picturesque spread that rivaled that of a *Better Homes and Gardens* layout. Freshly painted walls, newly polished hardwood floors, and rooms filled with an abundance of color danced with vibrancy, and both men were duly pleased with their efforts. Shepard was hopeful that his new family would not find anything about their former family home disrespectful, not wanting to initiate any tension between Clarence and his siblings. Delighted by the changes they had made, Marguerite had already given them her seal of approval, and this had greatly eased Shepard's nervousness. In the upstairs bedroom he and Clarence shared, the man paced nervously, fluffing the bed pillows every other moment.

In the distance he heard the doorbell, and then Clarence's voice as he welcomed the first of their guests. Inhaling deeply before making his way down the stairs, Shepard shook with anticipation, and was immediately relieved when Marguerite stood at the bottom of the stairwell, her arms opened widely to great him.

"Hi, Shepard."

"Hey, there."

"Figured I'd come a few minutes early. I knew you'd both be nervous."

Clarence laughed. "I wasn't nervous until Shepard started shaking. You'd think he'd never had a dinner party before."

Shepard rolled his eyes. "Not for your family. I'm supposed to be nervous."

Marguerite laughed with the two men. "It's going to be just fine. Don't you worry." She looked around, noting all the new changes since the last time she'd been there. "The place looks wonderful. I can't believe it's the same house. It's so much lighter and airier," she exclaimed.

Clarence wrapped an arm around Shepard's waist. "It is great. I wish we'd done something like this before Mama died so she could have enjoyed it."

"Now you know she would not have allowed you to do a thing to this house with her in it."

"I know, I know. But it would have been a challenge to try," Clarence said.

Marguerite smiled. "So is everyone coming?"

The two men looked at each other. Clarence cleared his throat as Shepard excused himself into the kitchen to check on the food.

"All the family is supposed to be here. Even Dexter."

Marguerite dropped her gaze to the floor. "Oh."

"Are you surprised? He is family. He's Shepard's family."

"No. No," Marguerite said, gathering her thoughts. "I figured you would be inviting him."

"Are you going to be able to handle it?"

"Yeah, no problem."

"Even with Leah and Patricia and Miss Minny and Delores butting in? Because you know they are going to be butting in."

Marguerite frowned. She exhaled deeply. "I don't have much choice, do I?"

Her uncle smiled widely. "That's my girl. You'll do just fine."

"He sent me flowers the other day."

"Really?"

"Yellow roses. My favorite. He also called. He wanted me to know that he would be waiting when I was ready to talk to him."

Clarence grinned brightly. "That's a very good sign. So there is still some hope there for you two."

Shrugging, Marguerite rose to her feet. "I don't know, but I'm trying to be positive."

Before Clarence could respond, the doorbell rang again, interrupting his thoughts. Marguerite moved toward the kitchen. "I'll go see if I can relieve Shepard," she said, waving her uncle toward the front door.

Minutes later, when she and Shepard returned, the room was spilling over with commotion. Leah and Patricia were standing open-mouthed in awe as they marveled at the many changes the two men had made to the structure. Family members were moving in and out of each room making themselves comfortable.

"Hey, Marguerite," they called, reaching out to hug her and Shepard. "Hey, Shepard."

The noise level was at an all-time high as Shepard pulled them from room to room, giving them a tour of the home's new interior.

"This is wonderful," Leah exclaimed, her hands clasped tightly in front of her.

Patricia tapped both men on the back. "You two have done a great job."

"It's so fancy," Miss Minny piped in. "Why you do it so fancy?"

"They likes fancy, Ma," Delores responded, answering for them.

"It's not fancy, Miss Minny, it's comfortable," Clarence said, escorting her to an oversized chair in the living room, "We just wanted it to be comfortable and homey for everyone. This is still the family home."

Miss Minny nodded her gray head. "Look fancy to me."

As if on cue, the crowd began to separate, as the men made their way to the back of the house and the women were left sitting in the living room.

Marguerite made herself comfortable on a large cushion on the floor.

"Where's your boyfriend?" Delores suddenly questioned. "He comin'?"

Marguerite hesitated. She should have known Delores would be the first one to mention Dexter. Before she could respond, her Aunt Leah voiced the very words Marguerite had been thinking.

"Delores, you are always worrying about someone else's man. Have you managed to find a man of your own yet?"

"Don't want me no man."

"Don't want one or can't get one?"

Delores flashed her cousins a look of disgust, rose haughtily from her seat, and exited the room toward the kitchen.

"How have you been, Miss Minny?" Patricia asked.

"I'se been just fine. Thanks the Good Lord every day. Every morning I get up and reads the obituary and if my name ain't there, I knows I can thank the Lord for another blessed day."

The women chuckled. "That's good, Miss Minny."

Marguerite could feel Leah and Patricia staring at her. Leah finally asked the question, expecting more of an answer than the one Delores had gotten. "So how are you and Dexter doing, Marguerite?"

Marguerite shrugged. "As well as can be expected, Aunt Leah."

"He is such a good man. I like him a lot."

"I do too," Patricia added. "I was hoping we'd be having us a wedding soon."

"Whose wedding?" Miss Minny piped in, trying to adjust her hearing aid so that she could hear better. "Who gettin' married?"

"No one," Marguerite responded, raising her voice slightly. "No one is getting married, Miss Minny."

"I thought you was gettin' married," the elderly woman said, turning to get a better view of Marguerite. Marguerite sighed in exasperation. At that moment, Clarence came to the rescue.

"Dinner's ready if you women are ready to eat."

He met Marguerite's look of relief with his own be-mused smile.

Marguerite jumped to her feet. "Yes, we're ready."

"Who cooked?" Leah asked.

"You know your brother didn't do any cooking," Patricia said with a laugh.

"I'll have you know I did too do some of the cook-ing."

"Oh, yeah? Like what? Cut up the salad?"

Clarence swatted at Patricia's head. "I'm a very good cook."

"Mama use to say you couldn't cook your way out of a TV dinner." Leah laughed.

"Mama was talking about you."

Marguerite fell back as the women made their way into the dining room. The light bantering be-tween them continued, and laughter filled the air. Looking out the front window, Marguerite won-dered what was keeping Dexter and if he was going to bother to show up at all.

Marguerite barely filled her plate with food, nervous anticipation waffling throughout her mid-section. She watched as the family piled large styrofoam plates with red potato salad, macaroni salad, fried chicken, barbecued ribs, salad, rolls, and an assortment of other summer foods. The chatter in her head was starting to ache, and she could feel depression starting to take hold as she thought of Dexter and his apparent absence. Had he decided not to come knowing she would be there? she wondered. Every so often she would catch one of her aunts or her uncle stealing glances in her direction, and she would meet their inquisi-tive looks with a forced smile. Shepard suddenly appeared at her elbow, brushing a palm against her back.

"It's going to be fine. He said he was coming and he will be here. Something has just delayed him. Maybe he's having a problem with that car of his."

Marguerite nodded and continued to smile. "I wasn't worried. I'm sure he'll turn up soon enough."

Shepard brushed a kiss against her cheek. "I know you weren't, but I wanted to ease your mind anyway."

Minutes later, as Marguerite forced a sliver of tomato into her mouth and willed herself to chew it slowly, the doorbell rang. As Sharon and Randy came bouncing into the room, hand in hand, the tomato caught in Marguerite's throat. The disappointment came flooding across her face as quickly as her friends had rushed inside to greet her.

"Lord, Marguerite," Sharon exclaimed. "What's wrong with you? Is the food that bad?'

Laughter suddenly jetted from Margerite's midsection, and she fought to not spew the salad in her mouth onto the floor.

"Oh, fudge," she gasped, inhaling deep swells of air. "That's not funny, Sharon."

"No, it's not," Clarence said tapping lightly against Marguerite's back, "'cause I know this food is good. This is some great food." The room joined him in laughter.

Taking a sip from her glass, Marguerite washed her food down with sweetened tea, the sugary liquid pleasant against her tongue. Sharon and Randy grabbed plates and began filling them with food. The noise level in the room rose slightly as chatter again filled the room. Moments later when the telephone rang, Marguerite was wrapped up in the conversations, moving back and forth between one of Delores's tribulation stories and another about Randy's latest investment deal. Her uncle gestured at her to take the receiver, passing the cordless unit toward her. His eyes twinkled as his mouth curved up ever so slightly, an all-knowing expression gracing his face.

Marguerite rose from where she sat and exited into the living room. "Hello?"

Dexter's voice greeted her. "Hey, you."

"Hey, what's up?"

"I just called to let Clarence and Shepard know that I'm not going to be able make it. I'm stuck here at the office and I don't think I'm going to be able to pull away in time."

Marguerite could feel herself nodding. "Oh. I'm sorry to hear that."

"Are you?"

She sighed deeply, not wanting the disappointment to show in her voice. "Yes, of course I am. Shepard and Clarence are going to miss you not being here."

"Will you miss me?"

Marguerite smiled. "Is there anything you want me to tell your brother?"

Dexter chuckled lightly. "Not until you tell me first."

"Good-bye, Dexter."

"I love you, Marguerite. Bye."

Marguerite clicked the phone off and grinned, racing back into the dining room.

33

The air outside was damp, cold settling into the night as the last of the day's faint light pulled away from the earth's surface. It had rained most of the day; dreary, gray rain that had done little to brighten the Marguerite's mood. She wrestled two logs from the rear deck to the fireplace. She welcomed the warmth of a freshly lit fire, anticipating the rising heat that would mask the chill trying to settle in the room and her spirit.

Pulling her briefcase from where it rested on the table by the front door, she settled herself onto the sofa to review a series of documents about her next project. She was excited about this new marketing venture. If she could successfully pull off the advertising campaign she'd presented to the board and stay well under the budget she'd been allotted, she knew a promotion to vice president would be assured. It was a surefire winner if executed properly, and it would have her name all over it. She smiled slightly.

Time passed quickly and when the doorbell rang, she was surprised to see that she'd been working for well over an hour. Her stomach, though, attested to the fact that it was late and not having eaten since breakfast, she was hungry. Rising from where she sat, she made her way to the front door and peered through the peephole. A large, black hand held a Papa John's pizza box in the view. Inhaling sharply, she pulled her hands through her hair, adjusted her powder-blue jogging suit as well as anyone could, then pulled the door open.

"I didn't think you were going to let me in."

"I haven't yet."

Dexter smiled, lowering the box level with his chest. "I come bearing food. Your favorite; sausage, mushroom, onions, and extra cheese."

"No hot wings?"

Sweeping his other hand from behind his back, he pushed a brown paper bag in her direction. "With blue-cheese dressing on the side. So what do you say? Can I come in?"

Marguerite grinned, opening the door to allow him entrance. "I could have had company. You should have called first."

"There's enough for everybody."

"That's not the point. I might not have wanted the interruption."

Dexter dropped his delivery onto the kitchen table as Marguerite reached into a cabinet for some plates. Striding over to where she stood, he leaned to whisper into her ear. "Brother must be able to do some amazing things," he said softly before leaning to kiss her lightly on the cheek.

Marguerite smiled slyly, noting the sudden rise in her body temperature. She stepped away from Dexter, who was grinning at her broadly. "And if he was, I would not have wanted the interruption."

Dexter laughed. "I hear you, girl," he exclaimed. "I know exactly what you mean."

Minutes later, they were sprawled in front of the fireplace inhaling the sweet combination of tomatoes, crust, and toppings.

"So what you working on?" Dexter asked, nodding toward the paper that lay on the sofa and the coffee table.

"New promotional project. They accepted my proposal and gave me full creative control."

"Congratulations. I am so proud of you."

Marguerite beamed. "Thanks. But how are things going with your expansion? I hear it's been keeping you very busy."

"My brother keeping you filled in, I see."

Marguerite blushed ever so slightly. "Not really. I do ask about you on occasion."

Dexter nodded, wiping at his lips with a paper napkin. "It's going exceptionally well. My whole staff has thrown themselves headfirst into the project, and everyone has worked extra hard to meet my demands. I just hired three award-winning Website designers and four additional tech staff. We're busy. We're challenged and I'm pleased."

"Very good," Marguerite said. "That's very good."

Silence engulfed them, rising warmly into the room as the fire crackled and snapped in front of him. They were both acutely aware of the energy that was passing from one to the other, and Dexter was suddenly embarrassed by the tightening of fabric across his groin. He rose, gathering the dirty dishes, hoping that Marguerite wouldn't notice.

"Well, thanks for sharing dinner with me," he said.

"Thanks for bringing dinner."

"I should be getting home. It's getting late and you look like you have a lot of work to get through."

Marguerite nodded. Glancing at the clock on the wall, she realized it had been just over an hour since he'd arrived. It only felt like minutes. The time had passed far too quickly, and she hoped the disappointment did not register on her face.

"You've got a long ride. Besides, I'm sure you need some rest."

They stood side by side, the moment awkward, as Dexter stepped in closer to her side. "May I kiss you goodnight?" he asked, his eyes pleading for permission to press his mouth to hers.

Marguerite blushed again as she leaned her chin upward, meeting his lips with her own. It was a soft caress as he brushed the curve of his mouth against hers, savoring the mild taste of Italian against her tongue. Marguerite inhaled sharply, reacting to the emotion that swept through her as Dexter pulled her in closer. The moment was surreal, spinning quietly out of control, until Dexter pulled away from her as easily as he'd stepped in.

The words were caught in his throat, the wanting in his eyes the only thing spoken between them. Brushing his cheek to hers, Dexter squeezed her hand slightly, whispered a faint good night, then headed out the door.

34

It had been well over a week since the last time Dexter and Marguerite had spent some time together. Both had grown fond of the impromptu meetings for lunch or dinner or their brief excursions to work out side by side at the gym. On this day, Dexter stood alongside a weight machine, peering anxiously at the front door. He had decided against leaving a message on her answering machine to let her know that he would be here. He didn't want to seem overly aggressive, knowing how she felt about being pushed. He'd been pleased when she'd called him to say she would indeed be coming, but that she might be late should he miss her. He'd replayed the message over and over, relishing the sound of her voice. John had called him crazy, and he was beginning to feel as if he were.

They'd been taking things ever so slowly. Dexter struggled not to press Marguerite for more. He'd been allowing their time to be an easy bantering of friendship, and Marguerite seemed to thrive on that. When she was ready, she would extend more. He was sure of this. He was respectful of how protective she was of her space. He was beginning to understand her anxiety and fears of abandonment. He was learning about her issues with trust and hurt, and he was working diligently to build her confidence in him and his commitment to the love he had for her.

He missed her when she wasn't with him. When they were together he was hungry for her. He could see in her eyes that she felt very much the same way. Today had been like every other day for the two of them. Thoughts of each other had occupied every empty moment of their time apart. Dexter struggled to bench-press the heaviness of metal weights over his head, but he could only think about Marguerite. Then, what little concentration he had was suddenly broken.

"Dexter? Dexter Williams?"

Dexter dropped the weight back onto its resting spot, and lifted his upper torso to see who stood over him calling his name. A slender woman in biking shorts and a sports bra smiled down at him, perspiration gracing the honey of her skin. She smiled sweetly, a look of obvious recognition on her face.

"I thought that was you. How have you been?"

Dexter grinned, reaching to pull the woman into a warm embrace. "Joy Harden. Long time, no see. How are you doing, woman?"

"I'm great. How are you?"

"I can't complain. Life is treating me well."

"I was here one day last week playing racquet ball with a friend and thought I saw you, but you were gone before I knew it. Do you come here often?"

Dexter nodded, peering around the room of the Sportplex. "At least three or four times per week. How about you?"

"Just joined. Work has been kicking my behind. I finally had to just stop and say time out for Joy."

"I know that feeling. So are you married, kids?"

"Not yet. I'm back and forth with someone special, though. But building my business has been the only thing getting my full commitment these days."

"Well, I don't have to ask how that's going. Every time I turn around, I'm seeing your name in the paper somewhere. Things seem to be going very well for you."

"They are. I'm playing in the big leagues now, and it feels really good. But what about you? Please tell me some woman has finally gotten you to settle down. I know you've stopped being that trifling brother I'd have to warn sisters away from!"

Dexter laughed. "Yes, Joy. I've slowed right up. I am madly in love with a wonderful woman, and hopefully she feels the same way about me."

Joy grinned. "Very nice. I would love to meet her."

Dexter glanced toward the doorway again. "I was hoping she'd get here tonight, but work seems to be holding her up."

"Well, maybe next time. Don't let me keep you any longer. I just wanted to say hello."

Dexter nodded, then suddenly the expression on his face went serious. "Joy, I need to talk business with you. There's something that I've been thinking about, and seeing you right now makes me think I need to give some serious thought to it."

Joy smiled again, the curve of her mouth lifting the lines of her face. "No problem." Reaching into an outside pocket of her leather sports bag, she pulled a business card from its space. "Here's my card. Just give me a call when you're ready and we can sit down and talk."

"Thanks," Dexter said, palming the paper between

his hands. "I'll call you before the week is out. Perhaps we can do lunch or even dinner depending on your schedule."

"I look forward to it. You take care now."

Dexter watched as the young woman walked toward the women's locker area, turning once to wave in his direction. The vibration of her hips was pleasing to look at as he and two other brothers watched her walk away. A short mocha-colored man with flaming red dreadlocks grinned, giving Dexter a thumbs-up. Suddenly self-conscious, Dexter nodded, then turned his attention back toward the front door.

35

Dexter waited patiently for Sharon to arrive. They'd agreed to meet at the Stamford train station at exactly eight o'clock, and he'd been sitting with the car idling since five minutes till eight. When he'd called Sharon and asked ever so subtly if she could keep a secret, he'd known she'd been intrigued. He also hoped that he could trust that every detail of the next three hours would not be played and replayed for Marguerite before he was ready. He smiled slyly as Sharon pulled her car into an empty spot three spaces down, locked the door behind her, and slipped into the leather seat beside him.

"Hi, there." She grinned. "I didn't keep you waiting too long, did I?"

Dexter shook his head, smiling broadly as he eased his vehicle out of the parking spot and into traffic. "Not at all. How are you doing?"

"I'm good. How about yourself?"

He shrugged. "I'll be better when I get my girl back."

Sharon laughed. "You two are going to make me crazy. So where are we headed?"

Dexter smiled. "You'll see."

Sharon sucked her teeth. "You make me sick."

As they made small talk about Randy and Sharon's wedding plans, Dexter headed north up Summer Street past the police station, the Ridgeway Shopping Center, and finally onto High Ridge Road.

"Where are we going?" Sharon asked again.

"North Stamford."

"Why?"

Dexter only smiled. The ride was a long one, seemingly to nowhere, as they drove through North Stamford and headed toward Pound Ridge and the New York state border. As Dexter studied the map that had been drawn for him, he wondered if he was doing the right thing. If maybe he should turn around and forget the absurdity of his thoughts. He wondered if Sharon would think him as foolish as he was beginning to feel. Tall hardwoods loomed in the distance as he turned right onto a newly cut road, the rich dark soil along the roadside nourishing budding vegetation. Although he enjoyed privacy and solitude, he was beginning to wonder if this was a touch too much even for his taste.

Sharon leaned forward in her seat taking in the view. "How beautiful," she muttered softly under her breath. Dexter studied the directions one last time before making one final turn toward the mailbox marker indicated. After turning onto another length of dirt road, cut just wide enough to allow a single car to pass, he continued down for another quarter of a mile before reaching a graveled circular driveway. The beginnings of an elaborate one-story structure loomed directly in front of them. The massive brick foundation outlined the perimeter of a six-thousand-square-foot building, and some impressive wall framing was starting to take shape. A crew of twenty was working diligently; cutting, lifting, and nailing wood roof trusses into place.

Parking his vehicle alongside a paneled pickup truck that boasted the logo of J.C. Harden General Contracting, Dexter slowly took in the surroundings. Sharon sat beside him staring just as intensely. A ten-acre lot of land had been neatly cleared for the construction. An additional forty acres of hardwoods bordered the property, and a four-acre stretch of pond loomed off in the distance. The view was breathtaking.

As they stepped out of the vehicle, Dexter inhaled deeply, filling his lungs with the cool morning air, and stretched the length of his large frame upward. Reaching back inside the car for his leather portfolio, Dexter checked his notes for the name of the site supervisor, then closed the door behind him.

Together, the duo strolled slowly toward the construction site, visibly impressed. J.C. Harden General Contracting was well known for superior work, and even in the home's initial stages, Dexter could see why. As he approached what would eventually be the front foyer, a small Hispanic man extended his hand, eagerly greeting him.

Dexter smiled warmly. "Good morning. I'm looking for Odilon Perez."

"Hello. I am Odilon. You must be Señor Williams," the man replied with a thick Spanish accent.

"Yes, and please call me Dexter. This is my friend, Sharon Donald."

"It is a pleasure to meet you both." The man smiled sweetly at Sharon as he extended his hand in her direction. "The office said you would be stopping by."

Dexter nodded. "Very impressive. I am thrilled to see it coming together so beautifully."

"We are pleased. We hope that you will be very happy with our work."

Sharon's mouth dropped open. "Dexter, this is your house?"

Dexter nodded. "Closed on the construction loan a few weeks ago. I'm hoping that it is going to be the home Marguerite and I grow old together in. Do you think she'll like it?"

Sharon shook her head in disbelief. "If she doesn't, I'll marry you. I like it."

Dexter laughed warmly. "Is J.C. around, by chance?"

Odilon smiled, then pointed toward the back of the house and a group reviewing a set of blueprints. "This way *por favor.*"

As they approached the group, Dexter was conscious of the eyes that took note of their steps. His black, patent-leather shoes moved securely across the wood sub-floor. Black slacks and a casual white crew shirt adorned his large frame, the white shirt a pleasing contrast to his dark complexion. His dress was impeccable, the clothes fitting neatly around the granite of his body. His stride was more of a strut. He knew his height and size were imposing, and he played on every inch of his grand stature. The crew paused briefly, acknowledging his presence. The new owner had arrived. Nodding their approval, they continued with their work.

In front of them stood two men, an older male and his mirror image, many years younger. Father and son, Sharon thought quickly, and not bad-looking either. She smiled sweetly, pacing herself behind Dexter. Between the two men, a woman was making notations on the papers before them.

"*Jefe*, Señor Williams is here, and this is Señorita Donald," said Odilon.

"Hello, Dexter." She grinned. "Ms. Donald, it's a pleasure," the woman said, extending her own perfectly manicured hand toward Sharon. "I'm Joy Harden, but please call me J.C."

"Nice to meet you," Sharon responded, a smile still plastered on her face.

"This is Douglas Reid, life long friend and my resident electrician, and his son Michael, our newest student intern."

"Hello," Dexter said as he and Sharon took turns shaking hands. "The house is going to be spectacular. I am speechless."

The builder smiled, turning her attention to Sharon. "Now, are you the wonderful woman he's building this home for?"

Sharon shook her head. "No such luck. She's my best friend, though."

"Lucky woman."

"You can say that again." The two women giggled like co-conspirators.

"Let me show you both around," J.C. said, passing the blueprints to the electrician and his son as they excused themselves. "It's much different in person than on paper." J.C. gestured for them to join her, then briefly diverted her attention when they were interrupted.

"*Jefe?*"

"*Sí?*"

Odilon asked her a question in his native language, which she responded to in perfect Spanish.

The man chuckled as he shook Dexter's hand one last time. "Good day Señor Williams, *señorita,* " he said, making his way to the other side of the building.

Dexter and Sharon smiled, answering in unison. "Thank you."

J.C. returned her attention to Dexter. "Have you chosen an interior designer yet? I need to meet with him very soon if you want everything to be tied in when this project is through."

Dexter nodded. "I think it's going to be Beverly. Sharon knows Marguerite's tastes better than I do, so I've had to let her in on my little secret so I can get her advice."

J.C. smiled at Sharon as the woman cut her eyes in his direction.

"Honey, hush," Sharon said, shaking her head.

"Well, Sharon, this is not your typical New England home," J.C. said.

Sharon raised an eyebrow. "What will be different?"

"Dexter is building a very large log home."

"Log?"

J.C. smiled at the look of confusion on Sharon's face as her eyes scanned the structure around her.

"Yes, log. The initial framing looks very traditional, but that's only for insulation purposes. Instead of traditional siding and sheet rock, these walls will be covered with a milled half-log on the exterior and interior."

"How large are these logs?"

"Sixteen inches in diameter," J.C. said matter-of-factly. "There will also be an extensive amount of stonework throughout the home, particularly in the foyer, and of course all the fireplaces will be masoned in stone or brick. All the floors will be hardwood except in the wet areas, which will be tiled, and the plans have terrazzo flooring in the kitchen. Have you ever seen a log home before?"

"A cabin at summer camp back in the early seventies. This will be my first large log home," Sharon answered, shaking her head slowly. "Are you sure about this?" she asked, looking over at Dexter. He laughed.

"We have over six thousand square feet of heated living space on one level," J.C. explained. "As you can see, the formal areas flow smoothly into each other."

Dexter interjected. "Sharon, I want the interior design to do much the same thing. I know Marguerite's tastes are somewhat traditional, but also a bit eclectic. I don't think she'd want frilly feminine, and I definitely don't want it to look like it stepped out of an issue of *Field and Stream*. I personally want an upscale vacation-lodge feel."

Sharon nodded, her expression serious for the first time. "Well, you definitely have a wonderful resort-like setting. Are you sure you don't want to let Marguerite in on this?"

Dexter shook his head. "I want it to be a complete surprise."

J.C. took a deep breath as though she were going to say something, but she didn't. Her attention was focused on the activity overhead. Dexter and Sharon followed her gaze toward the men struggling to secure a roof truss into place.

"Despacio! Despacio!" J.C. called out, a protective edge rising in her tone. "Slow! Take your time before you drop that thing or worse, one of you falls!"

"*Sí, jefe,*" one of the men responded.

Turning her attention back toward Dexter, J.C. handed him a cylindrical blueprint tube. "This is a set of floor plans for your designer to study. Have her look them over and then give my secretary a call to schedule some time for us all to get together to talk again. Meanwhile, walk around, familiarize yourself, and let me or Odilon know if you have any questions. Sharon, it was nice to meet you."

"Thanks, J.C., same here."

Dexter and Sharon watched as she scaled a ladder to the second-story level directing the crew with the truss placement. They watched as she struggled alongside them to ease the truss into place, then pulled a large hammer from the tool belt around her waist and proceeded to nail the thing in place. Sharon was impressed with the woman, having never met a female builder before. She punched Dexter lightly on the arm. "You go with your bad self. You must be some sort of crazy in love."

Dexter could only shake his head, watching the expression on Sharon's face as she watched J.C. swing a temporary piece of plywood up and into place and begin nailing it down. A nervous whisper kicked him full force, and as the two made their way back to the car, Dexter could feel his knees shaking just enough to throw off the smooth glide of his walk. It was either some sort of love or just plain crazy.

36

It had been a productive day, and Marguerite was pleased. As she pulled out of the parking lot of her office, she waved good-bye to the security guard and headed for home. The ride to 112 Meredith Drive, Unit C-12, would have been relatively short had there not been a tractor trailer hemmed up under the overpass between Main Street and the Route 85 bypass. Marguerite shifted her car into park as she and four other vehicles waited for the traffic to be rerouted around the obtrusive vehicle. Reaching for the radio, she turned up the volume, flooding the interior with Snoop Doggy Dog, then irritated by the noise, switched from the heavy rap station to one more soothing. Somebody's jazz reached out to stroke her brow, and she instantly felt better.

As she reflected over her day's activities, increasing thoughts of Dexter kept intruding upon her musings. They'd not spoken in so long, she felt as if she'd forgotten the vibrato of his voice. Forty minutes later, she was still thinking about Dexter as she finally pulled into the garage of her condo complex and parked.

The telephone was ringing off the hook as Marguerite made her way through the doorway. She cursed, remembering that she'd not turned on the answering machine. Slamming the front door behind her, she dove over the end of sofa to answer the call.

"Hello?"

"What did you think?"

"Excuse me?"

"Didn't you get my message?"

Marguerite shook her head laughing. "Sharon, you are too much, girl," she responded, easing around to sit comfortably on the sofa.

"I know I'm all that and a bag of chips. What I want to know is if you're interested in going to see this house with me or not?"

Marguerite stammered, a rush of color flooding her cheeks. "I don't know about this. Randy is going to have a fit if he finds out you are out house-hunting and decorating without him."

"Long as I got my prenup, he can have as many fits as he wants. So you coming?"

"Mmmm. You are so wrong. Now I'm sure this is a bad idea."

Sharon laughed again. "Look, I'm told this designer is super-talented and the best in the business. If that's so, I want her to do my house, and since you have such great taste, I want you to help me out."

Marguerite shrugged. "Well, I guess so."

Sharon suddenly changed the subject. "Have you called Dexter?"

"No, and why do you keep asking me that?"

"You haven't called him at all?"

"Not since the last time you asked."

"I swear, you are not making this easy for me."
Marguerite could feel Sharon rolling her eyes on

the other end of the telephone. She chuckled lightly as her friend continued. "Look, I'm picking you up at seven. We're meeting Beverly Stephens."

"Now who is she?"

"The designer. Duh!"

"Oh."

"She's having a private open house tonight for that new subdivision in Governor's Grove. Nothing fancy, just wine and hors d'oeuvres for select real-estate agents and potential clients. She invited us to come take a peek. This will give us a chance to see her work up close and personal. It will also give me a real feel for her taste and style. They gave her a multi-million-dollar budget and told her to do whatever she wanted. They say the woman outdid herself. She can't wait for the official opening so she can show it off to the public. From what I'm told, if this home had any flaws, Beverly has hidden every one of them and then some."

Marguerite listened as Sharon continued to extol what she perceived to be the woman's finer qualities. She was intrigued by her friend's sudden interest in home decorating.

"Okay. I'll be ready in an hour. I just need to get a quick shower and grab myself a sandwich."

"Great. Oh, before I forget, your cousin called me about us getting together for ladies' night. It's that time again."

Marguerite grimaced. "Delores gets right on my nerves. What day?"

"Friday, if everyone can get together. You don't have a date, do you?"

Marguerite laughed. "Good-bye, Sharon."

"Just asking. See you in a few."

* * *

Laughter filled the interior of Sharon's silver Volvo. The two women were in stitches as they made their way across town toward Governor's Grove. The vastness of their friendship spilled out into the open, flooding the vehicle with a warmth that energized them. They'd been each other's support group, cheering sections, crying posts, and anything else that was needed at the most pivotal events of their respective lives since before forever. Marguerite adored her best friend.

As they approached the brightly lit two-story home, Marguerite was not overly impressed. It was typical of the new construction for the area. She had been hoping to see something different for a change.

It was another beautiful evening. Clasped arm in arm, the two women made their way inside. Beverly Stephens, a petite brunette with raging blue eyes, greeted them in the doorway. "Hi, Sharon." She beamed, hugging Sharon warmly. "I am so glad you two could make it. This must be Marguerite."

Sharon raised her eyebrows slightly. "Hi, Beverly, and yes, this is my friend Marguerite."

"Hello and thank you for inviting me," Marguerite replied, extending a hand to the other woman.

The woman nodded as Marguerite's attention started to waver, her eyes taking in the foyer. "This is beautiful," Marguerite gasped, visibly impressed.

"Thank you. I am very pleased.

You two take your time looking around. You don't need the official tour. I'll catch up with you later," Beverly said as she waved in another arrival.

"Thank you," both women chanted in unison.

Sharon was still beaming. "Do I know how to pick 'em or what. You go look around. I'm going to go find me a chair near the food."

"You sure?"

"I know her work. This is for your benefit. Just take your time. I'm sure there's plenty for you to see. Then you can let me know what you think."

Marguerite allowed her eyes to flow slowly around the two-story foyer. The hardwood floor was covered by a large Moroccan rug in dark rich tones that seemed to reach up and outward toward the rest of the room. The walls were painted with a thick tawny patina. Its texture was full and inviting, making one want to reach out and touch it. An opulent English tapestry hung on the foyer wall.

Marguerite stepped down into the formal living room on her left, two oversized columns flanking the way. A rich burgundy was Beverly's color of choice, and she'd woven it throughout the entire downstairs, sometimes in subtle touches, sometimes with a bold, flagrant flair. The living room set was ornately detailed, hand-carved mahogany, upholstered in a thick red fabric. Varying shades of gold and cream accented the decor. The windows were trimmed in deep gold taffeta; reminiscent of a prom gown Marguerite had once worn. The paintings were original oils, very European, very expensive.

Extending off the living room was a glass-enclosed sunroom. A black baby grand piano sat pristinely off in a corner topped with a rich brocade fabric and floral arrangement. Dark gold cord woven around delicate gold lace trimmed the window tops, not disturbing the outside view. Musical instruments, a violin, flute, and clarinet, hung gracefully against the back wall. A ceiling fan spun quietly overhead, and Marguerite found the cool breeze pleasing. She couldn't help but take a seat in one of two gold corner chairs, their bottoms trimmed in a rich tassel. The pillows behind her back were burgundy and black, pulling their colors from the Oriental rug on the floor.

As she continued, Marguerite was taken by how smoothly the decor blended from one room to another. Sharon had been right. If any flaws existed in this house, they'd be lost behind Beverly's work.

As Marguerite entered the two-story family room and kitchen, she grinned at Sharon, who was huddled in intense conversation with Beverly. Marguerite lost her breath as she entered the adjoining kitchen. It was a kitchen she wouldn't have minded getting lost in.

Sharon interrupted Marguerite's thoughts. "You been upstairs yet?"

"No, I can't get over the downstairs. It's absolutely exquisite."

"She definitely outdid herself. I want to go look at the little girl's bedroom. Beverly says it's like nothing I've ever seen."

Marguerite nodded. "Lead the way."

Moments later, both women stood open-mouthed in the doorway. "I want this," Sharon said. "I would absolutely die for this room."

Marguerite nodded. If she had never before contemplated having a girl child, this room made her suddenly want for one. Beverly had added architectural detail where there was none. It was a magical garden of little-girl secrets. A headboard constructed from an old set of French doors highlighted the double bed. The glass had been removed and the frame had been painted white and aged. Painted vines crept slowly up the sides. Behind the bed, as if one were peeking out the door to the outside, grew a garden of blossoms. Meticulously detailed flowers had been hand-painted on the walls, pale greens and pinks flowing upward into a blue sky of cascading clouds. The furniture was white and simple, beautiful antique lines that were classically intriguing. The bed covering was a pale pink silk, the pillows white lace. In one corner, a child's swing hung from the ceiling, seeming to hang from the branches of a tree. A white whicker rocking chair filled with soft cashmere bunnies and teddy bears was the final touch.

"I want a baby," Marguerite said aloud.

Sharon laughed. "If I ever have any, you can have mine. I just want this room."

Their final stop was the master bedroom, a tantalizing combination of hunter-green and ivory. A king-sized four-poster bed beckoned one inside, and both women could easily imagine themselves sprawled across the mattress. A sitting area boasted a large palladium window that looked out over a backdrop of trees, and a full moon was peering inside. Beverly had masterfully played with rich vibrant colors, dark woods, and graceful touches of silks and lace. Both Marguerite and Sharon were sold.

"Okay. The woman is definitely hired," said Sharon.

"Who you tellin'."

"You know, if she doesn't make my home look better than this one, she's dead meat."

"Tell her."

"I will and so will you, friend. I'm glad you're going to help me." Sharon paused in the doorway. "Now tell me you didn't think about Dexter and that big behind bed over there."

Marguerite grinned. "Don't go there."

"Uh-huh. I knew it crossed your mind."

37

Construction on Dexter's new home had been completed, and he and Sharon had worked diligently to put the final touches on the interior decor. Without even knowing it, Marguerite had been a willing accomplice in decorating the oasis Dexter imagined for the two of them. Dexter marveled at just how well Sharon had managed to keep the secret, and Sharon herself was amazed at the restraint she'd shown.

Conversations between him and Marguerite had been more and more frequent. Dexter was thrilled when Marguerite had agreed to meet him to select a work of art for his condominium. He'd convinced her that he was redecorating the room John had once occupied.

Dexter opened the gallery door, his hand pressed against Marguerite's lower back as he guided her through the entrance. The flood to their senses was overwhelming as they stepped inside, scanning the length of the room. Marguerite gasped in awe, a panorama of wonderment before her. Bright natural light filled the open area, highlighting an assortment of paintings that lined the walls. Tables were lined with intricately detailed gourds in an array of colors, and the room was filled with texture. The colors were vibrant and exciting, and she felt intoxicated as she took it all in. Walking the blue-carpeted floor cautiously, Marguerite inhaled a soothing aroma of scented candles. Enya played in the distance, and the overall sensation was breathtakingly electric. She suddenly wished she could dance. The moment was sultry and ever so subtle, and she could feel her steps lighten as she examined each of the items before her.

It was the angel that captured her attention, the large abstract painting sitting at the forefront of the gallery. The piece was titled *Angel Angel*, by a North Carolina artist named Olivia Gatewood. The lines Marguerite saw were subtle, an eerie incandescence falling on the painted form. Marguerite could feel the figure rising, gossamer wings reaching out protectively, and without a word passing between them, Dexter knew that Marguerite had found the piece that would sit in their bedroom. Dexter smiled.

It was the woman who appeared from behind a screened wall that caught Marguerite's attention next, greeting Dexter with warm familiarity. A momentary wave of jealousy flooded her spirit as the two hugged warmly, the woman reaching up to press her lips against Dexter's.

"Marguerite, I want you to meet John's sister. Carolyn Patterson, Marguerite Cole."

"Hi." Carolyn smiled, embracing Marguerite warmly. "I've heard so much about you. It's a pleasure to finally meet you. We never got a chance to talk at the wedding."

"Thank you." Marguerite blushed. "It's nice to meet you. Your gallery is absolutely wonderful!"

"Oh, thank you. It's been a wonderful challenge,"

the woman gushed with visible appreciation. "So, did you find something you like, Dexter?"

The man nodded, grinning broadly. "I think Marguerite would kill me if I didn't take that painting up front there. What do you think, Marguerite?"

She smiled toward where he pointed. "I don't think he can lose with that one, but I'm not sure it's right for that bedroom."

Dexter nodded. "Maybe we should continue to look around."

Marguerite glanced again toward the angel.

Dexter smiled. "You want that piece for yourself, don't you?"

Marguerite grinned back. "Well, if you don't buy it, I might."

Carolyn laughed. "I will wrap, deliver, and hang it for the first taker. If you two want, we can even start bidding on it. The higher the better."

Marguerite rolled her eyes as Dexter laughed. "He'll take the painting," she said sweetly, "and if it doesn't work in his house, he can give it to me for mine."

Carolyn pinched Dexter's arm. "Cash, check, or charge?"

"Thank you," he said to Marguerite minutes later as they carried the wrapped package out to his car. "I can't tell you how much I appreciate all your help."

"Don't thank me. I was glad to help. I have to send Sharon here. She's been making a lot of plans for the new home she and Randy are getting. I know she'll love this place."

Dexter nodded, a secret glimmer in his eyes. "I'm sure she will," he said. "I'm sure she will."

38

Marguerite hesitated before picking up the telephone. She dialed quickly, fearful that she might panic and chicken out before completing the call. Pulling the receiver to her ear, she inhaled deeply, counting the rings on the other end. At the third ring, Dexter picked up, and the warmth of his voice embraced the nervousness she'd been feeling.

"Hello?"

"Hi, Dexter. How are you?"

"Hey, sweetheart. I'm good. How are you?"

"I'm doing really well. I was calling to see if I could treat you to dinner."

She could feel Dexter smiling on the other end of the telephone. "I'd like that. I'd like that a lot."

Marguerite grinned widely, pausing in momentary reflection. "Why don't I pick you up around seven o'clock and I'll wine and dine you in style."

Dexter chuckled. "Scared of you. Are you sure you don't want me to meet you halfway?"

"No. This is on me. I'll come there."

Dexter laughed out loud. "Whatever you say. I'll be ready."

"See you soon."

Marguerite briefly clutched the receiver to her

chest before dropping it back down on the cradle. A faint smile crossed her lips as she retreated into the bathroom for a hot shower. "Maybe I should have said eight o'clock," she mused, studying her reflection closely. Her usual crystal complexion was pale, her normal robust color faded. Puffy rings had settled comfortably under her eyes, giving her thin face a hollowed, starving-child appearance. Her full lips were cracked, dull, and dry, her mouth pulling at the edges as though she were in pain. "Lord have mercy," she said aloud, throwing up her hands toward the ceiling. As if responding, the light in the bathroom flickered ever so slightly, and Marguerite could not help but laugh.

Heaving a deep sigh, she sauntered back into the bedroom. Turning on the CD player in her bedroom, she inhaled the low drone of Muddy Waters as he moaned her newfound mantra, his lyrics promising that everything was going to be all right.

As if Miss Mae were coming in on cue, the overhead light in the bathroom flickered in time with the intoxicating beat. Marguerite watched the gentle twinkle that reached out to soothe her, and instinctively she knew that everything was indeed going to be all right.

Stepping into the shower, she let the warm water flow across her face, over her shoulders, and down the length of her back. Water had never felt so good, a subtle steam rising from the warmth of the fluid. Gripping a large bath sponge filled with lavender-scented body wash, she ran it along the length of her body, covering her full breasts and the flat of her stomach with suds. The music in the background was soothing, and Marguerite hung onto every word.

At precisely 6:54, Marguerite pulled into the parking lot in front of Dexter's house. Stepping out of the car, she adjusted the strap on her high heel, and smoothed the line of black panty hose up and over the curvature of a firm leg. Her calf muscles were rock-hard, and she was grateful that her recent hiatus from exercise had not softened her muscles much. The leopard-print silk dress that adorned her statuesque body fit like a glove. It felt good to be dressed, and she silently kicked herself for having stayed at her own personal pity party for as long as she had.

She had cleaned up nicely, and she was hopeful that Dexter would approve. She marveled at how patient he had been with her, and she was determined to right the wrong she'd brought upon them. She felt good about herself, and she wanted Dexter to feel good about her also. Running an index finger over her eyebrows, she smiled shyly as Dexter peeked out the window.

Dexter pulled the door open just as she reached to push the doorbell. "Hey, stranger," she said softly.

Stunned only momentarily, he stepped aside, grinning from ear to ear. "I do love myself some beautiful black woman," Dexter said, his chest pushed out, his eyes wide. "Yes indeed . . . yes indeed . . . beautiful."

Marguerite grinned back. "Thank you. I'll take that as a compliment."

Leaning to kiss her cheek, he nodded his head approvingly. "It's good to see you."

They both laughed nervously.

"So, what are you feeding me?" Dexter asked, pulling the front door closed and locking it securely behind them.

"Ribs. I've got me a serious taste for some ribs, corn bread, and greens."

Dexter laughed broadly. "I guess that means we're eating at Mr. Willie's Rib Shack?"

Marguerite smiled with him. "No. As a matter of fact, I'm taking you to someplace new. It's a new restaurant in downtown Wilton called Addison's. I hear it's a little more upscale than Mr. Willie's. Jazz and blues for some ambiance, and they actually give you those little wet napkins for your fingers." Dexter laughed again.

Dexter gently palmed the center of her back as he guided her to her car, which she had parked precariously in the fire lane in front of his building. Smiling up at him as she opened the door to let him in, Marguerite suddenly wondered why she'd been so hesitant to initiate contact with him. She missed him and being with him now, this close, brought her comfort she missed.

The man looked good in his double-breasted suit. Navy was a strong color on him, Marguerite thought, appraising the way the silk jacket sat against a paler blue dress shirt. His hair was cropped close, and Marguerite suspected that the cut was relatively new. The beginnings of a new beard and a full mustache, with a hint of silver speckled against black, adorned his face. Watching him made Marguerite breathless.

"I want you to know I canceled a date with John

and Debbie to go to dinner tonight. It was tuna casserole night at the Patterson house."

Marguerite laughed. "I'm flattered that you would give up tuna casserole for me."

"It's only because you're special." Dexter's grin widened.

Marguerite revved the engine, then pulled the vehicle out into the line of traffic. The conversation between them was light and upbeat as they bantered back and forth. Their comfort levels continued to rise.

A small body of water glistened in the distance as they drove over a small bridge into Ridgefield. The sun was setting neatly behind it, light reflecting off the water. "Prime for skinny-dipping, don't you think? We could dip our feet in, get wet, and be dressed again before anyone saw us. You game?"

Marguerite choked, coughing and laughing at the same time. "I am not interested in getting my feet or any other part of this body wet, thank you. You are crazy."

Dexter laughed with her. "Can't fault a man for trying."

Cutting her eyes in his direction, Marguerite sucked her teeth. "So you say."

Dexter eyed her smugly. Too smugly, Marguerite thought as she swatted a hand against his shoulder. "How's work going?" she asked as he chuckled lightly.

"Busy as all get-out. I'm really pleased with the progress. The forecasts look really good and everyone is really excited about the new prospects."

"I am so happy for you. I know how badly you've wanted this."

He nodded. "Thank you. I feel like it's quite an accomplishment for me."

As she parked, Marguerite leaned a manicured hand on his thigh and squeezed it gently. "You should be very proud of yourself. Now let's go eat. I'm hungry."

Seated at a corner table next to the window, Marguerite ordered two large platters of ribs, corn bread, baked beans, collard greens, and candied yams. Dexter hadn't realized just how hungry he was until the food was placed in front of them. A gallon of iced tea later, both sat back content, bellies filled to the point of discomfort.

"Lord, I'm too full," she said, rubbing the flat of her hand slowly across her stomach.

Dexter nodded, sucking the last drop of barbecue sauce from a rib bone. "But you feel good, right?"

"Yes," Marguerite droned slowly. "I do feel good."

He smiled. "Then that's all that matters."

Marguerite smiled with him. Her mood had lifted with the weather, the light drizzle that threatened earlier having given way to a clear evening. Outside, the sky glittered with stars, a quarter moon beaming at the edge of the darkness.

"Can I get you two anything else?" the waitress, a petite girl with crimson and gold braids, asked, twisting her order pad and a ballpoint pen between her small hands. "Maybe some coffee or a piece of our pecan pie?"

Marguerite groaned, shaking her head. "No, honey," she said with a grin. "You're going to have to roll me out of here as it is."

"How about you, sir?"

"I'll take a cup of coffee, please, and why don't I just try a real small piece of that pie. Thank you."

The woman nodded, did an about-face, and disappeared into the kitchen. A moment later, she was back with Dexter's coffee, a hunk of pie topped with fresh whipped cream, and the bill. Placing it all easily on the table, she smiled, then said she'd be back for the check when they were ready.

Marguerite watched as Dexter poured a large dollop of milk into his cup, then spooned in five sugars. She shook her head. "You want some coffee with that sugar?"

He laughed lightly, then suddenly turned serious on her, swirling his spoon about in his cup.

"So, are you finally ready to talk to me, Marguerite? Are you ready to clear the air between us yet? Are you ready to tell me?"

A pregnant pause filled the space between them. Marguerite heaved a heavy sigh, raising a hand to tuck a strand of hair behind her ear. She leaned back against her seat, fiddling with the napkin still resting in her lap. The silence between them grew as Dexter sipped his coffee slowly, waiting for her to speak.

She took a deep breath, inhaling the deep aroma of barbecue, before she spoke, choosing her words carefully. "I've been scared, Dexter, and that fear has made me push you away. You deserve so much, and I've been petrified that I can't be all that you need me to be. I've also been scared that once you realized that, you'd leave me, you wouldn't want me, and I figured I'd get hurt. I didn't want to risk being burned."

Not commenting, Dexter raised his cup to his lips, taking another sip of his coffee. Marguerite continued. "You have always been so secure with our relationship and so secure about your love, and I didn't know how to deal with that."

"Whoever told you I was secure? Without you catering, pampering, and making me feel like I owned the world, I didn't know what to do with myself."

Marguerite smiled. "I know you want to talk about this, Dexter, but I don't know if I'm ready to say what you want to hear, the way you want to hear it. I don't want to hurt you any more, so please let's not make this evening too serious. Please? Let's just enjoy each other's company. Nodding, Dexter pulled a platinum Visa card from his wallet and placed it on the table.

"Oh, no, you don't," Marguerite interjected, handing his card back to him. "This one's on me. I won't have you telling John and Debbie that not only did I keep you from that tuna casserole, but that I made you pay for the meal too. I can hear you now."

Dexter laughed. "That's right. I would definitely talk about you, girl."

The two laughed loudly as they made their way out of the building and back to the car. As Marguerite leaned to open Dexter's door, she did an about-face, pressing herself against the front of him. Wrapping her arms about his waist, she kissed him greedily. Dexter gasped for air when she finally released him.

"Dexter, you mean more to me than you will ever know. I made you a promise and I intend to keep it. Please, just trust me. I swear I won't disappoint you."

Neither Dexter or Marguerite could stop grinning as they made their way home.

39

Marguerite sat nervously behind the steering wheel of her car. She'd dropped Dexter off an hour ago, had driven around the block a few times, then had returned to sit in front of his door. In the distance, she could see a faint light on inside, and every so often she imagined movement behind the sheer white curtains that hung in the front window. Her breathing was rapid, and she felt as though her heart were about to burst. Inhaling deeply, she sucked in the cool air being emitted from the air-conditioning system in the vehicle. It had only been sixty minutes since she'd last talked to Dexter, his pronouncement of love still ringing in her ears. It felt like an eternity. *"Do it,"* a loud voice whispered over her shoulder. *"Don't just sit there, go knock on dat boy's door and tell him."*

Stepping from the car, Marguerite adjusted her clothes, pulling the form-fitting dress down across her thighs. Reaching up, she ran her palms along her hair, smoothing the silky strands flat against her head and adjusting the elastic band that held her shoulder-length ponytail. She could do this.

She could not remember ringing the bell. In fact, there was no recollection of the time that had passed between her first step and when he swung the door open wide, a look of surprise gracing his face.

"Hi."

"Hi," she whispered, wanting to turn and run.

"What are you—?"

"Can I come in, please? I need to talk to you," she said, interrupting, her eyes silently pleading.

As he nodded, opening the door wider to permit her entry, she welcomed the familiar scent of him that greeted her nostrils, easing her nervousness.

"I hope I'm not interrupting. You don't have company or anything?"

Dexter laughed. "No," he said shaking his head. "I was just cleaning the bathroom," he finished, showing her the cleaner and rag in his hands.

She smiled meekly, twisting her hands in front of her. "You never know what someone could do after an hour's gone by. You know?"

Putting the cleaner on the table, Dexter motioned for her to take a seat. Dropping heavily into the chair being offered, she suddenly felt like a small child come to confess her crimes. The voice over her shoulder pushed her on. *"Tell him."*

"Dexter, I've missed you so much."

Dexter rose from his seat, sauntering over to stand by the window.

Marguerite continued, the words spilling out quickly. "I'm sorry. I never meant to hurt you. There were just things that were too painful for me to deal with, and I didn't think I could handle sharing them with anyone. I've kept so much of it bottled up for so long that I really believed it was better for everyone if I kept it locked away."

She took a deep breath.

He turned to stare at her, his face expressionless. "I would have helped you, but you didn't trust me," he said. "I can't be with a woman who doesn't trust me."

Marguerite nodded. "But I do trust you. It's me I didn't believe in." She hung her head, fighting not to let her tears intrude upon her thoughts. "Dexter, for a very long time I felt as though I was not worthy of any man's love. I resisted you for as long as I did because I truly believed that once you got to know me, that you would see what I saw in myself. I didn't think I could handle that kind of disappointment. I didn't want to know that kind of hurt ever again. When you said you loved me, I just kept waiting for the dream to end."

"It wasn't a dream. It was a reality and you pushed me away." He paused. "Why are you here now? What do you want to tell me?"

Marguerite met his eyes. "I want to tell you that I love you. To tell you I miss you. To ask you to forgive me, to give me a second chance. To show you how much I want to be with you. To show you how much I want to share with you. I want you to know how much I need you. I love you."

Dexter turned away from her, staring back out toward the parking lot. He inhaled deeply, tears welling in his eyes. His smile returned.

Crossing over to where he stood, Marguerite rested her hand on his arm, pressing her cheek into his back. *"Say it again. Don't leave that boy standin' dere like dat!"*

"Dexter, I love you. I don't want to lose you. Not now, not ever."

Turning, Dexter pulled her into his arms, pressing his lips hungrily against hers. The familiar feel of him was overwhelming. Tasting him sent waves of shock throughout her body, and she was barely able to contain herself. As he hugged her, his eyes closed tightly, she fought against spilling the flood from her own eyes.

Finally speaking, Dexter pushed her away, holding her at arm's length. "We've got a lot of rebuilding to do. There's a great deal we need to discuss. I don't know if we can go on from here, but I know I want to. I have always wanted more from you than you were willing to give."

Marguerite nodded. "I want to give you all of me there is to have. I'm just asking that you let me prove it."

Dexter stared at her, wanting to take as much of her in during this brief glance as he could manage. He finally nodded, kissing her again, allowing his hands to roam across her back. "I have missed you so much."

"We've got a lot of things to talk about."

"First," Dexter said, nodding his head his head in agreement, "let's get the cleaning finished." Returning to the table, he picked up the cleaning fluid and tossed her the rag.

Pulling her into his arms again, he hugged her tightly. "Then I want to hear all about what happened with you and this guy and anything else you think I should know about. Okay?"

She nodded, kissing his cheek. As she nuzzled her head under his chin, absorbing the warmth of his arms around her, the voice over her shoulder caressed them both.

"*I do swear, chile. You always did like dem pretty mens. Now me, I needed an ugly man like yo' papa here. . . .*"

40

"I'm scared to death," Marguerite stated, tears welling in the depths of her eyes. "And I don't know what it is I'm scared of. It makes absolutely no sense to me."

Shepard nodded as Clarence passed her a tissue. "Have you spoken to my brother? Does he know that you're afraid?"

Marguerite shook her head. "I can't tell him. He will think I'm a complete fool."

Clarence cleared his throat. "I'd have to agree, Baby Girl, 'cause it sure doesn't make any sense to me."

Shepard laughed, shaking his head in Clarence's direction.

"It is perfectly okay for you to be scared," Shepard said. "What is not okay is for your to hold all that emotion inside. You need to talk with Dexter. You need to let him know what you're feeling and what you're thinking. Communication is the essential key to any relationship. Without it you are lost in the water."

Clarence rolled his eyes. "Oh, please. Where is all that talking supposed to get them? She just needs to suck it up and go for the good sex. Good sex is all she needs. Is that the problem, Baby Girl? Is Dexter lacking in the good-sex department?"

Marguerite laughed, wiping at her eyes. "No. That is not our problem."

"Well, then, it doesn't sound like you have a problem to me. Just sounds like you're being nervous over a lot of nothing. Besides, it's not like he asked you to move in with him or to marry him. You two just have a thing going on. No big deal. Sit back and enjoy it. You spend far too much time worrying about what ain't happened yet."

Shepard threw up his hands in exasperation. "Do you ever take anything seriously?"

"I took you seriously, didn't I?"

The two men glared at each other momentarily, then burst into earnest laughter.

"He's right," Clarence said finally, gesturing in Shepard's direction. "You need to talk with Dexter."

Shepard nodded. "Then you need to go have good sex," he added.

The duo giggled. "See how well it works?" Clarence said.

As they regained control, the laughter dying down to a low ebb, her uncle wrapped his arms around her shoulder. "How's that project going?" he asked.

"The pressure is on. I've got a dozen deadlines to meet and we're struggling to keep it under budget."

"Taking up a lot of your time, huh?"

"Too much."

"Doesn't leave much left over for you and Dexter, does it?"

Marguerite shrugged. "The last few weeks have

been the worst. We've barely had ten minutes together. Between my thing and his rollout we're both on overtime, functioning in high gear."

"So maybe your problem has more to do with the pressure you two are under and the fact that you haven't had much time together. Maybe what is frightening you is that you want and need him around more. Perhaps the issue isn't you being afraid of the relationship, but you being afraid of not having the relationship?"

On the other side of the room, Shepard nodded slowly, a wry smile gracing his face. Marguerite looked from one to the other and back again, suddenly sensing that her uncle was probably right. She missed Dexter. Although they spoke daily, she missed his presence. She wanted to drop her exhausted body into bed at night and have him there to catch her. She wanted to wake up in the morning with him beside her, and send him off to tackle his day as she left to do battle with hers. She suddenly knew what she needed and what she feared most.

Marguerite jumped to her feet. "I'm sorry but I've got to go. There's something I need to do."

Clarence and Shepard rose with her. "Are you okay?" Shepard asked.

She grinned, wrapping her jacket around her shoulders. "I will be. I will be very soon."

An hour later, Marguerite parked her car in a visitor's space in front of Dexter's office building. His vehicle was parked neatly, lined in a clean row beside seven other automobiles. Marguerite took a deep breath and headed inside.

Carol greeted her warmly. "Hello, there. How are you?"

"I'm fine, Carol," Marguerite said, hugging the woman warmly. "Is Dexter around?"

"He's in a board meeting, but he should be out any minute. Was he expecting you?"

"No."

"I can let him know you're here."

"No. I'll just wait in his office for him. Please don't interrupt him. I know how busy he is."

The woman nodded. "That man works too hard. I tell him every day he needs to slow down, but does he listen to me?"

The two women laughed.

"You just make yourself comfortable. Can I get you a cup of coffee or a beverage?"

"No, thanks. I'm fine."

Opening the door to Dexter's office, Marguerite inhaled the scent of him, the warm aroma flooding through her spirit. Thirty minutes later, as she peered out the window down into a courtyard, she finally heard his voice on the other side of the door. She turned in nervous anticipation as he crossed the threshold into the room.

"Hi," he said, striding over to her side. "What are you doing here?"

Marguerite leaned up to kiss his lips. "Hi. I wanted to see you. I needed to see you."

Dexter smiled, dropping the folders he held on the desktop. "You okay? There's nothing wrong, is there? Nothing else you need to tell me about your past that we haven't discussed?"

Marguerite paused before answering. "I need to talk to you. I wanted to ask you something."

Dexter sat on the leather chaise, pulling Marguerite down beside him. "What?"

Marguerite inhaled deeply, the warm breath calming the nervous flutter that rose through her midsection. Dropping to one knee in front of Dexter, she took his hands between her own. Kissing the edge of his fingers, she inhaled again, then lifted her eyes to gaze deeply into his.

"Dexter Williams, I love you. I love you with all my heart. Will you marry me? Will you take me as your wife and allow me to love you forever?"

Dexter grinned, dropping to his knees beside her. Wrapping his arms around her, he pulled her close, kissing her deeply.

"I thought you'd never ask. Yes. I want that more than anything else in this world."

41

The family was scattered throughout the house. Marguerite hung her jacket on a hook in the hall, then poked her head into the living room. "Hey, everyone," she called out, waving at Miss Minny and Delores. Her Aunt Leah gestured in her direction.

"Hey, Baby Girl. You finally made it."

Dropping into a chair, Marguerite kicked her shoes off into a corner. "Finally. Never thought I'd get done today."

"How's the project coming?" Pat asked.

"We finished today. Came in well under budget and it looks great. I'll get feedback from the executive board on Monday morning."

"Very good. We are so proud of you."

Clarence called her name from the doorway. "Hey, Baby Girl. When did you get here?"

"Just walked in."

He nodded. "Food's on the stove. The rest of the crew is in the den. The game hasn't started yet."

Marguerite lifted her body from her seat.

"Oh, and congratulations." Clarence grinned.

Marguerite smiled. "Thank you."

Her aunts caught the look that passed between

them. "What's going on?" Pat asked. "What are we missing?"

Marguerite shrugged. "Nothing. He was just talking about the project, I guess."

Pat glanced at her brother, then to Leah. "Sounds fishy to me."

"Me too," Leah chimed in.

Making her way out of the room before Delores thought to add her two cents, Marguerite gave her uncle a good pinch when they were out of earshot. "Thanks a lot," she said with a grin.

"What I do?"

Marguerite sucked her teeth. "You know exactly what you did. You are always trying to start something."

"Not me."

On the other side of the house, the men sat huddled around the television set. Dexter rose to plant a kiss on Marguerite's face. "Hey, beautiful."

"Hey, yourself," she replied, rubbing her palm against his back.

"You want to get in on this bet, Marguerite?" Shepard asked.

"I sure do. I'll take the Patriots for seven."

"You're kidding, right?" John snorted from the recliner in the corner. "The Patriots?"

Marguerite's hands flew to her hips. "What is wrong with the Patriots?"

"Nothing if you like a losing team."

Marguerite cut her eyes toward Dexter. "Tell your buddy that in the Cole Family house we pull for the Knicks, the Patriots, and the Yankees. And if his Southern Tennessee self can't handle that, then he needs to get out."

The room laughed.

"You heard my woman." Dexter grinned. "Put your money on the Patriots."

John shook his head just as Debbie and Sharon entered the room, their hands loaded down with two full plates of food.

"Hey, woman!" Sharon said. "Better get you a plate before it's all gone."

Marguerite nodded, settling on the sofa beside Dexter.

"All gone? All that food in that kitchen, we should be able to eat well for a month," Shepard snorted. "Where you getting all gone from?"

Sharon laughed. "These skinny women eat more than you think." She pointed at Debbie. "Look at that plate."

Debbie blushed. "She's right. We do eat well. Especially when we can get food this good."

Marguerite shook her head again.

John jumped up, reaching to turn the volume down on the television. The noise in the room rose threateningly. John pushed his palms into the air in front of him. "Hold up a second. This won't take but a minute. Dexter and Marguerite have something to say."

"Wait a minute," Clarence piped in, turning to shout into the next room. "You all better come in here quick. Dexter and Marguerite have something to say."

Dexter laughed heartily as Marguerite sat stunned. She glanced from one anxious face to another as everyone turned to stare at her and Dexter. Sharon grinned broadly, a low "Mmmmm" rising from her midsection.

"Okay," Clarence said as the other women took seats and made themselves comfortable. "We're all here."

Marguerite looked up at Dexter as he pulled her to her feet. She could only roll her eyes and chuckle lightly as he wrapped his arms around her.

"You folks are too much," Marguerite said.

"Well, you got something to say or not," Delores said snidely. "I was just about to tell Mama and them about my new boyfriend."

"Hush, Delores," Miss Minny scolded. "Let them chilen speak."

Marguerite looked about the room and smiled, leaning closer to Dexter. "Well, we want you all to know that. . . ."

Clarence jumped excitedly to his feet. "We're gon' have us a wedding," he announced loudly. "Our Baby Girl is getting married!"

The room erupted into cheers as the family grinned from ear to ear.

In the corner, Miss Minny swiped a wrinkled hand over her eyes. "Is that all? Lord, we knew that long time ago. Yo' granny been done told us all befo' she left this world. Told me befo' she was sick that you was gon' marry that pretty boy. You need to be tellin' me something new." The woman sighed.

"What you want us to tell you, Miss Minny?" Marguerite asked, looking up at Dexter as the others giggled.

"I thought you was gon' tell us about the baby comin'. Mae said you promised her at least a dozen befo' I goes on to heaven. Now I don't know what you waitin' fo', but you better hurry up 'cause I'm getting ole'."

Marguerite laughed. "Yes'm, Miss Minny. "We'll get right on it."

42

On October sixteenth, Dexter picked Marguerite up into his arms and carried her over the threshold of their new home. Marguerite was in awe of the log structure that would be her home.

Her grandmother's white wedding gown fit neatly against her frame, the antique lace falling in soft folds at her feet. Dexter looked resplendent in his ebony tuxedo. She kissed him lightly as he set her easily onto her feet.

"It's beautiful," she gushed, looking excitedly around her.

He grinned broadly, his perfect white teeth gleaming at her. "We can change anything you don't like."

Marguerite was thrilled as she moved from room to room. "What's not to like? I love it all. It couldn't be more perfect."

Dexter beamed. At the foot of the steps, he held out his hand gesturing for her to follow him. Hand in hand, they ascended the circular staircase. They were regal as they climbed the stairwell of their new home. King and queen of their own private oasis. Guiding her down the hall, Dexter swung open the double doors that led into the master bedroom.

As Marguerite stepped inside behind him, the view took her breath away.

Hundreds of white candles shimmered in low incandescence around the room. White and yellow rose petals led a path toward the king-sized bed adorned in satin and lace. The rich scent of lavender filled her nose, and Marguerite inhaled deeply. Above the bed, *Angel Angel* peered down upon them, blessing the room with her presence.

Tears filled Marguerite's eyes. The words caught in her throat. She reached to press herself against Dexter's body, wrapping her arms tightly around him. "I love you," she whispered. "I love you so much."

Dexter leaned down to kiss her forehead, clasping his arms about her. "I love you too."

"So what next?" Marguerite asked coyly, pulling lightly at the buttons of his tuxedo shirt. "What do we do now?"

Dexter grinned, grabbing her hand and pulling her excitedly down the hall. Rushing into a room at the other end, he smiled widely as Marguerite's face filled with glee, her expression priceless.

"We promised Miss Minny a dozen babies to put in this nursery before she goes to heaven. I guess we better hurry up and get started."

Marguerite laughed as Dexter swept her up into his arms and led her back to their bedroom. As he laid her down onto the bed of rose petals, she could almost hear her grandmother's laugh in the distance. The warmth of all that love smiled down upon her.

"That's right. Now all you needs is some babies to be rockin' on yo' chest."

Dear Friends,

The magic of putting pen to paper and manipulating phrases into coherent sentences has been my passion since I was twelve-years-old and doodling poetry in the margins of my junior high school science book. I have always believed that a great writer could change a reader's world. It's why I strive to be a great writer.

The stories I write come from the depths of all I believe in. I believe in family. I believe in miracles. I believe in love. I believe that all we have the ability to fulfill our dreams. I hold steadfast that the power of prayer can overcome any obstacle. I believe that without the profound wisdom, guidance and love of a higher power, I could not believe and, then, I could not write.

Thank you for your support. I hope that you enjoy my story. I hope that my words can change your world, if only for a moment.

Much love,
Deborah Fletcher Mello

ABOUT THE AUTHOR

Deborah Fletcher Mello is a writer, poet, and inspirational speaker whose experience encompasses twenty-plus years of scripting technical documentation for corporations worldwide. Born and raised in Stamford, Connecticut, she now calls Hillsborough, North Carolina home, where she resides with her husband, Allan Mello, and son, Matthew.

More Sizzling Romance From
Gwynne Forster

__Obsession	1-58314-092-1	$5.99US/$7.99CAN
__Fools Rush In	1-58314-435-8	$6.99US/$9.99CAN
__Ecstasy	1-58314-177-4	$5.99US/$7.99CAN
__Swept Away	1-58314-098-0	$5.99US/$7.99CAN
__Beyond Desire	1-58314-201-0	$5.99US/$7.99CAN
__Secret Desire	1-58314-124-3	$5.99US/$7.99CAN
__Against All Odds	1-58314-247-9	$5.99US/$7.99CAN
__Sealed With a Kiss	1-58314-313-0	$5.99US/$7.99CAN
__Scarlet Woman	1-58314-192-8	$5.99US/$7.99CAN
__Once in a Lifetime	1-58314-193-6	$6.99US/$9.99CAN
__Flying High	1-58314-427-7	$6.99US/$9.99CAN

Available Wherever Books Are Sold!

Visit our website at **www.BET.com**.

Arabesque Romances
by *Roberta Gayle*

__Moonrise   **$4.99US/$5.99CAN**
   0-7860-0268-9

__Sunshine and Shadows   **$4.99US/$5.99CAN**
   0-7860-0136-4

__Something Old, Something New   **$4.99US/$6.50CAN**
   1-58314-018-2

__Mad About You   **$5.99US/$7.99CAN**
   1-58314-108-1

__Nothing But the Truth   **$5.99US/$7.99CAN**
   1-58314-209-6

__Coming Home   **$6.99US/$9.99CAN**
   1-58314-282-7

__The Holiday Wife   **$6.99US/$9.99CAN**
   1-58314-425-0

Available Wherever Books Are Sold!

Visit our website at **www.BET.com.**